LAURA M.

KISS
~~MARRY~~
KILL

Enjoy!

HODDER &
STOUGHTON

First published in Great Britain in 2025 by Hodder & Stoughton Limited
An Hachette UK company

The authorised representative in the EEA is Hachette Ireland, 8 Castlecourt
Centre, Dublin 15, D15 XTP3, Ireland (email: info@hbgi.ie)

1

A CIP catalogue record for this title is available from the British Library

Hardback ISBN 978 1 399 72967 3
Trade Paperback ISBN 978 1 399 72968 0
ebook ISBN 978 1 399 72969 7

Typeset in Sabon MT by Hewer Text UK Ltd, Edinburgh
Printed and bound in Great Britain by Clays Ltd, Elcograf S.p.A.

Hodder & Stoughton policy is to use papers that are natural, renewable
and recyclable products and made from wood grown in sustainable
forests. The logging and manufacturing processes are expected to
conform to the environmental regulations of the country of origin.

Hodder & Stoughton Limited
Carmelite House
50 Victoria Embankment
London EC4Y 0DZ

www.hodder.co.uk

For my parents, Cecilia and Murray

Chapter 1

'Hello, there.'

It was a rather avuncular way to start, but Sara tried not to mind. The previous candidate had been much worse than avuncular – you only got five minutes with each man yet he had nonetheless managed to get his penis size into the conversation. What he had expected her to say she didn't know. Was she supposed to (figuratively) admire it, like a prize marrow at the village show?

'Hello,' she said. 'I'm Sara.'

'Nice to meet you, Sarah.'

'It's Sara actually – like the shop Zara, but with an S.'

'Zara,' he repeated.

'Yes, you know the high street shop?'

'I'm not much of a shopper, Zara.'

'No, it's . . .' Oh, what did it matter? He'd be gone in . . . she sneaked a look at the big digital clock set up on the bar . . . four minutes and thirty-five seconds. The clock sat next to a glossy sign bearing the name of the dating agency, *Kiss, Marry, Avoid*. The name had been chosen, her friend Angela had told her when she founded the agency ten years ago, to illustrate that whilst they were committed to providing a high-quality, personal service, dating after fifty could be enjoyable, light-hearted. It wasn't all National Trust memberships and knitting by the fire – there was still fun left to be had.

As part of their profile, the daters were encouraged to share the celebrity they would choose for each category. Sara had chosen to kiss Hugh Grant (now, in his rumpled, anti-Murdoch warrior era, not the floppy, foppish years), marry Michael Palin (such a lovely man) and avoid Tom Cruise. She couldn't be doing with a man who took himself so seriously.

'I didn't get your name,' she said to her companion.

'Ah, that's because I haven't told you!' He laughed, happy to have caught her out.

'Yes, I know. And now I'm asking.'

'I see. I thought you meant I had told you but you hadn't caught it, or had forgotten it. Sometimes I do that if I've forgotten someone's name when I've just been introduced to them. I'll say "I'm sorry, I didn't catch your name". Useful trick.'

Four minutes and twenty seconds to go. Sara adjusted her position. The cinched waist of the dress that had seemed so flattering back in her bedroom was restricting her ability to take a full breath, and the new bra that had promised so much in terms of lifting and separating had her in such a tight grip she felt sure there would be angry welts on her skin when it came to the sweet release of removing it.

'It's Philip. And before you ask, my celebrity choices are kiss Scarlett Johansson, marry Emma Watson and avoid Jennifer Lopez. She seems rather high maintenance.'

In your dreams, Philip. Sara knew it was meant to be fantasy, but men who didn't pick age-appropriate celebrities to kiss and marry gave her the serious ick. The only one of Philip's who was anywhere near his age was the once he'd chosen to avoid, and the reason was pretty depressing too. In Sara's experience, men who used high maintenance as a derogatory term were looking for a quiet woman with no opinions who would be happy to nurse them in their old age.

'What do you do?' If she was actually attracted to someone she rarely asked this question, finding it to be the least interesting thing about a person. However, if she was sure, as she already was with Philip, that it was dead in the water, then it was useful. They would drone on and fill the remaining time and she could nod and smile in the appropriate places whilst surreptitiously casting her eye over the other candidates. Like most people who find themselves single in their fifties, Sara bore the scars of relationships past, along with the other wounds life had seen fit to inflict. The slow, painful death of her husband James from pancreatic cancer was the biggie, but there were other, smaller cuts too, from sources that appeared innocent, like a sheet of paper that slices into the top of your finger leaving a bloody trail on the pristine, white page.

'I work in plastic,' he said.

'Interesting,' she said automatically. 'What kind of plastic?' Tupperware was the one that sprang to mind. She imagined him spending his days colour coordinating it and neatly stacking it in size order.

'We're very big into sustainable packaging solutions at the moment.' She was right about the Tupperware! There was a portion of soup in her freezer in a plastic container that had been given to her late mother as a wedding present sixty years ago. What was more sustainable than that?

'It's a project management role. I manage a large team who are split across a variety of sites, which can be quite a challenge.'

As he bleated on and on about polymers and climate change, she became distracted by the tinkling laugh that kept ringing out from the next table. Sara wondered if the woman's 'date' was actually funny or if it was more of a nervous tic. She allowed her eyes to stray to the left, where they met the gaze of the dater opposite the giggler, a square-faced bear of a man with a neat, dark beard peppered with grey. His eyes widened as they met Sara's and he gave a micro-shrug as if to indicate that no, he didn't know what was so funny either.

'You'll enjoy *this*,' Sara's companion said, pulling her focus back to him. 'He said there was no way he could work with someone in a different country! What does he think I do, managing an international team?'

'Goodness,' Sara murmured, catching the bear's eye again. They both smiled.

Sara jumped as the bell rang to signal the end of this microdate. Philip shook her hand across the table.

'Good to have met you. I enjoyed our conversation.'

'Me too,' Sara said politely, deciding against asking whether monologue wouldn't be a better word for it. God, she missed James. She longed to be part of a couple again, but what she'd seen so far of the world of middle-aged dating made that seem a very remote possibility indeed.

Philip stood and moved one table to the right, joining a striking, dark-haired woman in a maroon trouser suit. Sara heard him say 'Hello, there' to her.

'Was he right?' The bearded man materialised in the seat across from her, filling it much more convincingly than its previous occupant had done.

'About what?' she said.

'Did you enjoy it?'

'The hilarious comment about working with someone in a different country, or the whole date?'

'Both, I suppose,' he said, eyes twinkling.

'I certainly know a lot more about the production of sustainable plastic than I did before, so that's something. I'm a bit disappointed in this date, though.'

'How so?' he said, unoffended.

'I assumed from the gales of laughter coming from your last table that you were going to be hilarious. You haven't made me laugh once yet.'

'Give me a chance! What sort of thing does make you laugh? Programmes? Comedians?'

'Victoria Wood is my all-time favourite. Nobody made me laugh like she did.'

As well as being true, this was also a test to see if he was one of those men who think women aren't funny.

'She was amazing, wasn't she? I miss her.'

'Me too.' He had passed with flying colours.

'I would have chosen her for my "marry" celebrity actually, but I felt weird about picking someone who wasn't alive.'

'Who did you choose?' she asked, almost reluctantly. She'd felt more of a spark with this man in the last two minutes than with anyone she'd met since she started dating, and she was unwilling to have it ruined just yet.

'My kiss is Nigella Lawson.'

'Of course,' Sara said, pleased. Not only was Nigella age appropriate, she had an almost indecent love of a good meal and had always seemed like someone Sara could be friends with. 'And to marry?'

'Emma Thompson.'

'Another good choice.' Sara was delighted. Whilst Emma Thompson was an attractive woman, picking someone famous for her incredible talent rather than her looks demonstrated his integrity, his desire for a real relationship. Emma Thompson was another one on Sara's mental list of celebrities she'd like to be friends with — warm, funny and a huge champion of women. He was ticking a lot of boxes.

'I struggled with the "avoid" category, it felt a bit mean,' he went on. 'In the end, I think I put something like "anyone who seeks fame for its own sake". Bit of a cop out, probably. Have you done a lot of this kind of thing?' He waved a hand around the roped-off section of the upmarket wine bar and assembled daters. The women ranged from the ultra-groomed to the defiantly bare-faced. Apart from one outlier in black jeans and a Nirvana T-shirt, the men were wearing chinos or their best jeans topped by a shirt that aimed to show a bit of personality without verging into full midlife crisis territory. As a group, they represented the ultimate triumph of hope over experience.

'A fair bit, yeah, over the last couple of years,' she said. 'With varying degrees of success. You?'

'It's my first time. Be gentle with me.'

Delivered in a less silly way it was a comment that could have put Sara off, but it made her laugh.

'See, I am funny!' he said.

'Hilarious,' Sara agreed. 'So you're . . . what, recently divorced?'

'You got me. Well, recent-ish — it was all finalised a couple of years ago. It's taken me this long to pluck up the courage to start dating.'

That sounded promising. She'd been on dates with men for whom the ink on the divorce papers was barely dry — and indeed with men who, despite appearances, were very much still married.

'Do you have children?'

6

'One daughter. Isabel. She's thirty now – blimey, that makes me feel old. I still feel about twenty-five inside, so it doesn't seem feasible that I have a fully grown adult daughter.'

Sara was relieved. If the daughter was thirty, she would have flown the nest and wouldn't be hanging about making it difficult for her father to date. She'd had a taste of that with previous men she'd been seeing.

'She lives in America, so I don't get to see her as often as I'd like, but we're close.' A plane ride away. Even better.

'And you? Are you divorced?' he went on.

'The other one,' Sara said. 'Widowed. Five years ago.'

'I'm sorry to hear that.'

'Run for the hills if you like,' she said, having been burned by men who couldn't deal with her widowhood, claiming she wasn't ready to date or who got upset because she refused to remove all traces of her late husband from the house.

'Certainly not,' he said. 'My dad died when I was six, and my mum met someone else a few years later. He was brilliant.'

'Sorry about your dad.'

'Thanks – I don't remember much about him, to be honest. Do you have kids?'

'Yes, but they were a bit older when James died. Almost grown up.'

'Still hard though. Worse, in some ways, to have had him their whole childhood. I didn't know what I was missing, and then when Mum met Stu, he became like a dad to me and my brother. He hadn't had kids of his own, but had always wanted them, so he was well up for being part of a family.'

'That sounds perfect. It's one of the sadnesses for me of Max and Jonny being fifteen and eighteen when we lost James. They

7

were young enough to still need a dad in lots of ways, but too old for anyone who came into our lives since to become a father figure to them. Not that anyone did, or has, but anyway it would have been too late and they wouldn't have wanted it. So they had to manage without. I mean, they are managing, brilliantly, but . . . it just makes me sad, especially when I see their friends developing proper adult relationships with their own fathers.' Her voice cracked. The grief that cut so sharply five years ago was duller now, but it still had the power to hurt her. 'James wasn't well by that point, but he managed to take Jonny to the pub on his eighteenth birthday for his first legal pint – it was this big thing, you know? But when Max turned eighteen he just went out with his mates.'

Luckily (as Sara was on the verge of tears) the bell clanged.

'Sorry, that got deep a bit quickly!' she said, brightly. 'You really will want to run for the hills now!'

'No, I promise I won't. I'd always prefer to talk about real things. There's only so much to say about sustainable plastic, right?'

'I thought so, before today.'

'I've enjoyed our chat,' he said, standing up. 'And, well, hope to see you again soon, I guess. I'm Nigel, by the way.'

Sara resisted the urge to throw herself on the ground and cling to his ankles, to stop him from moving on to the next woman who, Sara now recognised, was uncommonly beautiful – fine-featured, elegant and slender. Sara cursed her own curves. On a good day she might describe herself as voluptuous, but today her body seemed to stick out in all the wrong places. She couldn't recall the last time she'd had a truly meaningful conversation with a man, and although she told herself it was utter foolishness, she was overwhelmed with the feeling that he was meant to be in her life.

She arranged her face into a suitably welcoming expression to greet her next date, a hollow-eyed man in what she was rather afraid was a brown shirt, and tried very hard not to mind that the beautiful woman in the maroon trouser suit lit up like a beacon when Nigel sat down opposite her.

Chapter 2

'Oh no, no, no,' Angela said, lips pursed, pouring thick, murky coffee for Sara at her kitchen table. 'You're getting carried away. I won't allow it.'

'It's up to me, isn't it?' Sara said weakly, knowing the answer was a firm negative. Since the day twenty years ago that she and Angela had met at the nursery school gates, she'd been unable to withstand the force of Angela's personality. Together they had taken their children, Jonny and Lizzie, to the parks Angela favoured, bought them babyccinos in the cafes she approved of, chased after them at the toddler groups Angela deemed suitable. At first, Sara had found it overwhelming and considered distancing herself, but gradually she'd come to understand that underneath, Angela was struggling with motherhood and the only way she could cope was to thunder towards it, head down, like a bull at a matador.

'No, it isn't up to you,' she said. 'When you signed up to Kiss, Marry, Avoid, we agreed that your solo foray into the world of dating apps hadn't worked, and you wanted my help. I believe the phrase you used was "I am entirely in your hands". This is what I do, Sara. It's what I'm good at – the agency is my life's work. Let me help you.'

'But Nigel was the only one I really liked.' Sara's stomach fizzed at the memory of their eyes meeting over the table. It was an excitement of a kind she hadn't felt since she met her late husband James thirty years earlier, back when she'd still had optimism, and a waist. She'd almost given up hope of ever feeling it again.

'Why did you tick yes for Ben and Steve, then?'

'Because I knew you'd have a go at me if I only ticked Nigel,' Sara muttered.

'Yes, I would. I am,' Angela said crisply. 'Something I have learned in my ten years running a dating agency is that you never put all your eggs in one basket. You always, *always* have a back-up plan. Ben and Steve are nice guys.'

'Did you sign them up yourself?'

'No, not as such. Saskia found them.'

'Saskia? The twenty-five-year-old you've put on a verbal warning for discussing clients behind their backs?'

'Well, yes,' Angela said, embarrassed. 'She's actually on a written warning now, truth be told. She's got a real knack for finding new clients though.'

'Oh, that's alright, then! What have you put her on a written warning for?'

'I overheard her on the phone to a friend – it was not long after your speed dating session, actually – taking the mickey out of the daters for having the temerity to want to find love over the age of fifty.'

'Charming!' Sara's face burned. 'So because my husband died at the age of fifty, I'm meant to live the rest of my life alone, is that it? How can you possibly keep her working for you – finding love for the over fifties is literally your agency's stated aim!'

'I know, I think she'll have to go, but I've got to follow the proper process with the warnings and so on. If she puts another foot out of line, she'll be gone. Shame though, she may be wholly unsuited to the agency but she's brought me so much new business. Ben's an architect, for goodness' sake! And Steve's a . . . what is he again?'

'Something to do with finance? Or was it IT? They all blend into one after a while. I ticked them because they were the only ones who didn't obviously have massive personality flaws – or not ones which showed within the allotted five minutes.'

'None of our daters have massive personality flaws,' Angela huffed. 'We're very discerning.'

'Where's Helen?' said Sara. 'I thought she was coming.'

'She said she was, but I dare say we'll get a message cancelling any minute now.' Angela rolled her eyes. 'She wants to be careful, if she keeps on like this, we'll stop asking.'

'That's harsh. To be fair, it's not a new thing – she's always been flaky in the twenty years since we've known her.'

'Is that supposed to make it better?'

'No, but it might mean there's something else at play.'

'Like what?' If Angela's eyebrows had arched any further they would have blended in with her sleek, iron-grey cropped hair. Sara had always been jealous of Angela's style, and how unapologetically herself she was. Angela's hair had gone grey many years ago, in her early forties, and she had never considered dyeing it, whereas Sara still spent a small fortune every month getting her roots done. Her clothes, with their angular geometric patterns and asymmetric hems could have looked ridiculous on someone less forceful, but on Angela were relentlessly chic.

'I don't know . . . I've always wondered if it was some kind of mental health thing . . . anxiety or whatever.' Sara was fond of Helen, but she didn't rely on her the way she did on Angela.

'Does having poor mental health make you lose your manners?' Angela said.

'It could do. Anyway, you're all talk. You won't stop asking and you know it.'

'You're probably right.' Angela grinned. 'Right, back to these dates. Why didn't you tick any others? There must have been more than three you liked.'

'There was only one I liked, as I've told you, but you won't allow it.' Sara thought longingly of Nigel's rumbling voice, his warmth, the way he had listened to her.

'There were lots that ticked you though, you should give them a chance. What about Philip?'

'The plastic guy? Are you kidding? He was so boring.'

'I think he's rather sweet. Are you sure you're not finding excuses not to date them to protect yourself?'

'Yes, I'm sure.' It was hard enough dealing with other people's preconceptions of what it was like to date as a widow, without Angela joining in. Of course Sara missed James, but she desperately wanted to meet someone else, to be part of a couple again. Why would she be sabotaging it? 'I liked Nigel but for some reason you're not keen for me to see him again.'

'I'm very keen! I just don't want you to pin all your hopes on one man. It's better to keep your options open at this stage. Everyone does.'

There was a small, significant pause.

'Everyone?' said Sara in a small voice. 'So . . . Nigel didn't only tick me?'

'He was more discerning than a lot of the men we get who tick yes to everyone so they can find out who has ticked them. He only said yes to you and Leila.'

'Which one was Leila?' Sara asked with a sinking feeling that she knew exactly which one she was. Maroon trouser suit, flawless skin.

'She was on your right. Dark hair, attractive.'

'Yep, that figures.'

'Not as attractive as you.' Angela patted her arm supportively. 'And between us, a bit of a nightmare as a client. She's lovely, but incredibly scatty and one of those women who has poor judgement when it comes to men. I doubt it'll go anywhere. But I insist on you going out with Ben and Steve as well as Nigel – you're only ever going to get a flavour of someone in five minutes. You need to give them a chance.'

'Fine.' It was useless to argue.

'And don't forget, the speed dating is only a small part of our offering – we mainly do it to attract new clients. You'd be better off signing up for our bespoke matchmaking service.'

'Let's see how this goes first.' Sara didn't have high hopes. She'd experienced everything the online dating apps had to offer – ghosting, breadcrumbing, photos of men's genitals. Was using the agency really going to be any better?

The two women's phones pinged in unison.

'What did I tell you? That'll be Helen,' Angela said, picking up her phone. 'Yep, she's not coming.'

'What's her excuse this time?' Sara asked.

'She hasn't even bothered to make one up – says she's been held up and can't make it. I don't know what could be holding her up. It's not as if she works.' Angela sounded disapproving.

'Neither do I,' Sara said. James might not have been the most exciting man but he had been wise in his investments and thorough in his life insurance.

'And you're very reliable as a result! Although I sometimes wish my closest friends had more of an understanding of what it's like running a business, rather than being ladies who lunch.'

'I hardly ever lunch!' Sara was indignant. 'I mean, I eat lunch obviously, but usually it's a cheese and pickle sandwich at home. Hummus and pitta if I'm feeling really fancy. I know I was lucky that James left me so comfortably off, and it was a huge relief not to have to worry about money after he died, but to be honest, I'd love to have some meaningful work to do now, although I don't know what that would look like. I don't want to go back to recruitment – that's a young person's game – but who's going to hire a woman in her mid-fifties for a new career?'

'What about volunteering?' Angela suggested.

Sara grimaced. 'Sorting dead people's clothes in a charity shop, you mean? I don't know if I fancy that.'

'It's not just charity shops. There are galleries and things.'

'Didn't Helen volunteer at an animal rescue charity years ago?'

'That's right. Didn't last long, like everything she does. As you said, flaky. How long did she work at your recruitment place, back when we first met her? Six months? Get your phone out, Sara. I'm not letting you leave here until you've messaged Ben and Steve to arrange your dates. If one of them goes well, you can bring them to mine and Greg's silver wedding party next weekend!'

'Now who's getting carried away?' Sara muttered. 'I thought that was a low-key get together.'

'It is. Family and close friends. Plus any amazing new boyfriends of close friends that I introduced them to. Oh, and Helen's frightful mother.'

'You're kidding, why is she coming?' Sara said. 'Last time I saw her she somehow managed to imply that it was my fault James died.'

'How on earth could it have been your fault?'

'Apparently I should have noticed earlier that something was wrong. If I'd been more "on the ball" he would have been diagnosed earlier, had more treatment options.'

'That's absurd. Pancreatic cancer is famous for being diagnosed late – well, famous isn't the right word but you know what I mean. It's very common.'

Sara had faded during those last months of James's life, as caring for him became harder and more time consuming. Usually one to put on a good front, she had admitted to Angela not long before he died that she was almost at the end of her rope, and that while she was dreading his death, there was going to be relief too. Then she had cried and asked Angela not to tell anyone she'd said that. Angela never had.

'I said that,' Sara said, 'and then she said what about immunotherapy, why hadn't I asked for that? She'd read an article – in the *Daily Express*, naturally, so it must be true – that said there was growing evidence it was an effective treatment for pancreatic cancer and why hadn't I pushed harder to get him into a clinical trial? The worst of it was that these were all things I was regularly accusing myself of in the dead of night at that time.'

'I can't believe she said that to you. To be honest, I'm not madly keen on her coming either. She doesn't think much of Kiss, Marry, Avoid – she once told me the idea of women (specifically women, mind you) looking for love in later life was risible and degrading. The problem is she's staying with Helen and Brian, so I couldn't really tell them to leave her at home on her own. Now come on, get your phone out and arrange these dates. If you're very good, I'll let you message Nigel as well.'

Sara sighed, but obediently took out her phone. When Angela was in one of these moods, there was no point resisting, but privately, she felt that if she couldn't make it work with Nigel, she would be ready to give up the whole idea altogether.

✓

Chapter 3

Helen tried to calm her breathing, but it kept catching in her throat. She retraced her steps around the house, starting at the top. There were very few places it could be in the bathroom. Brian hated clutter, so she kept her personal toiletries neatly stacked in the cupboard in her bedside table. She opened the mirrored cabinet above the sink and lifted every item in it for the second time that day, standing on tiptoe to run her hand across the top of the cupboard. Nothing. She did the same with the cabinet under the sink, kneeling down and reaching around the pipework, then shuffled across on her knees to the toilet to root around behind the pedestal. In her friend Angela's house, she was fairly certain this would be an unsavoury activity resulting in an abundance of dust and grit (and worse) but here there was none of that – just a faint scent of bleach that lingered on her fingertips. There was nowhere else it could be in here. She looked at her watch and her pulse quickened. She only had forty-five minutes.

She half ran back to the first spare bedroom. She didn't have time to check and remake all the beds, and anyway she knew she'd done that thoroughly this morning – hoping that she'd find it there and be able to make it to Angela's for coffee with her and Sara. She had also climbed up the mini stepladder and felt along the top of every pelmet and curtain rail in the house.

19

Brian wasn't a fan of books – clutter again – but in this room he'd conceded that guests might want something to read. More realistically, he'd wanted to give the impression that visitors would be welcome. In reality they rarely had an overnight guest. Helen's mother was arriving later for her annual visit, but other than her no one had stayed in this room since that night Sara had stayed, not long after her husband died. Brian and Helen had no adult children flipping in and out of the nest at will, like Angela's daughter Lizzie did. Helen felt the usual tug of envy at the thought of that ongoing need, the umbilical cord between Angela and Lizzie that stubbornly refused to be severed. Angela moaned about it, but Helen suspected she was secretly proud of it, cherished it. The years had dimmed the hurt a little, so Helen no longer experienced that hot stab of pain on seeing a small child run to its mother crying after a fall, flinging itself into her arms, tear-stained face buried in her neck. These days it was more of a dull ache. Would Brian have been different if she'd been able to give him children? He'd been so disappointed, month after month, for all those years of trying. He'd had his sperm tested and it was firing on all cylinders. She'd had all the tests too and the doctors had said there was no reason she shouldn't conceive, but she knew he blamed her. He had never said it outright, but he would send her articles about how stress and anxiety impacted a woman's fertility. She'd tried her best to be less anxious, but the trying made it worse, if anything.

Earlier today she'd taken each carefully colour-coordinated book from the shelf and dusted every side, as well as the shelf itself. There was one thing she hadn't done though. She moved swiftly across the room and pulled the first book down, rifling through the pages, shaking it vigorously, her hands slippery.

Nothing fell out. She worked her way across the shelf, her heart sinking with each empty book. When she got to the last one, she pressed her lips together and lined them up neatly, ensuring that no speck of dust from between the pages had fallen on the shelf or carpet. She had never really expected to find it there.

In the boxroom there were even fewer options. She knew she had checked the bed and curtains thoroughly, the bedside table was empty and there were no rugs or flapping carpets, no pictures with loose frames, no ornaments with hollow cavities.

As Helen scurried into her and Brian's bedroom, a cold trickle of sweat ran down her back. She didn't have time to re-examine every nook and cranny in the house – she needed to think of new places she hadn't already looked. It wouldn't be in Brian's bedside table, would it? He kept the drawers locked – he'd never liked her going through his private things. She opened the wardrobe doors, surveying his neatly pressed suits, shirts and trousers, colour-coordinated and arranged by category (black tie, smart, smart-casual, golf). She'd already wiped the rails and dusted inside and beneath each pair of shoes. She gave each pair another quick shake upside down just in case.

Abandoning the bedrooms, Helen walked along the landing, scanning left to right like a searchlight. She went down the stairs, running her hands along the underside of the wooden bannister. For one glorious second her finger caught on something and she thought she'd found it, but it was only a splinter that forced its way insidiously under her skin, impossible to get out.

With half an hour to go, she spent a crazed ten minutes lifting, for the second time that day, every tin, packet and sachet in the grocery cupboard. Pots, pans, plates, cups, glasses – she'd scrutinised them all.

There were two more rooms to go – the lounge and the small downstairs shower room. She decided to tackle the lounge first, interrogating every item on the mantelpiece, bookshelf and sideboard, including their wedding photo. Brian stared proudly into the camera, his smile wide, the picture of a happy groom. Helen, young and slender in ivory silk, gazed up at him in an adoring fashion. She had been twenty years old when they met, working as a veterinary nurse in her first job after the diploma she'd done at the local college. Her mother hadn't wanted her to go away for university, and Helen didn't think she would have enjoyed it anyway. Brian had come in with a girlfriend and her cat, which had a nasty eye infection. The girlfriend had been impatient and short with Brian, and he had given Helen a rueful grin, which she'd found herself returning. A week later, she found him waiting for her outside after work. He'd finished with the girlfriend and hadn't been able to stop thinking about her, and could he take her for a drink? It was the most wonderful, romantic thing that had ever happened to her. He was her first boyfriend, her first everything. Five years older, he was experienced and debonair. He showered her with compliments and gifts, and told her she was the one he had been waiting for, the one he needed, the one who could make his life complete. When he asked her to marry him she couldn't say yes fast enough. There was the added bonus that it got her away from her mother's suffocating presence.

The first time he had really lost his temper with her was a few weeks before the wedding. She was late back from a night out with friends, and with no mobile phones in those days, had no way to let him know. She wasn't so very late, only an hour or so later than she'd said, and it had taken her a few minutes to understand that his silence when she returned home indicated fury, rather than indifference. He wasn't silent for long though, soon accusing her of having met someone else. She had cried and sworn there was no one else for her and eventually his anger burned itself out, leaving him penitent and loving, swearing he was just insecure because he loved her so much. She had felt like the luckiest girl in the world.

She looked inside and underneath Brian's golf trophies, including the largest one, a silver full-size model of the head of a 9-iron golf club set into a heavy, cylindrical base. She noticed that the baize around the base was loose and hopefully slid a finger inside it, but there was nothing.

She continued around the room, removing all the sofa cushions, unzipping them and feeling inside. This was risky because there was a chance she'd cut her hand, staining the cushions, which would be almost as bad as not finding it at all, but Helen was panicking now, her mouth dry. She lifted the Persian rug for the millionth time. She couldn't have accidentally hoovered it up, could she? There was nothing there, so she replaced it carefully, lining it up with the edge of the sofa.

A horrible sense of foreboding settled upon her as she went into the shower room. It couldn't be in here – it was as wide as the shower cubicle with just enough room for a toilet and minuscule basin. They rarely used it. She would never let Brian know, but she didn't always bother to clean it every day – she hadn't today beyond a cursory wipe over with a duster. There were no cabinets, no shelves, not even a loo brush. She dropped to her knees, searching frantically, hopelessly. Brian was due home in fifteen minutes, which would have been bad enough, but then she heard his car in the drive. He was early. She clapped a hand to her mouth. It had finally arrived – the day she had been dreading for their whole marriage.

Helen gripped the basin to pull herself up. The cotton of her sage-green capri pants pressed clammily against her knee and she noticed a dark patch about the size of a fifty pence piece. There must have been water on the floor. Helen hadn't used the toilet in here today and she was certain Brian hadn't either. It was in here. It had to be in here. She jerked the bifold door of the shower cubicle open. The shower tray gleamed white, the chrome trap cover clear and shiny as a mirror. Nothing, nothing, nothing. Brian's key turned in the lock and she gasped. As she bent down to dab ineffectually at the damp patch on her trousers with the hand towel, a flash of light caught her eye. She thought at first it was the overhead light bouncing off the chrome, but then she saw it – a sharp corner of metal peeping out from under the trap cover. She hurriedly put the towel back, aligning it with the rail, and dropped to her knees.

'I'm home!' Brian called from the hallway. The door of the shoe cupboard clicked as he put his brogues away.

With shaking hands she unscrewed the trap cover and there it was, winking up at her. The razor blade. She let out an inarticulate noise of relief, somewhere between a sigh and a sob.

It was when they got back from their honeymoon that Brian had introduced the idea that he would hide a razor blade somewhere in the house every day before he left for work. If she didn't find it by the end of the day, he would know she had been neglecting her housewifely duties. He had billed it as a game, sort of, and she had accepted it as such, grateful that Brian had a good job so she didn't have to work. She thought she'd soon be busy raising their children, but when that didn't happen, as he said it was the least she could do to keep the house nice and have a hot meal ready for him at the end of the day.

There was no time to clean out the trap, but as no one ever used the shower it didn't matter. She popped the razor blade into her pocket, whirled the chrome disc back into place, stood, flushed the toilet and went out into the hallway.

'Hello, darling.' She pretended to cough, surreptitiously wiping the sweat from her upper lip, before kissing him on the cheek.

'Oh dear,' he said, amused. 'Have you only just found it?'

'No, no. I was using the loo. I found it this morning.' She took the razor blade and laid it in his outstretched palm, the sore spot on the pad of her finger from the splinter throbbing.

He took a step back and looked down, frowning. 'What's that on your knee?'

'Just a bit of water – I splashed myself when I was washing my hands.'

'You'd better go and get changed before dinner. Your mother will be here soon.'

'Yes, of course, I'll go now.'

Up in the bedroom, Helen took a pair of tailored black trousers out of the wardrobe and sat down on the edge of her bed. Her heartrate was gradually slowing back down to something approaching normal. She chastised herself – she'd been too slow today. She must have spent twenty minutes sitting in the garden with her coffee. It could have been even longer if she'd allowed herself to browse online, but she couldn't risk Brian checking her screen time. At least she'd found the blade in the end, but she vowed to do better tomorrow.

Chapter 4

Sara had tried to set up a date with Nigel before the other two, but he was away working for a couple of weeks. So with Angela's dire warnings about eggs and baskets ringing in her ears, she had unwillingly arranged to meet Ben the Architect and Steve the Finance/IT/Whatever guy.

She was deliberately seven minutes late for Lucky Bachelor Number One, Ben, not wanting to chance having to wait alone in the pub. He was standing at the bar when she got there, four inches of his pint already gone. Perhaps he was early. Or nervous, although he didn't seem it, greeting her with an extravagant double kiss, joking with the barman as he ordered Sara's gin and tonic.

They took a seat in an alcove, out of view of most of the pub. Tunbridge Wells wasn't a large town, so there was every chance there would be someone Sara knew in here. Even though it was five years since she'd been widowed, there was always someone who thought she shouldn't be dating, that she was somehow sullying James's memory by refusing to live the rest of her life in widow's weeds, locked in perpetual mourning. Ben lived an hour away in Lewes (Angela had to cast her net fairly wide to get enough suitable candidates for her speed dating events), so she could have gone there to avoid scrutiny, but she preferred to stay close to home for first dates, in case something went awry.

'So!' Ben said. 'Tell me about yourself – what's your dating history?'

For a moment, she thought she had struck gold – a man who asked questions and was interested in the answers – but before she'd had a chance to reply, he shattered the illusion by bringing the question back to him.

'Are you a survivor of divorce, like me?'

'No, I was widowed five years ago.' She had told him that last time they met, but he had met a lot of women that night, so it was forgivable that he'd forgotten.

'I'm sorry to hear that,' he said perfunctorily. 'Dating at our age always makes me think of that rhyme about Henry VIII's wives: divorced, beheaded, died; divorced, beheaded, survived.'

'Beheaded? Have you met many women whose ex-partners met that fate?'

'Ha! No, I suppose not. Wish mine had been, though. Unfortunately, she survived. Survives.'

Aha. Sara was familiar with this variety of middle-aged dater. Ben was a Bitter Divorced Guy.

'When did you divorce?' she asked, already sure of the answer he would give.

'It's still all going through. It takes forever, as you know.'

As she thought. Not actually divorced at all.

'Not really,' she said pointedly. 'I'm widowed, not divorced.'

'Right, right, sorry. Well, I can tell you it's an absolute nightmare. They say it's one of the most stressful life events – worse than bereavement.'

'I somehow doubt that,' Sara said quietly, trying not to think about how she and James's brother had sat beside his dying body in the hospice, the gap between each breath getting longer and longer until there was no breath at all. She felt a rush of unjustified anger at James for dying, for putting her in this pub, with this man. For showing her what a good relationship could be, and making her want to find it again.

'No, honestly, it's dreadful. And it's so weighted in favour of women. I can't tell you how many men I know who've ended up living in a depressing flat, hardly seeing their kids, while their wife gets to keep the house. It's a joke.'

'Is that your situation?'

'Well, no, we're having to sell our house because the profits have to be divided fifty-fifty in our case.'

'That sounds fair,' Sara said mildly, enjoying the wave of frustration that washed across Ben's face. This was not her first Bitter Divorced Guy rodeo and she knew the script.

'Fair! If you think it's fair that the person who paid the vast majority of the mortgage only gets fifty per cent of the house, *and* has to give up half their pension, then yes, I suppose it's fair.'

'Why did you pay the vast majority of the mortgage?' Sara would bet her life on it not being because his wife decided to lie around eating grapes.

'I was working long hours to provide for the family – I'm an architect, it's a big job, you know, not a nine-to-five. Emily wanted to continue to work – she was a solicitor – but it simply wasn't practical. I wasn't able to commit to collecting the kids from nursery in time.'

'Of course,' she said soothingly. 'You had a Big Job.'

'Exactly,' he said, pleased she'd understood. 'If Emily had gone back to work, she would have been the one who had to leave early to collect them, or take time off if they were ill. It wouldn't have been possible for me, much as I'd have loved to do it. So we decided it was better if she gave up work until they were older.'

Sara bit back the words she longed to say: *So she gave up her career to support yours and bring up your children, but you don't consider that an equal contribution to the marriage?* It was tempting but she at least wanted to finish her drink.

'How old are they now?'

'Teenagers.' He heaved a weary sigh. 'Expecting lifts here, there and everywhere. They don't seem to understand that I have a life too. They've been known to ring Emily on my weekends to pick them up and take them places, if I can't do it. Unbelievable!'

Sara envisaged Emily getting the call from a distressed teenage daughter for whom not attending a party could be social suicide. She saw her stick her feet into her boots, put her coat on over her pyjamas (which she'd put on at 6 p.m. anticipating a night alone by the fire) and go out in the cold, driving all the way to Ben's bachelor pad and on to the party, biting her tongue until it bled in a monumental effort not to badmouth Ben to their daughter.

'Do you have kids?' he asked.

'Two sons. Max is at university in Bristol and Jonny works in London.'

'I went to Bristol! It's a great city. It's where I met Emily. She was studying law and I was doing architecture. It's a seven-year course – equivalent to medicine.'

Sara imagined him sweeping into a hospital room in a white coat with a stethoscope around his neck, a block of high rise flats languishing in the bed before him.

'How did you meet?' she asked, feeling a kinship with Emily. Sara had only been in Ben's company for ten minutes and she was already feeling brow-beaten. Goodness knows how Emily had coped.

'Through mutual friends. It took me ages to persuade her to go out with me. She was so bloody stubborn. I should have seen the warning signs.'

'Warning signs?'

'Everything had to be on her terms, all the time. The house had to be clean to her standards, no matter what my feelings were. And if she felt I wasn't adhering to those standards, whoo, there'd be hell to pay.'

Sara translated this classic Bitter Divorced Guy speak rapidly in her head: *I did absolutely nothing around the house, and when she asked me to help, I said I didn't see the mess in the same way that she did, and if she wanted it done in a particular way, that was her responsibility.*

'Everything changed after we had kids – even her taste in TV. Before, we'd enjoy watching things together – quality dramas like *The West Wing*, or historical documentaries – but after kids she was always watching this mindless trash – *Keeping Up With The Kardashians* was her favourite.' From his distaste he might have been telling Sara that Emily enjoyed disembowelling fluffy little kittens.

'I must confess I enjoy a bit of trash TV myself.' Poor Emily, wanting to relax after a long day at the coalface of early mother-hood and being forced to watch a documentary about Nazi Germany.

'As for sex, forget that.'

Ugh, were they here already?

'Having kids can put a dampener on that side of things,' she said. She cast her mind back to those long-ago days when she'd spent all day being touched and slobbered on and *needed* by her small children, her body no longer her own. The last thing she'd wanted at the end of the day was James pawing at her. Luckily he'd been very understanding, and when the kids were older they'd managed to get some semblance of their sex life back. Not swinging from the chandeliers, perhaps, but they'd had a set routine that left all parties satisfied.

'It wasn't so much about the sex itself,' Ben went on. Sara knew what he was about to say — it was in the script. He didn't disappoint her. 'It's the closeness, the intimacy in the true sense of the word, that you miss if you stop having sex.'

Sara wanted to ask if he thought there were any other ways of being close and intimate without sticking his penis into Emily's vagina, or whether if he'd done more housework and childcare and generally been more of an equal partner in the marriage, Emily would have been more inclined to have sex with him, but there was no point. Ben was too far down this particular track to be saved. Eventually he would meet someone who hadn't heard the script before and who would fall for it. This woman would shake her head and sympathise with how badly he'd been treated. She would tell her friends about Ben's nightmare, controlling ex-wife and his ungrateful, demanding children. The children would visit less and less, and when they were asked about their dad, they would roll their eyes and say no, we're not close. When his daughter didn't want him to walk her down the aisle on her wedding day, Ben would blame Emily for turning the children against him.

'And clearly, divorce is easier for women,' he went on.

'How so?' She wasn't sure the divorced women she knew would agree.

'Traditionally, men have found it hard to reach out and ask for help. Women surround themselves with support networks built from other women, so when something goes wrong in their lives, it's easy for them to access what they need. Men's friendships tend to be built around work, or specific hobbies and events.'

'Yes, that's true.' He had a point. 'They're not as good at keeping in touch with their friends either.' When she first met James he had lots of mates – a gang from school, a smattering from university, a few at work who he'd have the occasional pint with, a weekly five-a-side football game. But as they got deeper into parenthood, his social circle had dwindled while hers had expanded to incorporate mums from toddler groups and later, the school gate. As the children got older and needed them less, she had taken up new hobbies – yoga, a walking club – whilst James said he was too old for any of the sports he'd enjoyed as a younger man and too tired to learn anything new. He never phoned or texted his old friends and they were lucky if they saw each other once a year. At his funeral, she had overheard the remaining group vowing to meet up more regularly, but it was too late for James.

'Exactly!' Ben leaned forward, animated by a zealot's passion. 'They're so busy keeping up with all these expectations of what a man should be – strong, a provider – that they let other things, like friends and their own mental health, go by the wayside.'

'There might be something in that,' Sara admitted. Perhaps she had misjudged Ben. He had a point about men's and women's friendships – Angela and Helen had their faults but she knew they would be there for her no matter what. After she lost James,

they had quietly stepped up in their own ways, Helen bringing round food night after night and Angela keeping up a constant stream of messages and what Sara thought were supposed to be comforting quotes and memes, even if they sometimes missed the mark. 'I think I read somewhere that the single largest cause of death for men under fifty is suicide, which is shocking.'

'Yes, it is shocking. I'm so glad you agree. I've come across some opposition to my views on dates before.'

'Really?' said Sara. 'Surely nobody thinks the suicide of young men is a good thing.'

'No, but it's this idea that the pendulum has swung too far the other way.'

'What pendulum?'

'Feminism,' Ben said as if it should have been evident that they were talking about this all along.

'Oh, I see.' It was a pity, because she hadn't had dinner and a moment ago she'd been eyeing up the menu chalked on the board behind the bar. Fish and chips, maybe, or the shin of beef, although come to think of it she didn't know what form that would take. Did cows have shins? There couldn't be much meat on them.

'I don't have a problem with it, as such,' he went on. 'If you called it Equalism, I could get on board with it. Everybody should have equal rights, not just women.'

'I think the point is that historically women have been disadvantaged in almost every way, so feminism has been a matter of redressing that balance.'

'Historically, sure, but not anymore. Men are at a massive disadvantage in today's society.'

'What about the women in Afghanistan who can't go out in public without a male relative? Or in the UAE where a woman who reports a rape is running the risk of being criminalised for extramarital sex?' Sara had read a long-form article in the *New York Times* about it just the other day. 'Go to one of those places and tell me the world's not heavily weighted in favour of men.'

'That's completely different. I'm talking about Western society, not those backward type of places.'

There was so much wrong with what he was saying, she almost didn't know where to start.

'There's still plenty of inequality in this country.' She knew it was pointless, that she would never get through to him, but she ploughed on regardless. 'Men still outearn women, they outnumber them in positions of political power and in the boardroom. And women are still doing the lion's share of the domestic drudgery.' It was the mental load more than the scrubbing of the bathroom. Even James, who'd been fairly enlightened for a man of his age, would never have thought to book a dentist appointment or buy a present for a child's birthday.

'Aha, but that's their choice,' he said as if Sara had walked right into his trap. 'The reason women earn less and don't progress at work is because they choose to stay home with their children, upping the pressure on men to be the provider. You can't have it both ways.'

Sara thought about reminding him that moments ago he had told her how Emily had wanted to go back to work, but couldn't because his job was more important – but she couldn't be bothered. She was never going to change his mind, so instead she downed her gin and tonic, said it had been very nice to meet him but she must be going, put her coat on and left.

Ben wasn't overly disappointed, and she didn't feel as low as she had in the past after other bad dates. After those, she would go home and leaf through the old photo albums – their wedding, the boys' babyhood, family holidays – missing James with the same burning intensity as she had when he first died. But somehow she didn't think she would tonight. It took her a while to identify why that should be, but when she did, she knew she must never confess it to Angela: she didn't mind that the date had gone badly – in fact if anything she was pleased – because it cleared the way for Nigel. She had purchased six dozen eggs – free range, the fancy ones with the golden yolks – and they were all firmly in his basket.

Chapter 5

'Is that what you're wearing?' Helen's mother, Sheila, stood behind her, both of them watching in the bedroom mirror as Helen smoothed down the skirt of the fifties-style dusky-pink dress with matching jacket.

'Yes. What do you think?' Helen cursed herself for asking the question, knowing she would never get the validation she so longed for from her mother.

'It's a rather peculiar colour.'

'The colour is my favourite thing about it,' Helen said, surprised and relieved that it was the dress's shade that had been singled out for criticism, instead of one of her own shortcomings. 'Angela said that her bridesmaids wore this colour, so it's appropriate for the silver wedding party too.'

'It washes you out rather,' Sheila went on. Ah. There it was.

'It's a flattering shape though, don't you think?' Helen couldn't help but persist, the way you can't stop your tongue poking at a sore spot on your gum.

'It's certainly very . . . revealing. If that's what you're after.' Sheila adjusted her own high-necked blouse, which was tucked into tailored, forest-green trousers. Her nails were flawless, pearly pink ovals and her white hair was woven into an immaculate chignon.

'Revealing?' The skirt fell to mid-calf. Helen's hands went to the dress's neckline, which rested a good couple of inches above the area that would have shown any cleavage. 'It's not, is it?'

'I don't mean that sort of revealing – although heaven knows nobody wants to see that either,' Sheila said. 'It's this.' She reached forward and pinched the loose skin around Helen's collarbone. 'It's so crepey. Once you get to a certain age, you can't get away with anything other than a high neckline. Brian agrees, don't you?' she demanded, as Brian came in and opened a drawer filled with neatly rolled ties.

'There's something to be said for dressing appropriately for your age,' he said, selecting a purple and black striped tie from the drawer. 'You always do that wonderfully well, Sheila.'

'Thank you, Brian,' she twittered, patting her hair. 'Helen, you're so lucky to have a man who loves you enough to care about these things. Unlike your father, who never paid any attention to my appearance, even before his head got turned by that floozy in the haberdashery shop.'

'Yes, I know,' Helen said hastily, not wanting her mother to get onto her favourite topic, The Floozy from the Haberdashery Shop. 'You wait downstairs if you're ready, and I'll quickly get changed.'

'Good idea,' Brian said. 'And I'm not sure about that lipstick, while you're at it. Too bright against your pasty skin. Come on, Sheila, let's leave Helen to it.'

'You don't get haberdashery shops any more,' Sheila said as he ushered her along the landing, 'and perhaps it's just as well.'

Helen stared miserably at her reflection. A moment ago she'd felt quite good about it. There was no getting away from the fact that she was a fifty-five-year-old woman, but for her age, she'd thought she'd scrubbed up pretty well. Whilst he didn't want her to attract any untoward male attention, it was important to Brian to have a well-kept wife. The fit and flare style of the dress complimented her slim waist and hourglass figure, giving her what she'd thought a rather elegant air. Slowly, she took it off and hung it back in the wardrobe, putting on a plain navy shift dress which fell straight down from its high neck, disguising any hint of a curve. She took a cotton wool pad and doused it in makeup remover, dragging it across her lips, removing all trace of the bright lipstick she'd thought so striking.

In the car, she sat in the back in silence as Sheila prattled away to Brian in the passenger seat, and at Angela and Greg's house she followed them up the garden path, as if they were the couple and she their child.

H.

Brian rang the bell, but when the door opened it wasn't Angela or Greg, but their twenty-three-year-old daughter Lizzie, clad in a cropped vest top, huge, flapping flared jeans and trainers, her hair twisted into a messy knot on top of her head.

'Helen!' she cried in delight, diving between Brian and Sheila to give her an enormous hug. Helen squeezed her back, planning the damage limitation exercise she was going to have to implement at Lizzie prioritising her over Brian.

'This is my mother, Sheila,' she said as Lizzie released her.

'Lovely to meet you.' Lizzie leaned in to kiss her on the cheek. Sheila recoiled. 'And you must be Helen's dad,' she said brightly to Brian, holding out her hand, burned by Sheila's consternation at the over-familiarity of a kiss.

'No!' Helen said in dismay. 'This is my husband, Brian. You – you've met before, I'm sure.' It wasn't the first time this mistake had been made. Once at the pharmacy getting their flu injections, the young nurse had referred to him as 'your father'. He was only five years older than her, but he hadn't aged well, whereas she spent a considerable amount of time and money on skincare. Like Pilates, it was one of the things Brian didn't object to her spending money on, as if her youthful appearance reflected positively on him. Except today it had backfired.

'Oh gosh, sorry,' Lizzie said, mortified. 'I didn't recognise you at first – it's been a few years and I assumed because you and Helen's mum were standing together . . . I didn't look at you properly. I can see now that you're nowhere near old enough. I'm so sorry.'

'That's fine,' said Brian stiffly, a rictus grin firmly plastered to his face. 'Aren't you going to invite us in?'

'Of course, come through.' She led them through to the kitchen, her cheeks flaming. 'Mum!' she called to Angela. 'Helen's here.' As Angela came over and greeted Brian and Sheila, Lizzie turned to Helen, anguished. 'I'm so sorry,' she whispered. 'He looks fuming.'

'Don't worry about it.' Helen knew she would take some flak from Brian later, but Lizzie was the one person she couldn't be cross with. She'd been three years old when Helen first met Angela. Brian and Helen had been trying for a baby for eight years by then, and she was beginning to lose faith in it ever happening. She'd found it painful to be around babies and children – and around their mothers, casually wiping noses and kissing grazed knees better whilst chatting to their friends as if it were the most natural, normal, everyday thing in the world. But the first time she'd met her, Lizzie had come bowling up to her and demanded a story. Put on the spot, Helen had made one up about a little girl called Lizzie who had a pet unicorn. Lizzie didn't leave her side that day, and they'd been close ever since.

Angela had struggled with motherhood – Helen supposed it had been a form of post-natal depression, not that Angela had ever sought a diagnosis or support. She'd been only too happy to help Angela out when she could, looking after Lizzie so Angela could work, and those days remained some of her most cherished memories. She would take her swimming, to the park, up to London to visit the museums, never correcting strangers who referred to her as Lizzie's mother.

'Come and meet my boyfriend,' Lizzie demanded, as Angela took Brian and Sheila over to the island where Greg was vigorously rattling a cocktail shaker.

'I should check if Brian's alright . . .'

'He's fine. Dad's making martinis. I mean, of course he is, at two in the afternoon! Come on.'

'My mother will probably want a cup of tea,' Helen said, looking back over her shoulder as Lizzie dragged her towards a handsome, dark-haired, pale boy sitting on the battered sofa tucked into the corner of the kitchen. Helen felt the usual flicker of envy at how imperfect Angela's house was, with its mismatched cushions and drink rings adorning every surface. Angela never hoovered behind or beneath anything, reasoning that there was no point cleaning things no one would ever see, but it was more of a home than Helen's spotless, sterile house could ever be.

'This is Raf,' Lizzie said. 'Raf, this is my unofficial godmother, Helen.'

'Hello,' Raf said, remaining seated.

There was only room for two on the sofa, so Lizzie and Helen stood awkwardly in front of him.

'Nice to meet you,' Helen said. 'How long have you two been together?'

'Two months,' Lizzie said.

'Gosh, so it's still quite new.'

'Sort of, but it's been a bit of a whirlwind.' Lizzie stole a glance at Raf. 'He won me over!'

'Charming!' Raf said it as if it was a joke, but there was an edge that felt familiar to Helen.

'No, I don't mean it like that.' Lizzie's face fell and she sat down and took his hand. 'I meant . . . I wasn't necessarily looking for a relationship, but when you came along, how could I say no?'

'Aww, that's cute.' Raf kissed her on the forehead.

'Oh look, here's Sara – and she's brought Jonny! How lovely. I didn't know he was coming.' Helen turned to Sara who was coming over with her tall, athletic eldest son Jonny, the spitting image of his father.

'Great – he said he'd be here,' Lizzie said.

'When was that?' Raf asked.

'When was what?' Lizzie asked, confused.

'When did he say that?'

'We were messaging the other day . . .' Raf frowned and she blushed. 'You remember I told you about Jonny and Max. They're like the brothers I never had.'

'Yes, that's right.' Raf's reaction felt disturbingly familiar to Helen and her automatic response was to try and smooth things over. 'We all spent so much time together when the kids were young that they grew up almost like family.'

'I see,' Raf said coldly.

'Lizzie!' Jonny was bearing down on them, all blond hair and broad shoulders. When Lizzie didn't get up to greet him, he stooped down and tried to envelop her in a hug. She submitted to it but kept her distance, her arms rigid like a ballroom dancer maintaining a strong frame.

Helen excused herself, a seed of worry about Lizzie sprouting inside her. Brian and Sheila were talking animatedly, so she went over to the island, which was littered with bottles of spirits and sticky patches where Greg had been too free with the sugar syrup. He was pouring deep pink, frothy cocktails into gold-rimmed cocktail glasses for Sara and Angela.

'Helen!' he said. 'Can I make you a French martini?'

'Not for me, thanks. I'll have a sparkling water, if you've got it.'

'Ooh, this is delicious,' Sara said, taking a huge slurp. 'I'll have Helen's if she doesn't want it.'

'Now,' Angela said officiously, 'you are both coming to this dinner/dance thing to raise money for the hospice next Saturday, aren't you?'

'I don't know, Angela,' Sara said. 'I've got a ticket, so that's the important bit, isn't it? The hospice will still get the money whether I go or not.'

'Why wouldn't you want to come?' Angela regarded Sara hawkishly through her expensive, steel-framed spectacles.

'Everyone else will be in a couple.'

'Nobody cares about that, not at our age! We're not seventeen any more, joined at the hip to our boyfriends. Although, Helen does tend to follow Brian around like a lost lamb . . .'

'No I don't!' Helen said without much conviction.

'But otherwise,' Angela ploughed on, ignoring her, 'I hardly talk to Greg at these things! You'd barely know we were together!'

'But the thing is you *are* together,' Sara said. 'And so are Brian and Helen. You'll arrive together, and you'll go home together. If there's ever a point in the evening where you feel lost and don't have anyone to talk to, you can go and find each other. You have an anchor. And when you get home, you'll get into bed and laugh and gossip about what people were wearing, and what they said to you—'

'You've definitely got the wrong idea about my marriage there,' Angela interjected. 'If I'm not too tired I might pick up my book, and Greg's nose will be buried in YouTube videos about rail design or the collapse of communism or whatever it is he's so devoted to on there.'

'You're missing the point,' Sara said, her voice catching. 'You wouldn't understand. You've been part of a couple since you were . . . what, late twenties? It's exhausting, doing everything on your own.'

'Why don't you hire in some help?' Angela said. 'It's not as if you can't afford it.'

'I'm not talking about practical stuff, although that's hard too – every single thing that has to be done I've either got to do it myself or pay someone to do it. But it's more than that – it's not having somebody to do things with – and to do nothing with. It's not having anybody to help you make decisions. It's going home every single night to an empty house, an empty bed.'

'Sounds bliss,' Angela said. 'Everything exactly where you left it, no snoring keeping you awake – doesn't it, Helen?'

'It does rather,' Helen said, shooting a guilty look at Brian on the other side of the room. She had never lived alone, or even with friends, having gone straight from her mother's house to Brian's.

'Well, it isn't,' Sara said shortly. 'The world is set up for couples. Everything is easier when you're a pair. Things are cheaper: holidays, trips and social occasions are designed for two, and people know where to put you, mentally. When I was half of Sara and James, my social status was totally different to

Sara the Widow's. And James may not have been perfect, but he was there, pouring me a glass of wine at the end of a hard day and rubbing my feet on the sofa while I told him about it.'

'Sorry, I didn't mean to be flippant.' Angela had the good grace to be a little shamefaced. She should be more understanding of Sara. Along with Helen, Sara was one of the few people who understood that at her core Angela was quite insecure. 'Come to the hospice fundraiser though, it'll be fun. You might meet someone! I'll put my matchmaking hat on and sniff out all the single men and parade them in front of you.'

'Oh, alright.' There was never any real point standing up against what Angela wanted. She always got her way in the end. 'A parade, you say? Will they all be in costume?'

'They'll be in black tie, which is even better. I think you really get the measure of a man when you see him in evening dress.'

'Greg looks fabulous in black tie,' Sara said. 'He was so dapper at your fiftieth birthday.'

'Was he? What did we do?'

'Angela!' Sara said. 'It wasn't even six years ago. We went to that restaurant with the chef's table . . . you know . . .'

'In town?' Angela said.

'No,' Helen said. 'It's up the road . . . what's it called . . .'

'God knows,' Angela said. 'If you want something remembered, best not to ask a menopausal woman.'

'If it's boiling rage you're after, no problem,' Sara said. 'Or someone to lie awake at three a.m. listing pet peeves, faults, foibles and worries both major and minor, I am your woman. But if you held me up at gunpoint, I could not tell you the name of that restaurant that I have been to several times and that I drive past on a near daily basis.'

They all giggled.

'What are you laughing about?' Sheila popped up at Helen's elbow, placing her mug of tea on the island and looking disapprovingly at the cocktails.

'The dreaded menopause and associated brain fog,' Angela said.

'Oh, that,' Sheila said dismissively. 'We didn't have all that in my day.'

'You didn't have the menopause?' Sara asked.

'We had the change of life, but we didn't make all this fuss about it like you do. We were just glad all that business was over and done with. It's different for Helen, of course.' She nodded in her daughter's direction.

'What do you mean?' Sara asked, puzzled.

'You two got something out of it, didn't you?' Sheila said, as if it should be obvious. 'But this one didn't have children, did she? Such a waste. I would have loved to have grandchildren.'

Angela and Sara were taken aback. They had been there with Helen through all those hopeful, despairing years, for every late period and negative pregnancy test, every 'there's always next month', until the decision was taken that there would be no more months, no more hope. A different kind of life.

Helen, however, was thoroughly unsurprised. Her mother had never bothered to hide her disappointment at not being a grandmother, and she was used to feeling like it was all her fault. Instinctively she looked around for Brian, in case he was involved in anything she needed to step into or manage. Lizzie had disappeared and Brian was sitting on the sofa with Raf, the two of them deep in conversation.

Chapter 6

'I'll go to the bar – what are we all having?'

Despite having been silent in the taxi on the way there, Brian was now full of bonhomie. The hotel bar was crammed with mostly middle-aged people in varying degrees of finery and the air was abuzz with laughter and conversation.

'Greg – pint of something?'

'Yes, bitter please.'

Helen tried not to compare Greg, sleek and sharp in his suit that although Angela said was off the peg looked like it had been made for him, with Brian, in his made-to-measure tuxedo which somehow still managed to be ill-fitting. The cummerbund was a mistake, she felt, trying not to let her eyes stray to it lest he guessed what she was thinking. He had a horrible knack of knowing what was on her mind.

'What about you, girls?'

'Girls?' Angela, resplendent in full-length black taffeta with a lace overlay, turned on him ferociously. 'We're hardly girls.'

'He doesn't mean anything by it,' Helen said, trying to maintain an easy smile. 'It's just an expression.'

'A patronising, infantilising one,' Angela said. 'Don't you agree, Sara?'

'I can't get that bothered about it, to be honest,' Sara said, adjusting the bodice of her floral dress, which had become mysteriously tighter since she last wore it. She had thought it was rather pretty in the dim light of her bedroom earlier, but now it felt all wrong, more suited to a summer wedding than a black tie evening event. Even Helen was more appropriately dressed in her plain navy shift dress, boxy and high at the neck. 'I'd probably say I was going for drinks with the girls if I was meeting you two.'

'I'm pretty sure I've heard you do the same,' Greg said to Angela.

'Exactly!' Helen said gratefully.

'No need to fight my battles for me, Helen,' Brian said in a manner the others might have described as genial, but to Helen's trained ear was anything but. 'I'm a big boy – or can I not say that, either, Angela?'

'You can call yourself whatever you like as long as you hurry up and get us a drink. Champagne, I think? The hotel are donating a percentage of their bar takings to the hospice so it's all in a good cause. We may as well get a bottle – you'll have some won't you, gir—' She stopped herself.

'Girls, were you going to say?' Brian said sweetly.

'Touché.' Angela laughed. 'Just go to the bar.'

'Your wish is my command.' He threaded his way through the throng. Helen breathed a sigh of relief. If things had gone wrong this early in the evening, she didn't know how she would have got through the rest of it. It was exhausting, always being on the alert for a remark that Brian could take the wrong way. She knew the others thought she was pandering to him, but she saw it as smoothing his way, making his life easier, and she was happy to do it. He could be so wonderful to her, did so much for her, and put up with so much. Just before he reached the bar, he stopped and greeted a tall, elegant man in an exquisitely tailored dinner jacket.

'Oh God, it's Patrick,' she said, more to herself than anyone else, but Angela caught the words.

'Who's Patrick?'

'Chair of the golf club committee. Brian's obsessed with him – hero worships him almost, although I'm not entirely sure the feeling's mutual. Oh – don't tell Brian I said that, will you?' Helen wished she could swallow her words. She should never have been so indiscreet. Brian would hate it if he thought Angela had seen anything of his soft underbelly.

'Of course not,' Angela said.

'What's *she* doing here?' Sara shot evils at an attractive, dark-haired, olive-skinned woman encased in a column of flowing fuchsia silk who stood alone on the other side of the room.

Angela followed her gaze.

'Oh! Leila. She's a widow, like you. I think her husband died in the hospice. Have a heart, Sara.'

'I do. I just don't want her stealing my man. Alright, alright, I'm joking!' She put out a hand to ward off Angela's reply. 'I know he's not my man and I've only spoken to him for five minutes, and most importantly I must not put all my eggs in his basket. You don't need to tell me again.'

'Who is she?' Helen asked. She often found herself chasing her tail in conversations between the three of them, having missed some vital component.

'You'd know if you hadn't flaked out on our coffee last week,' Angela said, poking her.

'Sorry, I got held up in traffic, I think it was . . .' What excuse had she given?

49

'Yeah, yeah,' Angela said dismissively.

'Don't worry about it,' Sara said. 'Leila is one of Angela's clients. She was next to me at the speed dating and she got a match with the one guy I really liked – Nigel, his name is. As you can see, she's deeply ugly.'

The three women's eyes swivelled in Leila's direction. Her neck was swan-like, her features impossibly delicate, as she turned her head back and forth around the room, the soft lighting bouncing off her unfeasibly shiny hair.

'He matched with you too,' Angela said. 'That's how dating works – you try people out for size. She's all on her own, I'm going to invite her over.'

Before Sara could protest, she waved her arms to attract Leila's attention. Leila's eyes widened in recognition and she weaved her way through the crowds towards them.

'Angela, thank God!' she said. 'I was beginning to think I'd have to spend the whole night alone.'

'Lovely to see you.' Angela gave her a brief hug. 'This is Helen and Sara.'

Leila held out a soft, elegant hand with deep red, manicured nails. Sara gave it the briefest shake with her own pudgy, bare-nailed one.

'I know you from somewhere, don't I?' Leila said. 'Oh, I know it's . . .' she mouthed the last part of her sentence '*the dating agency.*' They were all of a generation for whom dating agencies had, years ago, carried an unmistakeable stigma, and the shadow of it still lingered.

'That's right,' Sara said. 'I was at the speed dating event the other week.'

'Sorry, I didn't know if I should say in front of everyone. Let's have a debrief later!' she said chummily, although filtered through

Sara's internal translator, Leila was expressing dismissive relief that Sara, in her too tight, flouncy and busily patterned outfit, which could only be described as a frock, was no real competition in the dating stakes.

'And Helen, is it?' Leila said. 'Nice to meet you. Are you here on your own too?'

'No, I'm with my husband Brian, he's at the bar.' They all looked over. Brian appeared to be berating a member of the bar staff, a young woman with her hair woven in a burnished gold plait around her head. Patrick, looking uncomfortable in the extreme, was standing next to him. Helen's chest tightened.

'And what do you do?' Leila asked.

'I don't work,' Helen said.

'Lucky you! Have you taken early retirement?'

'No, I haven't worked for a long time. I was a veterinary nurse originally.'

'How wonderful! You must have loved that.'

'I did, but when Brian and I married I moved here to Tunbridge Wells as he already had a house and I was living with my mother, so I . . . I had to leave that job. I worked in recruitment for a while, which is where I met Sara actually, and after that I spent some time volunteering at an animal shelter but then . . . life got busy, so I gave it up.'

'Kids, I suppose?' Leila said sympathetically. 'It's not easy juggling it all, is it?'

'No.' Helen flushed. 'We don't have children.' When she was younger she had thought that once her child-bearing years were past, people would stop asking, but it seemed it was endless. The next stage would be grandchildren no doubt, a brand new layer of unexpected hurt waiting to assault her.

'Gosh, sorry, I shouldn't have assumed. So veterinary nurse, animal shelter . . . you must love animals.'

'Yes, I do.' She had a natural affinity with them – had been known, in fact, when she worked at the vet's, for being able to calm even the most distressed and anxious pet.

'What do you have? I've got a cavapoo called Dennis, he's a clingy nightmare but I adore him.'

'We don't have any pets. Brian thinks . . . that is, they're such a tie.' She had thought that after the wedding the next stage would be a pet, but Brian had suggested they wait until their (at this stage imaginary) children were older before introducing pets. By the time it became apparent that the children were going to remain imaginary, he said pets were such a big responsibility – they wouldn't be able to jet off on holiday whenever they wanted, or go to a nice restaurant without arranging a dog-sitter. She'd agreed, as she agreed with everything he suggested, but she couldn't help but notice that they rarely did jet off on holiday, at either short or long notice, and she could count the number of times they'd been to a posh restaurant together on the fingers of one hand. Brian said her cooking was so good, why did they need to go out to eat?

'Oh, I see,' Leila said. 'Yes, they can be.'

'I'm Greg, Angela's husband.' Sensing the slightly awkward pause in their conversation, he stepped forward and shook Leila's hand.

'Ooh! You're so handsome!' Leila said. 'It's frightfully reassuring to see that Angela's snaffled herself a nice man, hopefully she can find one for me. Heaven knows I've done a bad job of picking for myself so far. They always seem so lovely at the start, but sooner or later I find out they're an alcoholic or a compulsive gambler, or married with five kids.'

'Yes, we need to have a chat some time about spotting red flags,' Angela said. 'Although hopefully we've done our due diligence at the agency and there shouldn't be any of that with our daters.'

'I'm back – finally!' Brian handed Greg his pint and took a sip from the large glass of red wine in his other hand. 'Patrick's here,' he said excitedly to Helen. 'Did you see? Put it on the table,' he barked at the woman with the plait who was trailing behind him. In one hand she carried an ice bucket containing an open bottle of champagne, and in the other a white linen napkin and three flutes. 'Not there!' he snapped as she went to put them down next to her. 'On this table here, where we're actually standing.'

'Sorry.' Her face flamed as she put them on the high table in the centre of the group. 'Would you like me to pour it?'

'Certainly not,' Brian said, with a laugh. 'It'd be all over the floor. You get back.'

She scurried away, leaving a slightly awkward silence in her wake.

'Who's this lady?' Brian asked, looking at Leila appreciatively.

'I'm Leila, a friend of Angela's.'

Brian took her outstretched hand and stepped forward, planting a kiss on each cheek. 'Delighted to meet you. Helen, do you want to pour the champagne?'

She lifted the bottle out of the ice bucket, wiping the bottom with the napkin to prevent it dripping. She began to pour into the first glass.

'Tilt the glass,' Brian said.

'Sorry.' She tilted it and prepared to pour.

'You hold it by the stem, not the bowl,' he said. 'How many times?'

'We don't care, Brian,' Sara said. 'Just give me a drink!'

'Of course,' he said. 'Sorry.'

Helen passed brimming glasses to Sara and Angela and then poured a third.

'Would you like some, Leila?' Brian asked.

'That would be very nice. I'll go to the bar and ask for an extra glass.'

'No need – take this one.' He plucked the remaining glass from Helen's hand. 'Helen can get another.'

'Oh – yes, right.' Helen set off for the bar. At the far end, behind the bar, a man in his late thirties stood polishing glasses. He wore a striped waistcoat and had long hair tied up in a bun and an elaborate moustache. He put down his tea towel and started towards her. Helen turned and leant against the bar, pretending to root in her handbag. Out of the corner of her eye, she saw him stop and serve someone else. She turned back and the young woman who had carried the champagne emerged from the back room behind the bar.

'Could we have another flute, please?'

'Sure.' She reached up and grabbed a glass, handing it to Helen.

'Thanks. Sorry if my husband was rude, he's been working very hard recently and he's a bit stressed.'

'That's OK,' the young woman said. 'I'm used to it, working in hospitality. He's by no means the worst I've had.'

Back with the group, Helen poured herself a small glass of champagne, taking care to tilt the glass and hold it by the stem, and joined Angela and Sara who were deep in discussion. She tuned out of what they were saying and listened to the conversation across the table, where the two men stood either side of Leila.

'As a financial advisor I come into contact with a lot of very wealthy people,' Brian was saying, 'and there's one thing I notice about all of them – do you know what it is?'

'No, what?' Leila said.

'Short arms, long pockets!'

'I'm sorry?'

'Can't reach their pockets – tight as anything. That's how they got so wealthy!'

'I see.' Leila gave a polite chuckle.

'I think it's more to do with the fundamental inequality of our society which sees the rich get richer and the poor trapped in a vicious circle of unemployment and depression,' Greg said. Helen had forgotten that he read the *Guardian*.

'Good grief, lighten up.' Brian had never liked Greg, not trusting a man who didn't play golf.

'No, you're absolutely right,' Leila said earnestly. 'I've done a lot of research on child poverty for my work, and it's harder than it's ever been to escape it.'

Helen took in Brian's crestfallen expression as Greg and Leila embarked upon an impassioned discourse about routes out of poverty that excluded him completely. She willed her eyes to stay away from his hands as they adjusted the ill-advised cummerbund. He would be upset if he thought she was judging his appearance – and fair enough too. Anyone would be the same. She had always known that you can't compare the inside of your relationship to the outside of other peoples'. Every marriage had its challenges, and one thing she had never doubted was the strength of Brian's love for her. He showed her every day.

Chapter 7

The volume level in the room had risen in direct correlation to the amount of alcohol being consumed. Glasses clinked and regular roars of laughter burst forth from one particularly lively group. They had taken their seats for dinner and delicious smells wafted through from the kitchen every time a waiter went in or out through the swing doors. Angela had managed to get Leila moved onto their table. It hadn't been a problem because they'd paid for a table for six anyway. Sara could have invited someone, but she didn't know who she would have chosen. She knew who she wouldn't have chosen though – the gorgeous woman who was planning a date with the potential love of Sara's life. Yet here they were.

Helen was fussing around Brian like an overindulgent mother with a particularly demanding toddler. He only had to look askance at a smudge of grease on his wine glass and she was calling the waiter over to bring a new one. Sara didn't know how either of them could stand it.

Leila and Greg were still embroiled in their private, animated debate, which was becoming increasingly voluble and had moved on to the merits of the various judges on *Strictly Come Dancing*. Leila kept leaning in to touch Greg's arm, laughing loudly and overlong at every joke he made. She wasn't crossing any lines, but it wasn't a stretch to say she was flirting with him. With any other couple, Sara might have wondered if Angela would be looking at this askance but she and Greg were so solid, they'd probably be laughing about it in bed when they got home.

Angela took her phone out of her bag and tapped away at it below the table.

'No phones at the table,' Sara said, only half joking. Angela's phone was basically an extension of her hand.

'Just responding to a couple of work emails.'

'It's Saturday night, surely they can wait?' Sara said.

'It's a dating emergency!' Greg said, having overheard Sara in a momentary lull in his and Leila's conversation. 'What shade of lipstick should I wear? Is it polite or over-keen to be ten minutes early?'

'Shut up, you,' Angela said without malice, putting her phone away. 'It's alright for you early retirees, nothing to do but pursue your many hobbies.'

Recently retired at the tender age of fifty-eight, Greg had taken up a variety of hobbies with an enthusiasm he had never shown for his career in railway design.

'What hobbies are they?' Leila asked.

'You name it, Greg does it,' Angela replied. 'He volunteers at the repair café in town, then there's ballroom dancing . . .'

'Ballroom dancing? Oh, I'd love to try that!' Leila said.

'I'll send you the details of the class I go to,' Greg said.

'He also spends a lot of time on his meat,' Angela said.

'Goodness me.' Leila smiled uncertainly.

'Yes – procuring it from obscure vendors, hanging it, smoking it, barbecueing it.'

Leila was spared having to respond to this by the waiters arriving at their table and presenting each of them with an elegant arrangement of asparagus spears, parma ham and a perfectly round poached egg.

'This looks lovely,' Helen said. 'Imagine poaching all those eggs, I can't even manage one.'

'You can say that again,' Brian said. 'It does look nice, although . . .'

Sara caught the panic that flashed across Helen's face. Brian touched the rim of the plate with a fingertip.

'As I thought. What is the bloody point of going to all that effort to make a warm starter only to serve it on a cold plate?'

'Shall I send it back?' Helen twisted round, searching for a member of staff.

'Don't be ridiculous,' Brian said. 'I'm not saying it has to be sent back – please don't make me out to be some kind of tyrant. I'm simply saying that if you're going to serve hot food, the plate has to be hot otherwise by the time it gets to the diners, it's getting cold.'

Leila picked up a spear and dipped it into her egg. The yolk oozed out lazily across her plate. She took a bite.

'It's fine. Not piping hot, but definitely not cold. I suggest we dig in. Unless you did want to complain?'

'No, absolutely not,' Brian said. 'I don't know why Helen suggested it.' He attacked the poor poached egg viciously, stabbing the asparagus into it with unnecessary force. Helen reddened. It would be easy to conclude, Sara thought, that Brian was, in fact, some kind of tyrant, although she did suspect he would calm down a bit if Helen simply made less of a fuss of him.

'How are you finding dating, Sara?' Leila asked.

'You know, up and down,' Sara said stiffly. She thought the etiquette was that they wouldn't talk about this glaring thing they had in common over the dinner table. 'Of course, Kiss, Marry, Avoid is very good,' she added loyally, nodding towards Angela. 'I've done some online dating in the past but that was very hit and miss. Mostly miss.'

'Tell me about it.' Leila rolled her eyes. 'At least with the speed dating it's harder for men to pretend to be something they aren't.'

'Yes,' Sara agreed. 'Plus it weeds out those men who frequent the apps but have no interest in meeting up.'

'Ha, yes, the ones who won't commit to a coffee but are dying to know what you're wearing,' Leila said.

'I always reply very literally to those,' Sara said. '*Cargo trousers, walking boots, a fleece.*'

'That's brilliant, I'm going to start doing that,' Leila said, giggling.

'They're all married,' Angela said. 'They're on the apps to inject some excitement into their dull lives. We do our very best to ensure we don't have any of those at the agency.'

'Then there are the ones who do want to meet up, but for an ONS, NSA,' Leila continued.

'A what?' Helen said, bewildered.

'One Night Stand, No Strings Attached,' Leila said. 'There's a whole new world of acronyms these days – gone are the days of seeking someone with a GSOH. Now it's all MBA and FWB.'

'Married But Available and Friends With Benefits,' Sara translated for the table. Brian winced as if he'd trodden in something unpleasant.

'I also have to deal with a side order of casual racism,' Leila went on. 'I can't tell you how many times a man has told me in thrilled tones that he's never dated anyone Indian before. I mean, apart from the fact that I'm British and my heritage is Iranian, not Indian, why do they think telling me that they're basically dating me as part of a fetish is going to be attractive to me?'

'How ghastly,' Sara said.

'And the age ranges they put down!' Leila went on. 'There was this one guy, Sebastian, who I met early in my dating journey. I'd been messaging him for a few weeks.'

'Rookie mistake,' Sara said. 'Always meet as early as you can – no point wasting time messaging someone who makes your skin crawl in person.'

'Absolutely – that's what we always say at the agency,' Angela piped up. Sara reminded herself that Leila represented Angela's bread and butter.

'He said he was fifty-nine, he looked handsome in his photo and more than anything else, he knew how to use punctuation correctly.'

'*Swoon*,' Sara said.

'Is that a big thing, then?' Greg asked.

'Oh yes,' Sara said. 'There's so much bad spelling and moronic text speak out there, it's the biggest ick ever.'

'I'd do well in that case,' Greg said. 'I'm a stickler for the correct usage of a semicolon.'

'That's true, you are,' Angela admitted with a grin.

'Anyway,' Leila went on, 'I was so excited getting ready for our first date – I pulled out all the stops. But when I got there, I swear he was seventy-five if he was a day, and so different from the out-of-date photo he'd used on the app I wasn't even sure it was him.'

'Yup, been there,' Sara said.

'But I thought, maybe I shouldn't be so ageist, let's see how it goes, keep an open mind. He insisted on getting a bottle of wine rather than two glasses – another mistake because then I was trapped there. We were about a third of the way down the bottle when he referred to Elton John as a poofter. It was noisy in there and I thought I must have misheard him, so I asked him to repeat himself. "You know, a poofter. A shirt-lifter," he said. "We're supposed to be alright with it now, but it's not natural, is it?" I nearly choked on my rosé!'

'The assumption that you share their outdated views is almost as offensive as the bigotry itself,' Sara said. 'I don't know why we're bothering. These men are either married, coming out of a horrendous divorce or have a personal issue so massive that it's no surprise they're single.'

'Hey!' Angela said. 'That's not true. I've got lots of nice, genuine men on my books who've been unlucky in love – or been widowed, like you two. And they have stories to tell too – it's not only men who are a nightmare.'

'Fair enough,' Leila said. 'I look forward to meeting some of these wonderful guys.'

Was she thinking of Nigel? It was a shame Sara had cast Leila as the villain in her story, because she found herself warming to her. It would be nice to have a single pal in the same situation. Angela and Helen were all very well but they had no idea what it was like to date as a middle-aged woman, despite Angela working in the industry. Most of her other friends were coupled up with varying degrees of happiness. But unfortunately Leila had unknowingly disqualified herself from the position of Sara's single friend by virtue of her romantic interest in Nigel.

'I do think you're both brave,' Helen said. 'Putting yourselves out there like that. If I ever found myself in that situation I don't think I could do it.'

Married friends always said this to Sara, the implication being that finding yourself single in later life was a fate worse than death.

'Charming!' Brian said with ostensible jollity. 'What's happened to me in this fictional scenario? Have you upgraded to a younger model – like that young buck behind the bar with the ridiculous hair?'

'I don't think he'd be interested in me,' Helen said with a nervous laugh. 'I'm almost old enough to be his mother.'

'Almost? That's interesting. Also interesting that you instantly knew which man I was talking about.'

'There's only one man behind the bar,' Sara said with the absurd feeling that Helen needed to be defended. Brian couldn't actually be upset about this.

'I was thinking more if I was . . . widowed,' Helen said.

'So you're killing me off now!' He looked around the table as if for confirmation that he was being roundly abused. Greg was deliberately impassive. Angela's attention was drawn to a row going on at a neighbouring table. Leila was clearly wondering what the hell she'd got herself into, and wishing she'd stayed put on her original table, even if it was populated by total strangers. 'Good to know you're lining up potential successors.'

'No, I said I *wasn't*,' Helen said, her voice strained. 'I wouldn't. I love you. I would never want anyone else if I was to lose you.'

'I hope you're not implying I didn't love James,' Sara said. 'And I'm sure Leila loved her husband too.'

'Of course,' Leila said. 'I felt desperately guilty when I started dating, like I was cheating on Ali.'

'Me too.' Sara forgot for a moment that Leila was her nemesis. 'Did you ever dream that he had come back and was upset at you for meeting other men?'

'Did I? I still do, regularly! I had one the other night where I was on a date that was going really well, and Ali walked into the bar and came and joined us at the table. He didn't speak, just stared at me accusatorily.'

'So you see it's hard enough, Helen,' Sara said, 'without our friends judging us too.'

'I wasn't judging! I only meant for me I don't think it would be the right thing, and I know that Brian wouldn't want it.'

'What on earth do you mean?' Brian said. 'I've never said that.'

'Not in so many words, but you do sometimes say when it's a celebrity who's lost her husband . . . "she didn't wait long did she, her husband's still warm in his grave", that kind of thing . . . he didn't say that about you, Sara, of course.' She was like a cornered animal, her eyes darting back and forth between Sara, Leila and Brian.

'I don't recall saying anything of the kind.' Brian's voice was like ice. 'Please be assured, Sara – and you too, Leila – that I would never think less of anyone for seeking love again after a bereavement, despite what my wife has suggested.'

'No, I – sorry,' she said to Brian, and then 'sorry' again to Sara and Leila in a whisper. 'I think you're both wonderful and Brian does too.'

'No need to speak for me,' Brian said with a mirthless smile. 'I think you've done enough of that for one evening.'

Chapter 8

'I'm sure they don't think badly of you – they know you never said those things about *them*, of course you didn't, you wouldn't, you'd never say something like that about our friends, never . . .' Helen twittered.

'You're sure, are you?' Brian hissed under his breath so that the taxi driver, who was singing along quietly to the Beatles on the radio, wouldn't hear. 'I saw the way they were looking at me. How dare you tell them I said those things about widows not being allowed to seek love again? I never said any such thing.'

He certainly hadn't phrased it so prettily, but the substantive point had been the same. Shameless was the word he had used, Helen thought, and possibly even hussy. And it hadn't been an anonymous celebrity, it had been Sara herself he had denigrated. She had patently never loved James, he had said, if she could move on so easily, and wasn't there something unseemly about a woman of her age seeking out male company? The accompanying sneer had let Helen know in no uncertain terms that it was horizontal company he was referring to. The silly thing was she hadn't minded when he said it – she'd liked it, in a way. It was reassuring to hear that he didn't like the thought of her meeting someone else, even if he was dead. It was his way of showing how much he loved her.

'No, I'm sorry, I know you didn't,' she said, wondering whether to put a pleading hand on his thigh. There had been times where a sexual advance in a situation like this had saved the day, but an equal number where it had made things worse. She decided to risk it.

Brian looked at her hand in disgust, as if she had defecated on his trousers.

'Is that your answer to everything?' he said. 'Do you think that's the best way for you to seek forgiveness for lying about me to our friends? You made me look a fool – no, worse, a monster – and in front of Patrick too. He might have overheard!'

Helen withdrew her hand, a sheen of sweat coating her face.

'No, no. You made it very clear. *I* made it very clear – that I had misspoken, I mean, that you hadn't said those things. They believed me, I know they did.'

'Believed you? Are you seriously still persisting in this fantasy that I said those things? It's no surprise your friends don't like me, if this is how you've been misrepresenting me.'

'They do like you. I haven't, honestly. Please, Brian, I'm sorry.'

'That's enough.'

He looked fixedly out of the car window. Helen stared anxiously out of her side – he'd be even angrier if she looked at him. She was almost holding her breath, worried that any noise she made – a sigh, an exhalation of any kind, would be miscon- strued as a sign of rebellion. Under a streetlight, a young woman was entwined with her boyfriend. He bent to kiss her, his hands snaking possessively round her waist. She was about the age Helen had been when she and Brian got married. Helen had an unaccountable urge to jump from the moving car and drag her away from him, telling her to run far away and never look back.

When they arrived home, Brian handed over the fare.

'Thanks very much,' the taxi driver said glumly, surveying in dismay the exact amount shown on the meter, and not a penny more.

Brian, seated on the pavement side, stepped smartly out. Helen scooted over the back seat to get out after him, but he slammed the door shut in her face, so she returned to her own side and prepared to get out into the road, which after all was very quiet at that time of night.

'Are you alright?' the taxi driver asked.

'Yes,' she said, puzzled.

'Only your . . . husband, is it?'

'Yes.'

'Seemed a bit angry with you. I mean, I see all sorts in the cab, and I dare say you're fine, just had a rough night, but I always think it's worth asking, in case I'm the only person who does.'

Helen blinked back tears. 'That's very kind.' She tried to keep her voice absolutely steady. 'In this case you've nothing to worry about, we're both a little tired, that's all, but I appreciate your concern.'

'You're the boss,' he said equably. 'Have a good night.'

'You too.'

Helen climbed out into the road and walked around the back of the taxi.

'Been out on the razz?' Their next-door neighbour Moira, barefoot and wrapped in a velour dressing gown under which Helen suspected she was naked, opened her front gate and dragged her wheelie bin out into the road. They were about the same age, but she seemed to Helen to live the life of a much younger person, always off on nights out or weekends away with her friends. Brian had always disapproved of her.

'Well, not really . . . we've been at a fundraiser for the hospice,' Helen said as Brian unlocked the door and went into the house without acknowledging her. 'I'd better get in,' she said. 'Sorry about Brian, he's a bit tired.'

'That's fine.' Moira looked at her curiously. 'Is everything alright?'

'Yes, of course! Why wouldn't it be?'

She hurried after Brian into the house, putting her shoes neatly in the shoe cabinet and hanging her coat on its allotted peg. She could hear him running the cold tap in the kitchen for his night water, so she joined him, helping herself to a glass from the cupboard and waiting behind him at the sink as he filled his own. Once he had turned off the tap, he stood there at the sink, perfectly still, unspeaking, with his back to her. A creeping tendril of dread unfurled inside her. It wasn't unusual for Brian to choose not to speak to her, but this silence had a sharp edge to it that bit into her flesh.

'Brian? Could I get some water, please?' she said, tremulously.

'Thirsty work, was it?' he said, still facing away from her.

'The benefit? I suppose so. I've had a bit too much champagne.' She attempted a chuckle, although there was nothing funny about this. It was a familiar game Brian was playing. She should have known there was nothing she could do to pull it back, yet every time she was foolish enough to hope that there was something she could say to stop the tide.

'Not the benefit. Your little chat.'

'What chat? With who?'

'Your friend in the taxi.'

For one wild moment, Helen thought she was losing her mind. There hadn't been anyone in the taxi with them, had there? The others had all made their own ways home. Unless . . .

'Do you mean the taxi driver?'

As soon as the words were out of her mouth, she knew they had come out wrong, with a laugh behind them at the absurdity of the accusation. He whirled to face her.

'Is something funny? Did you and he have a good laugh about me after I'd got out of the car? You were nattering away very happily.'

Her mind raced. It had only been a matter of seconds, but there was no way she could reveal the true nature of her discussion with the taxi driver, centring as it did around an implied criticism of Brian. For a second, she considered whether it would be more palatable for Brian if she and the driver had been engaging in a flirtation.

'He was just . . .' She groped around for anything that would sound vaguely plausible. 'He noticed I'd dropped my phone in the footwell.'

'Really? Your phone?'

His eyes burned with a fearsome intensity.

'Yes.' She reached down to her silver evening bag, as if showing him the phone would be stone-cold proof of her faithfulness. The clasp was shaped like a shell. As she popped it open, her stomach dropped and she had the sensation of falling, fast, as if she'd been pushed from a cliff. Her phone wasn't in there. She hadn't taken it – Brian had suggested she didn't bother as they were going to be together all evening and he had his with him. How could she have been so stupid as to forget?

'Where is it?' Brian asked.

'Sorry, I meant to say he thought I'd dropped my phone in the footwell, but it wasn't mine.' The glow from her face could have lit the gas stove. 'It must have been whoever was in the cab before us.'

'Why are you lying to me?' he asked, almost conversationally, as if he was asking her how her day had been.

'I'm not.' She made a heroic attempt to control her breathing, keeping it slow and steady instead of allowing her lungs to take the agitated little puffs they wanted to. 'Shall we go to bed? It's late.'

69

'You'd like that, wouldn't you?' he said, his words slurring, their faces inches apart. She strove not to wince at the stale garlic and wine fumes that emanated from him. 'Go to bed with your boring old husband, thinking about the taxi driver – or would it be the barman from the hotel? Who knows with you?'

She was caught between the twin traps of Brian's nonsensical accusations. If she agreed to sex with him, he would accuse her of using it to fantasise about other men. If she refused, he would bring out his age-old complaint that she was frigid, unfeeling, not a proper wife. Not that she had ever seriously refused him. She was frightened that if she did, he would disregard her and do it anyway and she had never been ready to face up to what that meant. Instead she had acquiesced and feigned enjoyment and done her best to dissociate herself from the proceedings.

'I'm going to go up,' she said, finally admitting defeat. She couldn't influence what happened next, only endure it. She left the room and climbed the stairs. In the bathroom she removed her makeup and brushed her teeth robotically. In the bedroom, she took off her modest dress and hung it in her section of the wardrobe. Underwear went in the washing basket, as per Brian's rules. If she ever allowed herself to fantasise about living alone, wearing the same bra on two or more consecutive days was one of the highlights. Instinctively she wanted to truss herself up in long-sleeved, high-necked pyjamas, the drawstring tight around her waist, but even if she had a pair it would only be another black mark against her, so she put on a cream silk nightdress and lay on her side, motionless beneath the duvet. As Brian's footsteps ascended the stairs, Helen drew her knees up towards her chest, closed her eyes and prayed that he would believe she had already fallen asleep.

Chapter 9

Sara could hardly believe she was here again, sitting in the same pub, sipping on the same old gin and tonic. She'd been sorely tempted to cancel her date with Steve the Finance/IT/Whatever guy, but one, Angela would have done her nut and two, she wasn't superstitious but if she played along and went on her agreed dates, the universe might make Nigel everything she hoped he was and let things work out between them.

He was late, which wasn't a good start. She saw him now, searching the bar for her and making his way over. He was wearing the same outfit as he had been at the speed dating – band T-shirt, black jeans and leather jacket. He wasn't what she would describe as her usual type, but as Angela would no doubt say, that didn't seem to be working for her, so why not try something different?

'Sorry I'm late, I couldn't find the pub, never been here before.'

'No problem,' she said politely, although these days that couldn't possibly be a valid excuse, with everyone having an interactive map of the world in their pocket.

'Can I get you another?' he asked. When she declined, he went to the bar and ordered a pint of some extravagantly named real ale – it sounded like Bishop's Footmuff but Sara could have misheard. He paid in cash, extracting a large handful of change from his jeans pocket and counting out the exact amount.

'Do you do much dating?' she asked, once they had dealt with the question of whether they were well (very well, thank you, both of them) and asked after each other's days. It was a useful question for weeding out wrong'uns early on.

'A bit,' Steve said. ' I like Kiss, Marry, Avoid because you don't have to have an online presence if you don't want to. I'm not on the apps, of course.' He ran a hand over his close-cropped grey hair.

'Why do you say of course?'

'Do you realise how predatory their privacy practices are?' He leaned towards her across the table as if the apps themselves were lurking in the shadows of the pub, ready to pounce. 'Think about the data you're explicitly sharing with them, for starters. Your gender, sexual orientation, location data, political affilia-tion, religion, hobbies and interests. Then if you're sharing photos or videos they have access to those too.'

'I'm never quite sure why that matters so much,' Sara confessed.

'I see. You're one of those "privacy is gone, deal with it" types.' He nodded knowingly. 'I bet you click "Accept all" on websites multiple times a week, but have you ever read what you're accepting?'

'Well, no.'

'So you don't mind that the dating apps are sharing or selling your personal information, and don't guarantee you the right to delete that data?' He took a swig of his murky ale, warming to his theme. 'You don't mind that they – and when I say they, I mean actual human beings – are reviewing your so-called private direct messages, ostensibly to train their automated tools?'

'I've never given it much thought,' she said weakly.

'Perhaps it's time you did. These platforms don't operate in a vacuum – they work with other companies and services that receive information about you. They collect precise geo-location information about you which can then be leaked and sold, leaving you massively vulnerable to security risks.'

'So what you're saying is, Big Brother is watching me?' Sara tried to inject some levity, but it backfired.

'Absolutely,' he said. 'That book was a pretty accurate prediction of the world we're now living in.'

'I see. How do you know so much about it?'

'I used to be the UK head of data security for one of the top tech companies in the world, before I saw the light.'

'Which one?'

'I'd prefer not to say. If you name some, it'll likely be among them.'

'Google? Facebook, or whatever it's called now – Meta, is it? Amazon? Apple? Microsoft?'

'One of them,' he said. 'Don't ask me to elaborate.'

Sara hadn't been going to. She couldn't care less.

'So you see, I'm alright,' he continued. 'I know all their tricks. I know how to protect my privacy, how to do what I want and need to do online without leaving a trace.' That explained why he hadn't been able to find the pub. 'But you?' he went on. 'They know everything about you. Where you've been, who you've communicated with, what you've watched and searched for online. You've given up all control – all your rights.'

'I dare say you're right,' Sara said placatingly. 'But isn't it too late? The horse has bolted and the stable door is flapping in the wind.'

'You'd be surprised,' he said, revelling in his superior knowledge, as IT experts have been doing since computers were invented. What did these men do before the computer age? Take pleasure in instructing others on how to lay out the animal skins in the cave to best effect, or the best method of lighting the fire? *No no, you don't want to put them by the door. Don't lie the sticks flat, prop them up against each other.* 'I couldn't make you as invisible as me, but I could go a fair way towards achieving it, if you're interested.'

Sara politely declined, and made her excuses as early as she could without seeming unforgivably rude. Steve wasn't as bad as Ben, but he was relentlessly single-minded to the point of obsession about this hobby horse, and she wasn't ready to be consigned to a lifetime of him trotting out his theories on the subject, even if there were some truth to them. Steve was obviously disappointed, but took it well, reminding her that she had the number to his vintage, non-internet-enabled phone, should she ever change her mind.

Walking down the street, she became aware of an older couple who had stopped on the pavement in front of her. The woman said, 'See, I told you we wouldn't be late.'

'Are you kidding me?' the husband said incredulously, as Sara navigated her way around them. 'The only reason we weren't late is because every single thing about our journey went to plan. If one part of it had been in the slightest bit delayed, we would have been late.'

'Well, we weren't though – that should make you happy,' the woman said.

'Happy? Nothing about this makes me happy. You know not leaving enough time stresses me out and ruins my enjoyment of things, yet you make no attempt to be timely.'

Maybe she was better off staying single. There would be a peace to it. She could spend more time walking, doing yoga – or take a leaf out of Greg's book and learn something new. If anything, men and women became more set in their ways as they got older – would a relationship involve more compromise than she was willing to offer?

She continued on down the road, past a cosy, candlelit restaurant where a couple about her own age laughed together over bowls of pasta. She was pierced by envy. That could have been her and James if he hadn't bloody died. Were some of the men she had met right when they said that she wasn't ready to date, that she was too scarred by her bereavement, and self-sabotaging as a result? But no, she wasn't sabotaging the fledgling relationship with Nigel. They had a dinner planned when he got back from his work trip next week. It wasn't her fault – it was just that decent men were rather thin on the ground. Nigel was the first one she had met, the only one she had been able to see a future with. She vowed to do everything in her power to make it work with him.

Chapter 10

'What are you doing?' Angela said, as Greg rooted through the drawer that housed everything in the kitchen that didn't have its own place. 'I thought you were going out. Helen and Sara are coming over.'

'Don't worry, I'm going in a minute. I'm just looking for a tote bag.'

'Why are you looking in there? There's loads in the bag of bags in the utility room.'

He disappeared through the door and she listened to him banging around, followed by a silence as he took his time over selecting the most appropriate bag. The middle-aged, low-stakes version of the silence of the lambs: the rustling of the carrier bags. A

'What are you going out for, again?' she asked when he reappeared with a black cloth bag embellished with a pig that had once held their Christmas turkey.

'I'm going to meet this dealer in East London. Cash only, no questions asked.'

'Dealer?' Angela asked, alarmed.

'Yes. He's got this unbelievable brisket. I'm meeting him near Spitalfields market – he supplies some of the stalls there, but he saves the best stuff for his private clients. Are you going to say anything to Helen about how Brian behaved the other night?' he asked.

'I'm not sure. What do you think?' She valued Greg's perspective on these matters, finding him to be fair, thoughtful and clear-eyed.

'I think it's worth bringing up. I've never liked him – always found him very overbearing – but the way he spoke to her at the hospice dinner was something else. Made me feel very uncomfortable.'

'I know. I've always thought they had a bit of an odd relationship, but we spend so little time together as couples I've never given it that much thought. If you and he had been friends, and we'd seen them more as a pair, I might have seen what was going on earlier.'

'Don't blame me!' he said, pulling open his special drawer to make sure none of the crucial ingredients for his spice rub were running low. 'You don't like him either – you've always said you prefer to see Helen and Sara on their own.'

'That's true.' They had always been three women friends who happened to be married, as opposed to a set of three couple friends. 'I think it made things easier for Sara when James died. It would have reinforced what she'd lost if we'd been used to spending time as a six.'

The doorbell rang.

'I'll let them in on my way out,' he said.

Greg and Sara exchanged pleasantries in the hall, then the front door slammed behind him.

'Hiya,' Sara came in, unwinding a long, striped scarf from around her neck. 'Where's Greg going? He was very cagey.'

'He's going to meet his meat dealer on a street corner in London. Don't ask.'

'I thought it might be something medical so I didn't like to pry.'

'Why on earth would you think that? If it was something medical I'd have said.'

'Not necessarily,' Sara said airily. 'What if it was erectile dysfunction?'

'His erectile is fully functioning, more's the pity.'

'More's the pity? Isn't that a good thing?'

'I suppose so, if I can be bothered. It's not exactly anything I haven't seen before.'

'I guess so, but there's a comfort in that, isn't there? That familiarity. I still miss it. It's part of the reason I want to meet someone else. I'm not dead yet.'

'I know. Sorry, I didn't mean to sound ungrateful. You know I love him really. I thought you were bringing Helen?'

'I was, but she texted to say she'd make her own way, and might be late. As per.'

Angela rolled her eyes. 'Do you think we should talk to her about the other night?'

'I don't know,' Sara said. 'What would we say? Don't you think your husband's a massive arsehole? We could push her away altogether.'

'What if he's more than an arsehole though?' Angela had heard enough stories from her clients about their nightmare ex-husbands to be on the alert. 'What if she needs our help?'

'What, you think he's hitting her?' said Sara, appalled.

'No, I don't think he'd do that. But I've always thought he was a bit dismissive of her. He could be abusing her, you know, emotionally.'

'Now we have to say something,' Sara said. 'Imagine how bad we'd feel if it turns out she's desperate for someone to ask her and we didn't bother.'

'I'll feel terrible if that's the case,' Angela said. 'She was so amazing to me when Lizzie was little and I was struggling. I hate the thought that she's been in trouble herself and I did nothing. Do you really think we could have missed the signs, over all these years?'

'If you think about it, how much time have we spent with him, with them as a couple? I don't really know him at all. And Helen doesn't talk about him much.'

'That could be a sign in itself,' Angela said. The doorbell rang. 'Hold on, here we go.'

She went to answer the door and seconds later, led Helen into the kitchen.

'Sorry I'm late, the traffic was dire.'

Sara and Angela exchanged a look.

'What?' Helen said. 'It was — there's roadworks by Tesco's again.'

'I know, I got stuck in them too,' Sara said.

'Why don't we all sit down?' Angela put a cafetière of coffee and three mugs on the table.

'Yes, good idea,' Sara said.

Helen pulled out a chair and sat down. 'How did the date with the IT guy go? Steve, was it?'

'It was a no go,' Sara said. 'He was once really high up in one of the big tech companies doing data security stuff, but it's left him with this massive bee in his bonnet about how our every move is being tracked by Big Data firms — apart from his, of course, because he knows how to evade them, leaving no trace of himself behind.'

'Sorry to hear it didn't work out,' Helen said.

'Yes, well, never mind ...' Sara trailed into silence and looked at Angela.

'Why are you both being so weird?' Helen said.

'Fine, I'll go,' Sara said after a pause in which it seemed no one might say anything ever again. 'Angela and I wanted to talk to you, Helen, after the other night at the hospice benefit.'

'Talk to me about what?'

'Brian,' they said in unison.

Helen gave a breathless laugh. 'What about him?'

'The way he was with you,' Sara said. 'We were worried that he was . . . this is awkward, so I'm just going to say it . . . we worried he's a bit controlling or . . . abusive. It's not the first time we've noticed it, but it was the worst we've seen it. He's very dismissive of you, and you're always so anxious to appease him. It doesn't seem like the healthiest dynamic.'

'Oh gosh, you've got it all wrong!' Helen said. 'That's just the way we are with each other – you and Greg are the same, Angela!'

'I know what you're saying,' Sara said. 'They do bicker, but that's different. It feels more . . . equal.'

'And I wouldn't describe what I saw at the benefit as bickering,' Angela said. 'You're not yourself around him, Helen. It always feels like you're managing him, or managing the situation to avoid inflaming him.'

'No, that's not the case at all. Brian can be a grump, I know. He doesn't always get people's humour, and sometimes I try to make up for that and it gets a bit . . . much, but to say he's abusive . . . that's beyond the pale. He's never laid a hand on me! I know you might not always see it, but he adores me.'

'We're not suggesting he doesn't, or that he's hurting you physically,' Sara said. 'We don't want to upset you, we're worried about you, that's all.'

'Since when?' Helen said with uncharacteristic fire. 'Have you been discussing me behind my back for years? Poor Helen, whatever shall we do about her?'

'No, not at all,' Sara said. 'I promise, Angela and I have never had this conversation before today. It was only what we saw at the benefit, wasn't it, Angela?'

'Yes.' Angela squished down her natural instinct to slag Brian off. If they weren't careful, all they would do was push Helen away and further isolate her. 'If you say everything's OK, we believe you, but I hope you know that if ever there is anything you want to talk to us about, we're here. No questions, no judgement. Right, Sara?'

'Absolutely. Now, onto the more important question of what I'm going to wear on my date with Nigel.'

Helen shrugged, still smarting from the perceived attack.

'A wedding dress?' Angela said. 'I mean, you might as well at this point.'

'Ha ha. No, it's got to be something that's amazing but as if I haven't tried too hard. It would also be handy if it had magical powers that could make me look better than Leila.'

'Whatever you wear, you cannot tell him that you know he's going on a date with her later in the week.'

'Angela!' Helen was shocked out of her mood. 'Did you tell her? That's so unprofessional of you.'

'She weaselled it out of me,' Angela muttered. 'She should be in the secret service.'

'I literally asked you once if you knew whether they were going on a date and you said yes,' Sara said. 'And you told me his surname.'

Obviously Sara had subsequently done a deep-dive Google search on Nigel Peters, but it hadn't yielded much in the way of results. Either he didn't do social media, or his name was too common for her to elicit the correct search results. She'd briefly toyed with the idea of asking Steve the Data Guy to see what he could find on him, but had quickly dismissed the idea as inappropriate.

'You're one of my best friends,' Angela said. 'What else am I going to do? Lie to you?'

'I know, and I'm grateful. It's good to know what I'm up against. She'll be using all her wiles on him, so it's useful to be prepared, although I'm not sure I have any wiles to speak of.'

'Nor does she!' Angela said. 'She's really nice.'

'Yes, I thought she was lovely,' Helen said. 'You looked to be getting on well at the benefit, bonding over the dating stuff.'

'Ugh, what is this, the Leila appreciation society?' Sara had conveniently wiped from her memory the enjoyment she had got from talking to Leila over dinner. 'You're supposed to be on my side.'

'It's not a matter of sides, Sara,' Angela said. 'I hope things work out for you with Nigel if that's what you want.'

A

'It is what I want! You know it is!'

'You haven't even been on a date with him yet. You're putting the cart before the horse. You shouldn't—'

'I know, I know. Put all my eggs in one basket. You've only told me about a million times. Now, can you make yourself useful and let me ransack your wardrobe in case there's something I can borrow?'

'Alright. Are you coming, Helen?'

'No, I'll be in the way, you go.'

They bustled up the stairs to Angela's bedroom, still talking and sparring.

Helen sat in the kitchen, staring unseeing out of the glass doors at a squirrel worrying away at the nuts in the bird feeder. Her right hand was balled into a tight fist, and if you'd looked at her closely, you'd have seen that she was digging her nails into her palm, trying to stop the tears falling.

Chapter 11

Sara checked the time again. How could it be taking this long to get from one side of Tunbridge Wells to the other?

So sorry. Still stuck in traffic, she texted Nigel.

An ambulance siren sounded and began weaving its way through the cars behind them. Her driver edged the taxi up onto the pavement to let it pass.

Think it's an accident, she added.

'Could we go a different way?' she asked the driver. 'What about round by Upper Grosvenor Road?'

'It's even worse that way,' the driver said, indicating the satnav on his phone on the dash which was spidered with red. 'Satnav's still saying this is the quickest route.'

Her trousers were digging into her waist and her armpits were damp. The angora sweater had looked so soft and alluring in the mirror, the jumper of a woman you would want to spend time with, possibly even take in your arms, but she was stifling now. The driver had the heating turned up full blast. She opened her window a crack.

No worries, Nigel texted back.

They continued to inch up the road. Every so often a car in front of them would lose patience, execute a three-point turn and zoom off in the opposite direction. Sara sat rigid in the back, her body taut with stress. Eventually the traffic started to move and they reached the scene of the accident, where the police had arrived and were directing traffic around a white saloon car with a crushed bonnet which appeared to have been driven into a wall.

The police officer waved them through and finally they were moving at speed. Sara took a compact mirror from her bag and checked her reflection, immediately wishing she hadn't bothered. Her cheeks were flushed and sweat beaded on her forehead. She patted it with a tissue and wiped the mascara shadows from beneath her eyes, thinking miserably about Leila. She wouldn't turn up forty-five minutes late for her date with Nigel all sweaty and red-faced. She would float coolly in, stunning but appropriate, her unblemished face glowing.

Sara paid the taxi driver and clambered out, glad of the cool air. As she adjusted the waistband of her trousers, she saw Nigel standing outside Sorrel, the restaurant they had chosen, in smart jeans, a gingham shirt and a navy jacket, a wool overcoat draped over his arm. He was taller than she remembered, his beard darker.

'Sorry,' he said, walking towards her. 'They wouldn't hold our table any longer. They had people turning up who hadn't booked and eventually they turfed me out in favour of someone who was ready to order.'

'I'm so sorry,' Sara said, crushed. 'There was an accident on St John's Road, everywhere's gridlocked.' Would he suggest calling the whole thing off?

'Don't worry about it – it looked a bit posh for me anyway. It's one of those places that lists the components of the dishes, rather than describing them,' he said. '*Burrata, peach, pickled radish.*'

'Are you more of a *fishfingers, bread, ketchup* man?' she asked.

'I can do both!' he said. 'Although there's not much that beats a jacket potato with cheese and beans.'

'Food of the gods,' Sara agreed. 'So . . . do you want to rearrange, or . . .?'

'No! Of course not.' Some of the tension in her shoulders eased.

'I'm not sure where else we could go around here,' she said doubtfully. 'We could try to make our way back into town, but I don't fancy our chances in this traffic.'

'You mentioning fishfingers has given me an idea – there's a chippy across the road. We could get fish and chips and sit on the common? Unless you think it's too cold, in which case – well, I don't want to make you feel uncomfortable so please say if you'd rather not – but my house is ten minutes' drive out towards Penshurst, so away from the traffic – we could take them back there.'

'Oh . . .' Sara hesitated. It was against all the rules of online dating – meet in a public place, let someone know where you are – but her gut told her she didn't need to worry about any of that with Nigel. He was safe.

'Honestly, it's fine if you don't want to.'

'No, that sounds great,' she said, putting the rules to the back of her mind. 'It's too cold to sit outside.'

They ordered and collected their cod and chips, and then walked to where he had parked his gleaming, black BMW.

'This is very plush,' she said, settling into the butter-soft leather seat.

'I do have a weakness for luxury cars, I'm afraid. If I'd known I'd be giving you a lift, I would have brought the Jag in an attempt to impress you.'

Sara didn't care about cars, particularly, but a flame ignited in her at the thought that Nigel was keen to make a good impression on her. They drove through Bidborough and out into the countryside. Before they reached the next village of Penshurst, Nigel slowed and turned down a gravel track into woodland that she'd never noticed before, despite having driven along this road numerous times. The night was inky black outside her window, but the beams of the headlights swept over a small white sign with the word Claricoates on it. A seed of doubt unfurled within her, prickling down her spine. Where was he taking her? A large shape emerged from the woods to her left and she gasped as Nigel slammed on the brakes to avoid it. It was a deer, its antlers silvery under the headlights.

'I'll wait, there's usually another one,' Nigel said, and sure enough, a doe trotted out after her mate, disappearing into the woods on the other side of the lane.

'I didn't know there were any houses down here,' Sara said nervously, as he set off again, slower this time.

'Only mine,' he said, looking across at her briefly. 'Oh God, don't worry, my house really is down here, like a proper house. I'm not taking you to some creepy cabin in the woods. I'm so sorry, I should have thought about how it would feel for you as a woman. Please don't worry, I'm not an axe murderer.'

'No, no, I didn't think you were,' Sara said, not wholly reassured.

'And now I've said murderer, that's made it worse. Look, shall I run you home? We can turn straight around.'

They came to a halt in a circular driveway, softly lit all around by LED lights in the flowerbeds. To her left was a triple garage, presumably housing the Jaguar, and ahead was one of the most beautiful houses she had ever seen. Pure white, it was a nineteen thirties art deco dream, sleek and polished with curved lines and windows made from continuous bands of glass. It was like a house from an Agatha Christie TV drama where no expense had been spared.

'No, it's fine,' she said softly. The house was about as far from a creepy cabin in the woods as you could imagine.

'Wonderful. In that case, welcome to Claricoates.'

He negotiated a series of complicated locks on the wide, glass-panelled front door and they came into a large hallway with a shiny, herringbone parquet floor. There was one door on the right and then a flight of stairs with an ornate, iron balustrade leading up to the next floor. On the left, another staircase led down underground.

'This is beautiful,' Sara said.

'Thanks,' Nigel said. 'I'll give you a quick tour, if you like. This is my study.' He opened the door on the right. Sara took in floor-to-ceiling bookshelves, a huge mahogany desk and an opulent leather chair.

'And these stairs lead down to the basement.' He indicated to their left.

'What's down there?' she asked.

'Cinema room and the pool,' Nigel said.

'You have an indoor pool! Wow!' Sara was comfortably off herself, but this was on a different level and she had to stop her jaw from dropping open at every turn.

'Wait there and I'll pop the fish and chips in the oven to keep warm, then we can go down.'

Sara stood, gawping around her in awe until Nigel reappeared and showed her down the staircase. At the bottom, they turned left into an exquisite cinema room with two rows of huge, red velvet armchairs. The screen, which took up almost the entire end wall, was framed by matching velvet curtains. The brown and yellow geometric-patterned carpet was plush beneath her feet and the two side walls were taken up with a hand-painted mural in a sunburst design.

'Wow,' she said again. It was an inadequate word to comment on the beauty, the sheer opulence of his house, but she didn't know how else to react. She hoped she wasn't being too uncool.

'And through here is the pool,' Nigel said, taking her back into the hallway and through blue glass double doors.

Stone columns lined each side of the turquoise pool, its surface like glass. Subtle lighting – she couldn't tell where it was coming from – illuminated the mosaic panelling on every wall. At each corner of the pool, a bronze walrus stood guard, water spouting from its mouth.

'Bring your swimming costume next time!' he said. 'Don't get too excited though – I've got the house up for sale.'

'Why?' Sara said, aghast. 'It's so beautiful.'

'I know, but since the divorce I've felt it's much too big for one person – or even two, if I were to meet someone.' He gave her a little bow and a foolish smile spread across her lips. 'It's a family home – it should have a family living in it. Downsizing will enable me to release some capital too – I'd like to help my daughter out buying a property.'

'I think you said she lives in America?' Sara asked.

'Well remembered!'

Sara hoped he hadn't guessed that she had spent the last few weeks poring over every detail of their five minutes together.

'How long has she been there?'

90

'About five years. She works for a management consultancy and she had the option to relocate to Boston. She loves it there.'

'You must miss her.'

'Terribly,' he said, suddenly forlorn. 'I thought she'd come back, but it's starting to look as though she's going to make her life there. Right, shall we go and have these fish and chips?'

Sara followed Nigel back up the stairs, through the hallway and into a large kitchen, where he invited her to sit at a velvet bar stool by the island, which was topped with a thick slab of swirled marble. Three bronze orbs cast a mellow light onto the fish and chips as he served them up on geometric-patterned china, along with a chilled glass of white wine from the vast, American-style fridge.

'What is it that you do?' Sara asked. 'I don't think we got to it on our speed date.' What she was really asking was how the hell do you afford this extraordinary house, but she was trying, unsuccessfully, to play it cool.

'I was finance director for one of the big accounting firms in the City for many years. I semi-retired from that last year, but I'm still on various boards and doing consultancy work, so in actual fact I'm busier than ever.'

'Do you enjoy it?'

'Not really, but it's given me a good lifestyle. I can't complain. How about you?'

'It's a bit embarrassing to say,' Sara said.

'Ooh, intriguing!'

'I don't actually do anything. I told you I was a widow, I think.' Sara knew she had, but it would be interesting to find out if he had been listening.

'Yes — you said around five years ago?'

'That's right.' Goodness. That extremely rare thing – a man who actually listened. 'I was lucky that my husband was financially savvy so he left me fairly comfortable.' In fact, Sara was more than comfortable – she was a very wealthy woman indeed thanks to the various insurances, pensions and investments that James had set up, as well as the sizeable chunk of family money he had inherited from his parents, but she didn't usually divulge that on such early acquaintance. Not that it would matter to Nigel, given what she now knew of his lifestyle.

'And do you enjoy not working?' he asked.

'For the most part, yes. I'd always worked – in recruitment – apart from when the boys were very little. I stopped after James died – I was grateful not to have to worry about money, getting back to a job before I was ready.'

'How did he die, if you don't mind me asking?'

'Pancreatic cancer.'

'Oof.' He grimaced. 'A close friend of mine died of that a few years back. It's not a good one to get, is it? Not that any of them are,' he added hastily.

'It's OK. I know what you mean. You're right – it's often diagnosed too late for it to be curable, which turned out to be the case with James.'

'It was the same with my friend. I know his wife felt guilty – needlessly, wrongly – that she hadn't made him go to the doctors earlier.'

'I can relate to that,' Sara said. 'There was so much to feel guilty about. Should I have encouraged him to seek diagnosis earlier, could I have tried harder to get him into a clinical trial? The worst one was . . . oh, never mind. This is a bit depressing.'

She took a sip of her wine, which was one of the most delicious things she'd ever tasted.

'Don't worry. I think I said to you on our first date, I love to get into the nitty gritty of life, whether it's on a date or otherwise. It's so boring having the same old conversations about the weather and house prices. But only if you feel comfortable.'

'I feel the same.' Sara took a deep breath. She had never told anyone this before. 'There was this time, quite near the end of James's life as it turned out, he was on palliative chemo tablets. By that point he was struggling to keep on top of his medication, so I'd taken charge of making sure he took the right pills. I got to the end of the month's supply and I couldn't understand why I had so many tablets left. Then it hit me like a train – I'd been giving him the wrong dose for the whole month. It was meant to be two tablets per dose, and I'd only been giving him one. I could hardly breathe. I felt like I'd killed him.'

'Oh Sara, that must have been awful. But you know now that you didn't, right? I mean, it was palliative chemo, so there was nothing you could have done to save him at that point?'

'I know,' she said. 'But it was such a heart-stopping, harrowing moment, and he was so upset when I told him.' Her breath caught in her chest at the memory of it, a part of her still there in the kitchen, reeling, the pack of unused tablets in her hand. 'You might want to stay well away from me now I've told you that.'

'Indeed. The Black Widow.' Nigel rolled his eyes back in his head in a parody of death, and then immediately stopped. 'Oh my God. I'm so sorry, I don't know what made me do that. It was so inappropriate.'

Sara felt a giggle rising up inside her and bubbling out of her mouth. Nigel began to laugh too, horrified at first, but becoming increasingly hysterical. Every time one of them started to calm down, the other one would do the 'death' face and it would set them off again. Eventually their laughter subsided and they looked at each other, breathless on their bar stools.

'Your mascara's run . . .' Nigel reached out a hand. 'May I?'

She nodded, and he ran his thumb under her eye. It wasn't an obvious move, but he left a trail of fire where his thumb had been, and when he reached the outer corner of her eye, he didn't take his hand away. She tilted her head so it cupped her cheek.

'I'd really like to . . . if you don't mind . . .' He stopped, unsure of her reaction, but Sara had never been more sure of anything in her life. She slipped off the velvet bar stool and stepped towards him. Gently, he drew her in and their lips met. He was the first man she had kissed since James. She'd always secretly worried about what it would be like, should she ever find herself in this situation. Would she feel she was betraying James's memory – cheating on him, even? But as Nigel's lips met hers, soft at first, then increasingly urgent, there was no room for doubt, no question that this was what she wanted, needed. It felt right, like it was always supposed to happen. Long-forgotten sensations swirled and shimmied within her as he slid one hand round her waist and the other around the back of her neck.

When they came up for air, the world around her was changed, her life charged with possibility. Nigel leaned his forehead against hers.

'That was lovely,' he said.

'It was. Sorry if I got a bit deep before.'

'Don't ever feel you have to keep quiet about those kind of things with me – I'm not easily scared.'

'Thank you,' she said, and a burst of happiness popped inside her, a sensation she hadn't felt in as long as she could remember. 'So what's our next topic to be, the weather or house prices? Obviously I'll be straight on Rightmove when I get home, having a nose at this house.'

'You won't find it,' he said, settling back onto his bar stool. 'Not yet, at any rate.' He looked sheepish. 'I'm using this rather exclusive estate agent who doesn't put your house online. It's . . . well, it's a security thing.'

Sara found it endearing that he was embarrassed by his good fortune.

'This agent's books are full of wealthy people,' he went on, 'and they work personally with them to find them the right house. As well as the security aspect, it can end up with you getting much more for your house than if you put it up on the open market. At least, that's what they tell me!'

As he poured her a second glass of wine, she plucked up the courage to ask the all-important question.

'So, are you dating much at the moment?' Everything rested on the answer he gave. Sara knew he didn't owe her anything, that just because they had shared one kiss it was entirely reasonable for him to be having first dates with any number of different people, as indeed she herself had done recently. And yet she waited with bated breath.

'I'll be honest with you.'

She hoped he couldn't hear her heart thumping.

'I do have a date planned with someone later this week.'

Sara willed herself not to accidentally give away how completely this was not news to her.

'What about you?' he asked.

'I've had a couple of dates with men I met at the speed dating event, but I don't think they're going to go anywhere.'

'Good.'

'Good?' Sara's stomach leapt.

'I think so. You'll have to tell me what you think about this, but . . . in fact, why don't you tell me how you think this date is going first?'

For a second, Sara contemplated playing it cool, but she was too old for games, and she liked Nigel too much to risk losing him by feigning disinterest.

'I think it's going brilliantly,' she said. 'The best first date I've ever had.'

'Thank God,' he said, his face wreathed in smiles. 'Me too. I didn't want to say in case you thought I was the most horrendous bore. In that case, I'm going to cancel my other date.'

'Really?' Absurdly, Sara felt tears start up in the backs of her eyes. Nigel was prepared to give up Leila's smooth, olive skin, her curtain of shining hair, for her.

'Yes. Let's face it, how often do you meet someone you think you could build something with?'

'Hardly ever. Never.'

'Me neither. I don't want to mess that up by starting on the wrong foot, making you feel like I'm choosing between you and another woman. I choose you. Let's see where this goes. What do you say?'

Tearfully, inevitably, Sara said yes.

Chapter 12

'Remind me why we're having this dinner party again,' Greg said, buttoning up a pink and white pinstriped shirt dotted with small parrots. On anyone else it would have looked ridiculous, but with his lean, meat-fed body and handsome, craggy features, he just about got away with it.

'It's kind of a mea culpa,' Angela said from her seat at the dressing table, massaging primer into her own face, which was less craggy and interesting, more haggard and worn. 'I warned Sara one too many times that things were moving too fast with Nigel and she exploded. I've never seen her so angry.'

'How long have they been together now?'

'A couple of months. She said it was the first time she'd felt truly happy in five years, and why did I want to take that away from her. So I said I didn't, and then somehow I found myself inviting them to dinner.'

'But why are Helen and the dreaded Brian coming?' Greg buckled the wide leather belt he favoured when he was wearing his best jeans. Usually Angela ribbed him about it – *who do you think you are, Bono?* – but she was too focussed on trying to disguise the bags under her eyes.

'Partly because it feels less like we're putting Sara and Nigel under the microscope, but also because – although Helen denied this vehemently last time we tackled her about it – Sara and I are still worried that Brian's a bit controlling.'

'I wouldn't be at all surprised, but how does inviting them to dinner assist?'

'We want to make sure we always include her – in case he tries to isolate her from her friends. If we keep reminding her – and him – that we're here, we're not going anywhere, it might help.'

'Fair enough. You look very nice.'

'Don't be ridiculous,' Angela said, tugging at the loose skin under her chin. 'I look about a hundred and three.'

'You're *my* one-hundred-and-three-year-old,' he said, leaning down to plant a kiss on her cheek. 'I'd better go and check on that lamb.'

'Can you see if there's enough white wine in the fridge too?' she called after him. 'I guess we'll be having red with the main course, but in case anyone wants white?'

'I'm on it,' Greg said, bustling down the stairs.

Angela was putting the finishing touches to her makeup (glumly trying to banish the phrase 'like putting lipstick on a pig' from her internal commentary) when the doorbell rang. Greg answered it, and she heard Sara, overflowing with an excitement that bordered on manic, as well as a deep male voice, calm and mellifluous. She straightened her dress in the mirror and composed herself. Social events for her always had a slight edge, even ones like this with her closest friends. Growing up she had struggled with friendships, always too much for other people, too overbearing. She'd had friends, but she'd always felt like the outsider in any group, the least liked of any of them, the one always forgotten. She'd seen a post on Facebook recently, a university friend who had remarried and posted photos of her very cool wedding day in Margate. Until

then, Angela had believed that the others in that group had fallen out of touch with each other as much as she had, but there they all were, hugging the bride, raising champagne glasses, reminiscing over their enduring friendship. She'd felt a sharp sense of loss at the realisation that they had never really considered her part of that group. Becoming a mother had been like starting school again. She hadn't fitted into any of the mum cliques – not enough of an earth mother for the attachment parents with their slings and extended breastfeeding, not wealthy and chic enough for the ultra-groomed, Boden-clad, Land Rover set. It was only in her thirties when she met Sara, and subsequently Helen, that she understood what easy, uncomplicated friendship could feel like. Both women had seen that she was struggling with Lizzie and had empathised and stepped in to help without making a big fuss about it.

'Evening!' she trilled, heading down the stairs as Greg divested Sara and Nigel of their coats, and they handed over a bottle of wine and a battered box of liqueur chocolates that Angela was convinced she'd seen at another dinner party hosted by a friend of theirs last month. She hugged Sara and turned to Nigel.

'Hello, Nigel. It's lovely to see you away from the agency.'

He kissed her on the cheek.

'Likewise. I would have said it was a great opportunity for you to rate my skills on a date, but I'm hoping – in the nicest possible way – that I'll never have to use the agency again.'

Sara beamed and put her arm through his. 'Don't say that to Angela – she's very anti putting all your eggs in one basket. *Always have a backup* – that's your motto, isn't it?'

'For my agency clients, I do advise caution, yes. I've been in this game a long time. But for friends – which is what you are now, Nigel – I'm just happy for your happiness. Life's too short, I think that's the phrase I'm looking for.'

Greg maintained a neutral expression in the face of this blatant falsehood, but Sara was less restrained.

'You don't mean a word of that,' she said, laughing, 'but bless you for pretending.'

'Come through to the kitchen,' Greg said.

'It smells amazing in here,' Nigel said. 'What's on the menu?'

'I sourced a shoulder of lamb from a local farmer I know.'

'Is it from the farm shop out towards Groombridge?' Sara asked. 'I love that place.'

'No, no, no,' Greg said pityingly. 'You don't want to get meat there. This guy doesn't have a shop, he only sells privately to discerning customers.'

'They do these delicious cheese straws, though,' Sara protested.

'That's as maybe, but this lamb won't be like anything you've ever tasted before. I massaged my own spice rub into it before marinating it for twenty-four hours in onion, garlic, rosemary, thyme and red wine. It's been in the oven since this morning on a very low heat. I use a meat thermometer to keep it at precisely the correct temperature for maximum flavour and texture.'

'Alright Greg, they don't need to know everything about your special relationship with the poor lamb's shoulder,' Angela said. 'What's everyone drinking?'

Greg was delighted to find that Nigel was a fellow martini enthusiast and they were soon involved in a deep dive as to the ideal balance of vermouth and gin and how the different brands of vermouth impacted on the ratio. When the doorbell rang he was heavily involved in demonstrating his specialist lemon twist peeler, so Angela went to answer it.

'Hello, you two!' She couldn't tell if she was imagining the strain on Helen's face as Brian's whiskery cheek brushed hers. 'Come in. Sara and Nigel are here.'

'Marvellous,' said Brian, taking off his overcoat and handing it to Angela. 'I've heard so much about this Nigel from Helen, I feel as if I know him already.'

Helen gave a mirthless titter as Angela led them through to the kitchen where Greg was brandishing the cocktail shaker vigorously.

'Evening!' he said. 'I'm making martinis for Nigel and me, anyone else for one?'

'Not for us, thanks,' Brian said. 'White wine, please.'

'You sure? Helen?' Greg asked.

'No thanks – bit strong for me,' Helen said. 'White wine would be lovely. Only one though, I'm driving.'

'I'm Nigel – good to meet you.' Nigel held out his hand to Brian.

'Brian,' he said, grasping it and giving it the briefest of shakes. 'And this is my wife, Helen.'

Helen held out her hand to be shaken too but Nigel leaned in and kissed where her cheek would have been if she hadn't turned her head to such an extent that his lips met thin air.

'It's nice to meet you,' she said stiffly.

The others stood around the island as Greg put the finishing touches to the martinis, pouring them into frosted glasses and threading olives onto stainless-steel skewers.

'Cheers, everyone!' Greg held up his glass and everyone chimed in. 'And welcome to Nigel. It's great to have you here.'

'Lovely to be here. Thanks for the invite.' Nigel tipped his martini glass towards Greg and took a sip. 'That's delicious. You two should have had one,' he said to Brian and Helen.

'Better not,' Brian said. 'I'm playing golf in the morning. Need a clear head for that.'

'Indeed you do,' Nigel said. 'What do you play off?'

'Twelve. Do you play?'

'After a fashion. Not as well as you. I'm off eighteen, but rarely play to that, to be honest.'

'Nice to meet someone who plays at all – Greg here doesn't know a 5-wood from a 9-iron. We should have a game some time.'

'That'd be great, although I'm not even sure where my clubs are, it's been so long since I've played.'

'I've got some you can borrow,' Brian said. 'Are you a member at the Windell?'

'No, I don't have a membership anywhere at the moment. I'm a bit rusty – not sure how much fun it'd be for you.'

'I'll be the judge of that! We'll set it up. I might be able to get you in as a member – I'm on the committee. Patrick, the chair, is a very dear friend of mine.'

Angela, who happened to be looking at Helen at that precise moment, caught her in an almost indetectable eyebrow raise. It had been uncharacteristically indiscreet of her to have told them that Brian was obsessed with Patrick, and that she had a sneaking suspicion that the feeling was not at all mutual.

'Lovely,' Nigel said. 'Do you play any sports, Greg?'

'Not team sports, but I run, and I've taken up ballroom dancing since I retired last year.'

Brian snorted. 'That's hardly a sport.'

'It's a lot more physical than you think,' Greg said earnestly. 'Have you seen the professionals on *Strictly*? They're athletes!'

'I wouldn't call men prancing around in fake tan and high heels athletes. I might call them something else,' Brian said.

'This wine is delicious,' Helen broke in, desperately trying to prevent Brian displaying his unpleasant and bigoted views. 'Where is it from?'

'France, I think,' Greg said, 'by way of Waitrose.'

The conversation moved on, and ten minutes later Greg drained his martini glass and announced that dinner was ready, busying himself getting six small plates of smoked salmon sprinkled with dill out of the fridge.

'Would you like us to sit anywhere in particular?' Helen asked, the nervous tension that Angela had detected on her arrival making a reappearance.

'No, no, wherever you like,' Greg said, putting a plate of salmon on each placemat.

Sara and Nigel moved as one to the far side of the table, unable to stay out of each other's orbit. They couldn't keep their hands off each other. Nothing inappropriate for the occasion – a stray hair smoothed here, a hand on the small of a back there.

Helen moved gratefully to the left-hand end position next to Sara and prepared to sit.

'Actually Helen, could you sit the other end?' Greg said. 'It'll  be easier for me to hop up and down getting food and replenishing the glasses from this end.'

'Oh.' Helen looked in dismay at the other end, which would mean she was sitting next to Nigel. 'Or Brian could sit there? And I'll go on this side, opposite Sara.'

'Whatever you like,' Greg said, plonking a basket heaped with slices of fresh rye bread and a bowl of lemon wedges in the centre of the table.

'Goodness, Helen, why are you making such a fuss?' Brian said. 'Was there somewhere in particular you wanted to sit?'

'No,' she said, sliding miserably into the end seat next to Nigel. Brian sat next to her, shaking his head in what Angela thought was meant to be amusement, although she didn't quite buy it.

'This looks delicious,' Nigel said. 'Smoked salmon is one of my favourites.'

'Mine too,' Sara said, smiling at him dreamily. Angela decided she didn't want to know what that was about. 'It's amazing how many things we've got in common,' she went on. 'We both love olives, but hate anchovies! Isn't that weird? Most people either like them both or hate them.'

'I like both,' Greg said, scooping a glistening ribbon of salmon onto a slice of the dark bread. 'Whereas Angela likes anchovies and not olives – our relationship was never meant to be.'

'Like Romeo and Juliet,' Angela grinned.

'And when I worked for RPM in Victoria,' Sara continued undeterred, 'Nigel worked in the building right next door! He was literally in the next office block. We went to the same pub for after-work drinks. Imagine if we'd met then – life might have been very different.'

'Was that before you met James?' Brian asked.

'Yes. Just before.'

'You wouldn't have wished that any different, surely?' he said with a note of disapproval.

'No, of course not,' she said, flustered. 'It's a funny coincidence, that's all.' She tore a piece of bread in half and crumbled it onto her plate.

'And then we had another chance a couple of years later,' Nigel said, riding to her rescue. Sara gave him a grateful look. 'We were both at the same Oasis gig in Kentish Town.'

'Oasis. Ugh, what a bunch of oafs,' Brian said.

'You could have a point there, Brian,' Nigel said, 'but we were . . . what, mid-twenties? I thought they were amazing. What kind of music do you like?'

'I don't listen to music,' Brian said, in the manner of one saying they don't pull the wings off insects for fun.

'Not at all? What about you, Helen?'

'Well, Brian doesn't like it so we don't really have music on in the house.'

'For God's sake, Helen, when will you stop insinuating that I'm a despot who rules the house with a rod of iron? You're free to listen to whatever music you like.'

'Of course,' she said hastily. 'I suppose if I was going to listen to anything it'd be folk music – Joni Mitchell, Joan Baez, that type of thing.'

'Oh brilliant, I like that too,' Nigel said. 'Have you heard Phoebe Bridgers? She's a modern singer but very much in the mould of those two.'

'No, no I haven't.'

'I'll send you some song recommendations – in fact, I've got a playlist on Spotify that I could send you if you give me your number?'

'I don't have Spotify – please don't worry. I'll look her up. Phoebe Bridges.'

'Bridgers. There are some other artists on there you might like too though – Lizzy McAlpine, Indigo Girls. You can get a free version of Spotify. What's your number?' He dug his phone out of his jeans pocket.

'Why don't you send it to Sara and she can send it on to me?'

'Oh. OK.' Perplexed, Nigel put his phone face down on the table.

'Have we finished?' Angela broke the awkward silence that threatened to engulf them all, jumping up to clear the plates. Greg went to the oven to minister tenderly to his true love, the slow-cooked lamb.

The rest of the evening continued in a similar vein. Sara and Nigel, while apparently enjoying themselves, clearly couldn't wait until it was time to leave and they could be alone again, and Helen tiptoed around Brian as if he was an unexploded mine. Angela wondered whether she and Sara ought to have another word with her, but to be honest Brian seemed more exasperated by her fussiness than explicitly angry or controlling.

Nigel and Sara took their leave as soon as was decent, although not before Brian had taken Nigel's number and pencilled in some dates for a round of golf. There were no unseemly displays of public affection between Sara and Nigel, but it was unmistakeable that they were going to tumble into bed together the moment they got home. Brian and Helen lingered a little longer, but once there was no one to talk to about golf, Brian lost interest and they were soon saying their goodbyes with empty promises of a return invite. Angela couldn't think of a time when Brian and Helen had hosted them for dinner or even drinks.

'Phew,' said Greg when the door had finally closed behind them. 'I'm knackered, although in the end that was more fun than I thought it was going to be. Nigel seems like a good bloke.'

'He does. I hope she's not rushing into it though.'

'She'll be alright, she's got her head screwed on. Judging by the indecent haste with which they put their coats on, that's not the only thing getting screwed.'

'Greg!' He must have had more to drink than she realised. He was rarely salacious sober. She was considering if she had the energy for conjugal relations, or whether the large amount of wine and lamb swilling around inside her made it a bad idea, when she spotted a pink striped scarf hanging on the coat hook. 'Helen's left her scarf. I'll run out and see if they're still there.'

She plucked it from the peg and hurried out of the door, not staying to see whether Greg was relieved or dejected.

She was in luck – Helen and Brian were standing by their car, Helen digging around in her handbag. Angela was in the shadow of the house and neither of them had seen her. She was about to call out when something in Brian's demeanour stopped her.

'How can you have lost the keys, you stupid woman?' he hissed at her.

'I haven't, they're in here somewhere.'

'You've left them in the house – and I know why,' he said.

'No, no, they're in my bag.' She rummaged ever more frantically.

'You got distracted by your fancy man, didn't you?'

'My – what? No, Brian. Please—'

'Laughing away with him, swapping music recommendations. How very touching. You were dying to give him your number, weren't you?'

Angela watched in horror as Brian leaned in close to Helen, gripping her right wrist.

'I saw the way you were looking at him.'

'Please, Brian. Let me find the keys and we can go home.'

In one swift movement, he let go of her wrist, grabbed her bag and emptied it out all over the pavement. Helen dropped to her knees and scrabbled around scooping everything up – including the keys, it seemed, because once she had got everything, she unlocked the car. Brian stalked around to the other side without a word, got in and slammed the door. Angela shrank back further into the shadows and watched as Helen gathered herself. Her face twisted in anguish briefly, but she made sure to banish any trace of it before getting into the driver's seat.

Angela walked slowly back to the house, Helen's scarf still in her hand. She locked the door and went upstairs. She was longing to get Greg's perspective, to unburden herself, but he was lying on top of the covers snoring lightly, in boxer shorts and the parrot shirt, still wearing his glasses. She took his glasses off, turned off his bedside lamp and arranged the duvet over him as best she could. One of them may as well get a good night's sleep, and after the scene she'd just witnessed, it wasn't going to be her.

Chapter 13

'Are you not working today?' Sara asked.

'I'm working from home.' Angela seemed nervous, flitting around the kitchen, emptying the dishwasher and wiping down the surfaces. Sara had been grateful when Angela suggested a coffee at hers. Her news would be better delivered face to face, even if the thought of Angela's likely reaction made her stomach churn.

'Did you say Helen was coming?' Sara said. Whilst they all had their own individual relationships with each other, they generally met up as a three, all things being equal.

'Yes, in a little while,' Angela said grimly. 'She's popping by to pick up her scarf, but I told her to come a bit later than you. There's something I need to talk to you about before she gets here.'

'There's actually something I want to talk to you about too,' said Sara, her mouth dry.

'Is everything OK?' Angela said anxiously, sitting down heavily opposite her friend. 'Are you ill?'

It was a depressing reality, and one keenly felt by Angela herself who had been through breast cancer twelve years earlier, that at their age, any such pronouncement was likely to be a precursor to the speaker having had a worrying scan or blood test result.

'No, nothing like that. It's good news – at least, I think it's good news.'

'Why do you look so worried, then?' Angela asked.

'I'm not so sure you're going to agree.'

'Let's have it. Mine's definitely not good news – don't worry, it's nothing to do with health,' she said quickly, seeing Sara's worried face. 'But let's have yours before we get to it.'

'Well . . .' Sara took a steadying breath, 'you know things are going well with Nigel?'

'Yes. Oh my God, you're not getting married, are you?'

'No!'

'Thank goodness, because that would be madness. You've only been going out a couple of months.'

'Yes, I know. I know it's early days, but . . .' How to explain it to someone who'd been with their spouse for almost thirty years? Even though dating and relationships was Angela's business, on a personal level it was always going to be hard for her to understand how Sara felt about Nigel. Best to launch into it. 'We've been talking about moving in together.'

'What?' Angela said, horrified. 'When?'

'As soon as we can get everything sorted.'

'Who's going to move in with who?'

'He'll move in with me, but you don't have to worry, Angela, this is not about money. He's significantly wealthier than me – I've seen his house, for a start.'

Following their date, Sara had revised her Google search to include Nigel's job. This had been more successful than her previous forays, and thrown up various reports from business magazines about promotions he had gained over the years, including an article about his recent semi-retirement and the various boards he had subsequently been appointed to.

'Why aren't you moving in to this mansion then?' Angela asked.

'Claricoates is too big for two people − it's a family house. He'd already decided to downsize − the house has been up for sale for a while. We're going to do it all legally and fairly, so we both know what's what.' It was almost insulting that Angela imagined she was walking into this with her eyes closed. How naïve did she think Sara was?

'What about the boys?' Angela asked, changing tack. 'What will they think?'

'What about them?' Sara said hotly. 'Jonny and Max have been my *life*. Everything I've done over the last five years has been about supporting them, giving them opportunities and choices, ensuring that not for one second were they disadvantaged by only having one living parent.' After James died, Sara had squashed down her own grief, turning her focus like a laser beam onto the wellbeing of her boys. Friends said how strong she was being, but she'd wanted to ask what they thought the alternative was? Take to her bed and leave the boys to fend for themselves? The fact that they were both out in the world, independent, happy, was her life's proudest achievement, but now it was her turn.

'They really like Nigel, anyway.' The boys had come back for a weekend recently and had both given Nigel their seal of approval. Jonny, the eldest, had pronounced him a bloody good bloke, and Max, always the more sensitive of the two, had told her privately that it had been weird to see her with someone else, but that he was happy for her, and glad she had someone to look after her. 'They've left home, they're both settled and happy – it's time I did something for myself.'

'I wouldn't argue with that. But are you not rushing into things?'

'I knew you'd say that,' Sara said. Angela was nothing if not predictable.

'Don't be cross. I wouldn't be doing my due diligence as a friend if I didn't ask.'

'Fair enough. I understand you're looking out for me, but you don't need to worry. I've never been in a relationship that felt so right. I don't mean to be disrespectful to James, but it was never like this with him. I thought when people fell in love in the movies that they were exaggerating, that it didn't happen like that in real life, but it does. That's what this feels like.'

'That's all very well, but why the rush to move in? Why not enjoy this honeymoon period without any of the domestic trappings, the drudgery?'

'But that's the stuff I want! I want the everyday, boring things with him as much as I want the romance. It's so different with Nigel to any relationship I've had before – I can be totally myself with him. He sees who I am, he knows me in a way I'm not sure James ever did, even after thirty years together. It's like that scene in *When Harry Met Sally*, where Harry says that when you realise you want to spend the rest of your life with someone, you want the rest of your life to start as soon as possible. That's exactly how I feel. We're not getting any younger. Who knows how long any of us have got left? I don't want to waste any precious time.'

'Wouldn't it be more sensible to continue as you are for a bit, see how things go?'

'I'm fed up of being sensible! I've been so, so lonely since James died. I don't bang on about it because what's the point, but I can tell you it's no fun going back to an empty house day after day after day. I've carried on, and supported the boys and thrown myself into my hobbies and my friends and trying to build a new life, but it's hard.'

'I'm sorry,' Angela said humbly. 'I wish you'd let me help more – you always seem so strong.'

There it was again, her fabled strength.

'I am,' she said, 'but it's exhausting being the one on whom everything rests, not having anyone to pick up the slack if you have an off day. I was beginning to think I'd never meet anyone, and then here is this wonderful man, who adores me, looks after me, puts me first. Can you blame me for wanting to throw myself in head first? If it all goes tits up, so be it – you're welcome to say I told you so. Like I said, everything's going to be done properly, I won't be leaving myself vulnerable financially – and nor will he.'

'Fair enough,' Angela said. 'And for what it's worth, if it does all go wrong (and I really hope it doesn't) I won't be crowing over it. I'll be there to help you pick up the pieces.'

'I hope it never comes to that, but thank you,' Sara said, calming down. 'I appreciate it. Now, what did you want to talk to me about?'

'It's Helen,' Angela said. 'That's why I told her a later time than you to come over.'

'What about her? I noticed she was treading on eggshells around Brian at your dinner on Saturday, but I'm never sure how much of his annoyance is justified.' Helen was a bit of a fusspot, and in the throes of her new love, Sara was keen to give others the benefit of the doubt. 'Maybe that's just their dynamic, and we need to stay out of it.'

'No. After they'd left I realised Helen had forgotten her scarf, so I ran out to the car with it. She was rooting around in her bag looking for the car keys, and he was getting really annoyed with her.'

'That doesn't sound too bad.'

'It was – he was seething, not mildly annoyed. He was accusing her of flirting with Nigel.'

'What?' Sara laughed. 'That's absurd! I know Nigel's friendly but there was nothing untoward in it.'

'Exactly. It was completely unjustified. Then he grabbed hold of her and the next thing I knew he had emptied her whole handbag out on the ground. She found the keys, so he got in the car leaving her to scrabble around for all her stuff.'

'Do you think he was really, really drunk, and the next morning he would have been super apologetic?' Sara was clutching at straws, and she knew it. Brian hadn't had that much to drink, and even if he had, that wouldn't have excused this behaviour.

'No, I don't think so. Honestly Sara, it was horrible – worse than it sounds in the description. It was as if he hated her. And she was so frightened – I mean if Greg spoke to me like that, I'd be furious, but she was trying to appease him, like she always does. But I suppose now we know why.'

'What does Greg think about it all?'

'I didn't tell him. He was asleep by the time I got into bed, and in the morning, I wasn't sure whether I should tell him – whether Helen would want me to. He's out sourcing meat now.'

A memory assailed Sara. 'Do you think that was what was going on when I stayed with her and Brian that time after James died – d'you remember?'

Max and Jonny were both away for the night and Sara couldn't face being alone. Angela had a houseful of Lizzie's friends, so Sara had asked if she could stay with Helen.

'That's right,' Angela said. 'Wasn't she really off with you in the morning?'

'Yes. Brian had been away on the Friday night for work, so she and I had had a nice supper together, all very cosy and relaxed. But in the morning, I could tell she was trying to get me to leave. She didn't say it in so many words, but she was hugely on edge. I was pretty hurt at the time. It must have been because Brian was coming back and she hadn't told him I was staying.'

'But why would he have minded that? He wasn't even there.'

'I don't know.' Sara ranged further back in her memory, reframing events from their shared past in the light of this new information. 'Do you think that's why she left Star Recruitment? She never worked again after that, did she?'

Sara had met Helen around the same time she'd met Angela at the school gates. Helen had worked for Sara's employer, Star Recruitment, for around six months. She'd seemed to enjoy it, but one day had unexpectedly handed in her notice.

'I feel so ashamed,' Angela said. 'Helen's always been so supportive of me. I wasn't in a great place when I met her – well, you remember – and she was amazing. How could we not have noticed what was going on?'

'Don't beat yourself up. That's the nature of these things. These men are clever – they hide in plain sight. From the outside, a sadly put-upon husband with a fussy, nagging wife can look much the same as an abusive man and the woman he controls through making her feel like the one at fault. It's an old story.'

'So why didn't I twig? I've let her down.'

'Don't be so hard on yourself. I didn't see it either, but we know now. We have to talk to her.' Having had the light and colour poured back into her own life so recently, Sara was fired up by the idea of saving Helen from the prison of her marriage.

'I agree,' Angela said. 'Although it didn't do much good last time we tried.'

They heard a key in the front door, followed by shoes being kicked off and the door slammed, the sound echoing down the hall.

'Is that Greg back?' Sara said. 'That was quick, I thought he usually spent hours with his meat.'

'Mum!' Lizzie called from the hall. 'Where are you?'

'In the kitchen!' Angela called back, bemused.

'What's she doing here?' Sara said.

'I don't know.'

Lizzie came in like a whirlwind, her hair escaping from a messy ponytail, strewing items across every available surface – bags, coat, hat, scarf, phone.

'Is everything OK, sweetheart?' Angela asked. 'I wasn't expecting you.'

'No, everything's a mess,' Lizzie said, prostrating herself on the sofa like a tragic heroine. 'I can't believe I've been so stupid.'

Chapter 14

Lizzie had only just begun to unburden herself of her tale of woe when the doorbell rang.

'That'll be Helen,' Angela said. 'Can you finish telling me later, Liz? We need to talk to Helen about something.'

'Ooh brilliant, I want to tell her all about Raf too. I'll get the door.'

Lizzie flung the front door open. 'Helen! I'm so glad to see you! Come in!'

She led Helen, uncharacteristically casual and ungroomed in yoga pants and a sweatshirt, through to the kitchen.

'I can't stay long,' she said. 'I'm in the middle of cleaning. I just popped by to get my scarf.'

'You have to stay!' Lizzie said. 'I'm having a crisis.'

'What kind of crisis?'

'Raf and I broke up.'

'Oh dear. He seemed a nice young man,' Helen said. 'But as I said, I need to—'

'That was the problem!' Lizzie said. 'He *seemed* nice. But he wasn't. He started getting funny about me having male friends – even Jonny and Max, who are, like, practically *relations*. Then one night we were out and he accused me of flirting with the barman – I was literally ordering a drink!'

'I can see you're upset,' Helen said, 'but it sounds like you're better off without someone who behaves like that.'

Angela looked at Sara. The parallels with Helen and Brian were not lost on either of them.

'I know, I know, but I thought he was the one. I'm going to go and have a bath. Can we have a roast dinner tonight, Mum?'

'I haven't got the stuff in, and I've got a ton of work to do today.'

'Can't you go to the supermarket? I need the comfort.'

'We'll see,' Angela said. They both knew that she was already mentally running through the fridge and cupboards, calculating how many potatoes they would need and wondering for the millionth time whether, as Lizzie averred, cauliflower cheese was a vital component of a roast dinner.

Lizzie drifted upstairs, having somehow left the kitchen in utter chaos.

'You are lucky, Angela,' Helen said wistfully.

'I know, but I could do without it at the moment, to be honest,' Angela said. 'She doesn't appreciate me one bit. It won't be long before I'm hearing all about her friend Beatrice's mum, who despite being called Carol is known inexplicably as Bunty. Beatrice and Bunty are always going for spa days, or off for dinner and a show. Bunty's so caring, so empathetic, so full of wise counsel. I've never met the woman but I loathe her.'

'The poor thing's obviously frightfully cut up about this Raf, though,' Helen said. 'He sounds awful.'

'Yes, he does,' Angela said cautiously. 'Which leads me on rather neatly to what we want to talk to you about.'

'What do you mean? I've come to get my scarf. I don't have time for a coffee today.'

'Helen, if you can see that Raf's behaviour is wrong, I – we, Sara and I – wonder if you can see that Brian's behaviour towards you isn't quite right in a similar way?'

'Not this again! I explained after the hospice benefit, that's the way he is, there's nothing to worry about.'

'Yes, I know, but . . . after you came for dinner the other night, I saw what happened by the car. How Brian spoke to you.'

'You were spying on us?' Helen's face burned.

'No! You forgot your scarf – I came running out to give it to you, and I heard Brian accusing you of flirting with Nigel, and then he emptied your bag out on the ground.'

'He was . . . he'd had a bit too much to drink. He was ever so apologetic in the morning. Don't tell me you've never spoken to Greg like that.'

'I really haven't, Helen. I know Greg and I bicker, but we would never speak to each other with such hatred. It's not right, is it, Sara?'

'No, it's not. Look, Helen, I know this might be difficult to hear, but . . .'

'We're not going to be like you and Nigel, love's young dream. We've been together for thirty-five years.'

'James and I were together for thirty years, and he never belittled me, or made me feel like he hated me.' An unexpected wave of grief washed over Sara at the thought of James's quiet steadiness.

'Brian doesn't hate me. Sometimes he feels I don't appreciate him and he gets frustrated, but that's more my fault than his.'

'Helen, none of this is your fault,' Sara said, reaching for her hand. 'Please tell me you know that.'

'No.' She pulled her hand away. 'Some of it *is* my fault. You don't live with me. I can be a nag, a perfectionist. I'm not the easiest person to live with.'

'I don't believe that,' Angela said, 'but even if it were true, it doesn't excuse the way he spoke to you on Saturday night by the car. He was accusing you of flirting with Nigel.'

'Nobody likes their partner to flirt with someone else in front of them,' said Helen.

'But you weren't!' Sara was bubbling with frustration. 'You hardly spoke to Nigel – he said on the way home that he thought you were very quiet and he hadn't had much chance to get to know you.'

'Brian's just insecure – he can't help his anxieties. It's his way of showing love. If I can reassure him, make him feel better, I'm happy to do it.'

'Brian's about the least anxious person I've ever met,' Angela scoffed. 'He's trying to manipulate you – why can't you see that?'

'If you're going to have a go at me, I'll leave now,' Helen said, white-faced.

'That's not our intention at all,' Sara said. 'We want to help you.'

'You can't,' Helen said blankly. 'That is, I don't need help. And even if I did, I couldn't leave Brian.'

'Of course you could!' Angela said. 'Look at Lizzie – she's just walked away.'

'Don't be ridiculous, that's completely different. She's young. They've only been together a few months. Where would I go? How would I afford it?'

'You could stay with me for a start,' Angela said.

'What about Greg? He wouldn't want me moping around.'

'Of course he would. He loves you, and he basically does what I tell him.'

'But I couldn't stay with you forever, and there's no way I could afford to buy or even rent a place of my own. I haven't worked for years.'

'Brian's got a good job, though,' Angela said. 'You two must have plenty of money floating around. I presume you've paid off the mortgage on this place?'

'I don't know,' Helen said. 'Brian deals with all that.'

Angela and Sara exchanged an appalled look.

'What about bank accounts? You must have savings, investments?' Sara said.

'I don't have access to the bank accounts – I've never needed it. Brian gives me money to cover everything I need.'

'Helen, that's so wrong!' Angela said. 'It's financial control.'

'No, no, it isn't – he's very generous. He never minds me spending on clothes, or skincare or bits for the house. And it's his money after all. He's the one who works for it.'

'Not really,' Sara said. 'If the two of you made a joint decision that Brian would work and you would be responsible for the home, anything he earns is joint money. You have as much right to it as he does.'

'Yes, and I've told you, he's very generous. I've never had to go without. I appreciate your concern, but apart from anything else I'm too old and too tired to start again. And Brian would be lost without me. You don't see the side of him that I do – he needs me.'

'Do you need him, though?' Sara said. 'Really and truly? Don't you think you'd be happier on your own?'

'Have you been happy on your own, these past five years? You're always saying how hard it is being single.'

'That's a bit different,' Sara said, stung. 'James died.'

'I know. And now you've replaced him, so you can't have been that happy on your own.'

The words stabbed her like a dagger, even though she knew deep down Helen was simply lashing out because she felt cornered. 'I haven't replaced him, that's a horrible thing to say.'

'Brian always says that he and I are enough for each other, and that I'm too influenced by you two.' She looked from Angela to Sara and back again defiantly. 'And I'm beginning to think he's right.'

She stormed out without saying goodbye, leaving her two friends staring at each other miserably.

'What are we going to do?' Sara said. 'What if we talk to Nigel and Greg – one of them could have a word with Brian, man to man? Nigel's arranged to play golf with him next week, I could ask him to say something.'

'I don't think that'd help. It'd inflame the situation, if anything. Greg's never liked him anyway. No, I think we should keep this between ourselves for now.'

'Do you think we've made things worse, by bringing it out into the light?' Sara said. 'If she isolates herself from us, things'll be even worse for her.'

'I won't let that happen,' Angela said. 'From now on, I'm going to do everything in my power to support her. There has to be a way to get her away from him.'

122

Chapter 15

Helen closed her front door behind her, and leant against it for a second. How dare they ambush her like that? Comparing Brian to Lizzie's horrible boyfriend, insinuating that he behaved as he did towards Helen out of controlling narcissism, when she knew it was a manifestation of his anxiety? He only behaved the way he did because he loved her, despite all her faults, and she was happy to fall in with his way of doing things if it made him feel more secure in her love for him. It was the least she could do after all they had been through together, especially the years of disappointment as their shared dream of becoming parents had got further and further away with each negative pregnancy test.

She didn't have time to think about it though, because she hadn't found today's razor blade, despite having gone over the house with a fine-tooth comb. She needed to think outside the box – where hadn't she looked? As she straightened the rug on the floor of the hallway, a thought occurred to her. She'd checked under all the rugs, but what about the fitted carpets? Could he have wedged it down the side of one of those? The only room downstairs with a carpet was the lounge, so she checked there first, running her fingers along the edges, moving the furniture where necessary, but the carpet was tightly glued down and fitted neatly under the skirting boards. She still had an hour or so before Brian was due home, but she was running out of options.

Upstairs in their bedroom, she knelt down and started checking the left-hand wall. For a second, she saw herself as Angela and Sara would see her, a pathetic creature dripping in sweat (she must have a shower before Brian got home), panicking at the thought of her husband's reaction to her not having cleaned the house thoroughly. She almost allowed herself to believe that they were right, but she closed that thought down before it could take hold. If it was true, if they were right about her relationship, there was no way she could stay. She would have to leave, or try to, but what would Brian do then? How would he cope? How would he react? It was easier and less dangerous not to think about it.

She worked her way methodically around the room until she got to Brian's side of the bed. She pulled out his bedside cabinet, with its locked drawers – the one place she never looked for the razor blade – and saw that there, the carpet was not quite flush with the skirting. Was that a glint of metal? Her heart began to beat faster. Did she dare to hope that she'd found it? She reached down and fished around, her fingers meeting cold metal. She took it out, rejoicing, but her joy was short lived. It wasn't the razor blade after all. It was a tiny key. She stared at it, nestled in the palm of her hand. There was no doubt that it was the key to the locked bedside drawers, but the question was, what was she meant to do with it? Was she supposed to find it because he had, for the first time, hidden the razor blade in his private drawers? Or did he never expect her to have found the key, and would she therefore be invading his privacy if she used it?

She didn't have time to overthink it – she would open the drawers and if the razor blade wasn't there she would simply replace the key and hope he hadn't fixed up a trap that would tell him that she had been in the drawers.

Hands trembling, she slotted the key into the lock of the top drawer. It turned easily, and she opened it. There wasn't much inside, but she took everything out, searching for the razor blade. First were their passports, which she only saw on the rare occasions they went abroad, and even then Brian kept hold of them for safety. She flipped through them quickly but there was no flash of silver between the pages. Next were NHS cards in both their names – she'd never seen these before, but as there was nowhere to hide anything in them, she laid them aside. An envelope containing their birth certificates and marriage certificate yielded nothing, likewise a pile of paperwork relating to the house and Brian's pension, of which she could make neither head nor tail. The drawer was now empty, so she put everything back in order and relocked it.

Moving on to the lower drawer, for one horrible moment she thought the key didn't fit – had Brian hidden the other key elsewhere? But with a wiggle it slid into the lock and turned. This second drawer was deeper than the other one and contained multiple cardboard envelope files with labels like INSURANCE, INVESTMENTS, WILLS. She flicked through them all, only looking for the razor blade. Even if she'd had time to read the contents, she didn't think they'd make much sense to her. She thought of how shocked her friends had been when she told them she didn't know if the mortgage was paid off. Perhaps she'd been silly to let Brian handle all their financial affairs, but it was too late now. She wouldn't know where to start. The last folder was labelled MEDICAL. There was no sign of the razor blade, but she leafed through the contents, thinking here at least would be something she could understand. The more recent documents were on top – letters from the consultants who had treated Brian's in-growing toenail, investigated her mysterious stomach pains, operated on Brian's hernia, removed a basal cell carcinoma from her nose.

At the bottom of the pile was the letter regarding Brian's vasectomy. After ten years of trying for a baby, when Helen was thirty-seven, they'd made the heartbreaking decision to give up. Brian felt that at forty-two, he was getting too old for first-time fatherhood. He'd said it was time to accept that it wasn't going to happen for them. She'd mentioned other options – IVF, adoption – but Brian was adamant that it was their own, natural-born baby or nothing. It was his idea to get a vasectomy – once he'd made the decision that he was too old, he didn't want there to be any accidents. She'd had no choice but to agree. She ran her eyes quickly down the letter. The consultant, a Mr Madden, Consultant Urologist at their local private hospital, had written to their GP (copying Brian) saying he had seen this very pleasant gentleman who had requested a vasectomy. He went on to say that whilst they wouldn't normally advise such a young man to undergo the procedure, this particular gentleman was adamant that he didn't want children and had offered some very persuasive arguments, including various hereditary conditions in his family that he didn't want to pass on. On balance, Mr Madden was happy to go ahead with the procedure.

Helen frowned. Forty-two wasn't particularly young for a vasectomy, and what hereditary conditions? Her eyes flicked to the top of the letter, and her blood ran cold. She put it down as if it could bite her. It was dated 2nd February – thirty years ago. Five years into their marriage. Two years *before* they started trying for children.

Ten years. Ten years of trying and waiting and hoping. One hundred and twenty bloodied sheets of toilet paper, each one a knife through her heart. *There's always next month*, he would say. *At least we know there's nothing wrong with my sperm.* All the while safe in the knowledge that there was no chance of her falling pregnant. He had put her through ten years of that hell – had made her think it was her own fault, that if she could only relax and stop worrying about it, she'd fall pregnant easily. She'd watched friends fall away into the all-consuming world of motherhood, having less and less time to give to her. *Never mind,* Brian would say. *We've got each other – that's all we need, isn't it?* She had thought it bonded them, this joint tragedy of never becoming parents. But Brian had never wanted it at all – in fact had made sure it wouldn't happen. He had lied to her – not once, but over and over again. A lifetime of lies.

She didn't know how long she'd been sitting there on the floor when the sound of Brian's key in the door roused her from the stupor she'd fallen into.

'Hello?' he called, a note of displeasure evident at not finding her downstairs as he usually would on his return from work.

Not caring about the consequences, she left the medical folder lying on the floor, its contents spilling out, the drawer open, the key still in the lock. With the letter in her hand, she walked slowly down the stairs to the hall, where Brian demanded angrily why she had taken so long to come and greet him on his return from work. It was only as she held the letter out to him, demanding an explanation, that she realised that for the first time ever she hadn't found the razor blade. Brian had never told her explicitly what would happen if she didn't. She supposed she was about to find out.

Chapter 16

Amelia Edwardson, graduated three years ago. That made her as young as twenty-four. Angela closed down her CV. There was no point employing someone even younger than Saskia. She needed someone who could empathise with her daters instead of laughing at them, or worse, pitying them.

Saskia had already been on a written warning, but she'd banged the nail into her own coffin when Angela sent her an email asking what she thought of a female dater's new photos and Saskia had forwarded it to a mate with the comment *Can you imagine trying get a date when you look like this?* Unfortunately for Saskia, she hadn't forwarded it, she'd replied to Angela.

She opened up the next one. Hannah Coulter was a hardworking, confident, committed professional. She scanned down the CV to see what it was that Hannah was so professional in. Ah. She was six months out of university, and her only work experience was a part-time job in Starbucks. This was hopeless.

She was finding it hard to concentrate on the mediocre CVs anyway, her mind still on Helen's situation. She replayed the morning's scene over and over in her head. Was it a mistake to have confronted Helen in the way they did? Angela was so desperate to help her, but had she gone crashing in like a bull in a china shop in her usual overbearing way and made things worse?

She opened up a web browser and searched for advice for women leaving a relationship. There were multiple options. The National Domestic Abuse Helpline, Women's Aid, Women Against Abuse. Would any of these organisations be of any use if the woman in question was refusing to acknowledge the abuse? She clicked on a checklist for women leaving a controlling relationship. It advised opening a secret email, squirreling away funds if feasible and getting copies of as much financial documentation as possible. She was still looking at it when Greg came breezing in, bending to kiss her cheek.

'I bumped into Nigel in town,' he said. 'You didn't tell me he and Sara were moving in together!'

'I've barely seen you,' Angela said, closing the web browser. 'If you're not at your Italian class you're learning to play pickleball, and I'm swamped at work since I had to fire Saskia. Where have you been today?'

'Geocaching. Good for them, I say,' he said, swiping an apple from the fruit bowl and taking a huge bite.

'Do you? You don't think it's too soon?'

'Not really, but you clearly do. I hope you're being supportive.'

'Of course I am. I'm delighted they're happy, that's the *raison d'être* of my agency, but I don't see what the mad rush is.'

'When you know, you know, I guess,' Greg shrugged. 'Life's pretty short, as Sara knows only too well. I don't blame her for wanting to grab any happiness that comes her way. You could see at the dinner party how in love they are.'

'Blimey, when did you get so poetic? Much as I love you, I need to crack on with some work so can you leave me alone, please?'

When he'd gone upstairs, she opened up the browser again, this time searching for advice on helping someone escape an abusive relationship.: *Understand the dynamics of abuse*, the website advised. *Greater understanding of this will help you develop more empathy for the person who is experiencing it.* Angela experienced a tidal wave of guilt. Not only had she failed to notice what was going on Helen's life, when she did find out instead of showing empathy, she had barged in and told her how awful it was. Helen would be even less likely to confide in her now. If Angela was honest, Helen had probably been left with the impression that Angela and Sara thought she was weak and pathetic. *Your friend may be unwilling to talk – they may even defend their partner,* the website continued. *They may be ashamed and not want to admit that things aren't alright. Try not to judge them. Remain open and supportive.* She had handled this all wrong. She hoped that blundering in hadn't made everything worse.

When the doorbell rang, she closed the laptop and went to answer it. Helen stood there, her face in shadow. They hadn't yet switched on the outside porch light.

'Helen! Are you OK? Come in.'

'Not really.' She stepped into the hallway. Angela clapped a hand to her mouth. A dark red, mottled bruise bloomed on Helen's cheek.

'Oh, Helen. Are you . . . did . . . was it . . .' *Try not to judge.*

'Yes. It was Brian,' Helen said shortly. Her usual dogged defensiveness had been replaced by a cold, factual delivery.

'Oh, Helen,' she said again, taking her friend in her arms. Helen allowed the embrace, but didn't respond.

'Come through, sit down.'

Without asking, Angela poured them both a glass of wine from an open bottle of red and they sat opposite each other at the kitchen table.

'Has he done this before?' Angela asked. 'Hurt you, physically?'

'Once or twice,' Helen said. 'Never on my face, though. Too clever for that.'

'Where is he now? Have you . . . have you left him?'

'No. I can't just walk out. I told you. I've got no money, no access to the bank accounts.'

'You can't stay with him!' The words burst from Angela before she had a chance to check herself. *Remain open and supportive.* 'Sorry, I didn't mean to shout. I'm so glad you're here, that you're telling me about this. I'll help you in any way I can.'

'I had to come straight here and tell you. If I'd left it 'til tomorrow I would have lost my nerve.' She took a huge gulp of wine. 'You and Sara were right, everything you said earlier. I think I've got so used to the way he treats me it's become normal, but I've always known in the back of my mind that it wasn't right. I do want to leave him, but I need to be careful about it.'

'Absolutely,' Angela said eagerly. 'We can help with that. I found a useful checklist online for what documents you should try and gather before he knows you're leaving – I was looking for ways to help you. I'll send you the link.'

'No, don't do that. He . . . he checks my phone.' She gripped the edge of the table. 'That's not normal, is it?'

'No!' Angela must have sounded shocked because Helen's cheeks flushed. 'No, it's not,' Angela went on more calmly, 'but please don't ever feel embarrassed to tell me this stuff – you have nothing to feel embarrassed about. Where is he now? Does he know you're here?'

'No. He's gone to a golf club committee meeting. I mustn't stay too long. He'd be furious if he knew I'd let anyone see me like this.'

'What made you come tonight? Don't get me wrong, I couldn't be happier that you've opened up to me, but what prompted it? Is it because Brian hit you?'

'No. I – I – found something. Oh, Angela . . .' She put her face in her hands for a few seconds, composing herself. Angela waited, scared of upsetting the delicate balance of events that had led Helen to this point.

'I found the key to a drawer that Brian always keeps locked. There was a file of medical information inside. One of the letters was about his vasectomy. Do you remember I told you he had one? It must have been a couple of years after I met you.'

'Yes. You said that you'd tried for children for a long time, but had decided that you were too old and you didn't want any accidents.'

'That's right. Although it was Brian that said he was too old, rather than me. I was only thirty-seven. Anyway, today I found a letter confirming the procedure. He had it done twelve years earlier.'

'What?' Angela couldn't quite understand what she was being told.

'He had a secret vasectomy before we even started trying for children. I was never going to get pregnant. He's been lying to me all these years.'

'My God, why?' Angela had known Brian was a bastard, but this was on another level.

'I don't know. I suppose it was another way to control me. It's obvious to me now that he wouldn't have wanted children – he didn't like anything that took my focus away from him. That's why I've hardly worked in my life. I loved it at Star Recruitment. I was good at it. That's where I met Sara, and through her I met you – I wouldn't have any friends at all if I hadn't done it. But Brian felt it was impacting on our life together, and I wanted to please him, to make him happy. I thought he wouldn't mind me working at the animal shelter – it was only a few hours a week and it was all women that worked there at first. But then I mentioned that a male volunteer had started, and I knew straight away from his reaction that he wasn't happy about it. He'd never been physical with me back then, it was . . . it's so hard to explain the hold he had on me, why I didn't want to upset him. I know you must think I'm weak and stupid.'

'No, I absolutely don't. Sara and I will do everything we can to support you in leaving him. You can stay here as long as you want. You won't be alone. You must be careful, though. I was reading just now that women are most at risk of violence when they're leaving the relationship.'

'I need to go – I must make sure I'm home before he gets back.'

Angela walked Helen to the door and gave her another tight hug. This time she squeezed back. They weren't normally friends who hugged, but it seemed appropriate. Helen felt like a bird, light and delicate, as if Angela holding her too hard would crush her into tiny pieces.

'Where's your car?' she said, opening the front door for Helen and peering up the street.

'I walked. I needed the fresh air – actually, no, that's not true.' She screwed up her face as if willing the words out. 'I'm not going to lie to protect him anymore. I walked in case Brian checks the mileage on my car. He doesn't like me to go anywhere without telling him.'

'You're doing the right thing,' Angela said. 'I know it's not going to be easy, but your life will be so much better in the end, I promise you.'

As Helen walked down the street and turned the corner, out of sight, Angela swore that this time, she would not let her down.

Chapter 17

'I have this horrible feeling she's not going to go through with it,' Angela said, indicating left to turn into Helen and Brian's road.

'I don't know, she seems pretty determined. I'm still reeling from the fact that he kept his vasectomy secret all those years – and what about that thing with the razor blade? Unbelievable.' The extent of Brian's abuse had come trickling out of Helen over the last two weeks, to Angela and Sara's utter horror.

'He's an absolute arsehole,' Angela agreed. 'Did Nigel ever have that round of golf with him?'

'Yes, they've played a couple of times,' Sara said. 'Nigel seems to quite like him, which is going to be awkward when he finds out what's been going on.'

The two friends had decided not to tell their respective partners about Helen's escape plan until it was a done deal. Their focus was on keeping up the pressure on her (in the nicest possible way) to ensure she didn't have a change of heart. The fortnight had been spent planning her exit down to the minutest detail, when Sara wasn't helping Nigel move into her house. Whilst Brian was at work, Helen had taken every document from his secret drawers to the library and photocopied them, keeping them in an orange foolscap folder at the very back of the cleaning cupboard (a place Brian was very unlikely to go).

The one thing she still needed to get from the drawer was her passport, as to take that any earlier than today would have alerted him that something was up.

'I know.' They pulled up outside the house. 'Right, here we go.'

Helen opened the door, rigid with tension. She was stylish as ever in loose linen trousers and an elegantly draped cowl-neck top – old habits die hard, plus Helen had wanted everything to seem normal this morning before Brian left for work.

'Everything OK?' Sara asked.

'Yes, fine. I tried to be as natural as possible when he left for work, so I hope he didn't suspect anything.'

They followed her through to the kitchen. A large suitcase stood upright near the door, along with four smaller bags.

'Can I tell you something mad?' Helen asked.

'Always,' Sara said.

'After he left this morning, I started looking for the razor blade. Even though I knew I wasn't going to be here when he got home. It's so ingrained in me. Isn't that stupid?'

'It's not stupid,' Angela said. 'It's entirely understandable.' Sara was impressed with how the usually brisk, no-nonsense Angela had risen to the occasion once it became clear that what was called for was calm, measured support. 'Is this everything?'

'Yes. Apart from my passport, which I need to get from the drawer.'

'Right, let's get all this in the car,' Angela said, taking hold of the suitcase, 'and then you can get your passport and have a final look round for anything else you want to bring.'

Sara and Helen took two each of the smaller bags. Once everything was safely stowed in the boot, they came back into the kitchen.

'A final sweep to make sure you've got everything?' Angela said.

'Good idea. There's nothing in here – I'm not bringing any kitchen stuff. Let's check the living room.'

They went through and Helen placed the orange folder of photocopied information on the coffee table while she opened drawers and surveyed the shelves.

'There's nothing in here, let's have a quick squiz upstairs – oh!' She broke off, every trace of colour draining from her face at the sound of a key in the door. Sara froze, fear flooding her body.

'Helen?' Brian called from the hallway.

'In here,' she whispered, then again, more loudly, as there was no way he'd have heard the first one: 'In here.' ✓

The three women looked first at each other, stricken, and then at the folder on the coffee table. There was no time to hide it or to discuss their strategy because within seconds, Brian was upon them.

'Hello, ladies! This is a surprise – I didn't know you had plans with your friends today, Helen.' A

'She didn't,' Angela said, seeing that Helen was unable to speak. 'We dropped in unexpectedly for a cuppa, but decided we'd go out for coffee. You were going to get your scarf, weren't you, Helen? From upstairs?'

Helen left the room, shooting them an agitated glance over her shoulder.

'Are you not working today, Brian?' Sara said as normally as she could manage.

'Supposed to be, but I didn't feel well.' He beamed at them, seeming far from unwell. In rude health, in fact.

'Sorry to hear that,' Angela said. 'We'll take Helen out and leave you to rest. Ah, here she comes now.'

Helen came back in, even more upset than she had been before she left the room.

'I can't find it. My scarf, I mean. It's not where I left it.'

'Never mind,' Angela said. 'Worst case scenario you can always get another one. Shall we go?'

'But my . . . scarf,' Helen said.

'Which one was it?' Brian asked kindly.

'What?' she said, unable to meet his eye.

'Which scarf? Not the pink striped one – I saw that hanging on the peg as I came in.'

Helen was mute, her mind wiped empty by adrenaline.

'It wasn't a warm, woolly scarf.' Sara came to her rescue. 'More a decorative one. The blue one with the little birds, wasn't it, Helen?'

'A decorative one? How lovely,' Brian said silkily. 'It's nice to dress up for a coffee with friends, isn't it?'

'Yes, isn't it?' Sara agreed faintly. This was ridiculous. She had no reason to be afraid of Brian, yet her chest was constricted, her pulse racing. You could cut the atmosphere in the room with a knife.

'Let's go without it,' Angela said. 'It doesn't matter. Come on, Helen. I'll take this.' She picked up the foolscap folder and tucked it under her arm. 'Some work documents I need to drop off at the office.'

Helen took one last, desperate look around the room, as if seeking her passport would make it magically materialise. Sara took her arm and started to lead her out to the hallway. They were minutes away from being in the car, speeding away from Brian towards the safety of Angela's house.

'Helen,' Brian said in a low voice. She stopped in the doorway and turned.

'Were you looking for this?' He reached into his trouser pocket and drew out a small, black booklet embossed in gold. Her passport.

Helen went very still.

'Did you honestly think I didn't know what you were planning? You're my wife. I know you better than you know yourself.'

'It doesn't matter,' Angela said. 'Helen can get another passport. What matters is she's leaving you, and you can't stop her.'

'You've decided that, have you?' Brian said. 'Is that what you want, Helen?'

'I . . . well . . . I'm . . .' She dropped her arm from Sara's grasp.

'Please,' he said softly. 'I know I'm not perfect, but I love you. You have to give me a chance. Haven't we been everything to each other, over all these years?'

'Why was it that you were everything to each other?' Angela asked, with a dangerous edge.

'Helen,' Brian said, ignoring her. 'Please, don't do this to us.'

'Was it because you didn't have children?' Angela continued.

Brian stepped forwards and took Helen's hands in his. She kept her eyes down. Sara didn't like the hint of resignation she detected – surely she wasn't going to fall at the last hurdle?

'Because there was a reason for that, wasn't there?' Angela ploughed on. 'You had a vasectomy, didn't you?'

'That's private medical information,' he said tightly, 'but yes, since you ask, we'd been trying for ten years. I was getting too old to be a father. It was a decision Helen and I made together.'

'No, Brian,' she said. 'You had a vasectomy before you and Helen started "trying" for children. She was never going to get pregnant. You're a liar.'

Brian's face clouded over.

'We know all about how you've behaved towards her,' Angela went on passionately. 'You've got this wonderful woman and you've treated her like dirt. I can't believe I didn't see it all along. You're a monster.'

He dropped Helen's hands.

'How dare you speak to me like that in my own home?' he said to Angela. 'You're poisonous, both of you. Get out of my house.'

'We're not leaving without Helen,' Angela said. 'You might have been able to intimidate her, but you don't scare me − and you don't scare her any more either.'

'Helen isn't scared of me,' he said. 'Tell them!' he said to her.

Helen shook her head. Sara wasn't sure if she was refusing Brian's request, or agreeing with him that no, she wasn't scared of him. She prayed it was the former.

'She's petrified,' Angela said. 'You've been controlling her for years. We know all about it. But no more. It's over. She's leaving you and she won't be coming back.'

'I said get out of my house,' Brian said, incandescent with fury. He took a step towards Angela, but she stood her ground.

'With pleasure,' she said. She took hold of Helen's hand and tugged her nearer. Helen allowed herself to be taken out of Brian's orbit. Her shoulders lowered a fraction, but then Brian jerked her other hand, dragging her back towards him so roughly she almost lost her balance.

'Let her go!' Angela shouted. 'She's not your possession. She doesn't want you any more, Brian.'

He dropped Helen's hand and took a step towards Angela, towering over her. Because of her forceful personality, Sara thought of Angela as tall and physically strong, but in fact she was neither of those things compared to Brian. Sara tried to tell herself there was nothing to fear from Brian, but her feet were rooted to the spot. He took hold of Angela's shoulders and shook her and she stumbled backwards, dropping the orange folder on the floor, where it skidded under the sofa. Sara went to speak, but it was as if her mouth was glued shut.

'Don't touch her,' Helen said. 'Don't you dare touch her.'

'You've found your voice, have you?' Brian said. 'Nobody tells me what to do in my own house. You of all people should know that.'

Without taking his eyes off Angela, he raised his hand in front of her, fist clenched. Sara was still frozen, as if she was watching the scene play out from a great height, unable to influence events. Angela flinched and closed her eyes for a millisecond, anticipating the blow. Suddenly Helen launched herself on him like a wildcat, screaming at him to stop. Sara watched, stupefied, willing herself to do something, anything, as Helen grappled with Brian. It was only a few seconds but time seemed to stand still. Helen was smaller even than Angela – Brian didn't like her to go above a size ten – but her core strength was remarkable thanks to her daily Pilates sessions. Brian struggled to shake her off as she clung to him, trying to get him away from Angela. With immense effort he freed himself and pushed her away. She half fell into the fireplace, clinging to the mantelpiece to stop herself from falling. Brian turned back to Angela with a roar of rage, having lost all control. As if in slow motion, Helen grabbed a large, silver trophy in the shape of the head of a 9-iron golf club, swung it high into the air and brought it crashing down on Brian's skull. For a second he teetered, almost righting himself. He reached out to Helen but she stepped away, leaving him grasping thin air. There was a tremendous crash as his head hit the stone hearth, and then a terrible silence as he lay, unmoving, on the living room floor, a pool of sticky, dark red blood seeping from the underside of his head.

Chapter 18

Helen let the trophy fall from her hand. Her stomach swirled and her breath came in panicky little puffs. She didn't want to look at Brian's waxy visage any more but she couldn't tear her eyes away, afraid of what she would see on Angela and Sara's faces as they grappled with what she had done. He lay utterly still.

'Is he . . . ?' Angela said, but then his chest rose and fell, air hissing out of his lungs.

'Thank God,' Sara said. The gap between each breath and the next was agonisingly long, but Brian was indubitably still alive. 'I'll call an ambulance.' She took her phone out of her pocket.

'Wait,' Helen said, the word springing almost involuntarily from her lips.

Sara's thumb hovered over the keypad. 'What?'

'Never mind,' Helen said. 'Sorry, I just thought . . . no, never mind.'

'She's right,' Angela said. 'Let's not have a knee-jerk reaction. Let's make sure we're doing the right thing.'

'The right thing?' Sara said. 'There's no question about what the right thing to do is when someone's seriously injured. Is there?'

'But . . . this wasn't an accident, was it?' Angela said.

'No,' Sara said. 'It was self-defence. Brian was coming at you, he was going to hurt you.'

'That's not strictly self-defence, though, is it?' Angela said. 'Helen wasn't defending herself.'

'No, she was defending you against someone who was trying to hurt you,' Sara said. 'That's the same thing.'

Brian made a gurgling sound.

'Listen to him!' Sara said. 'We should call the ambulance.' She looked wildly from one to the other.

'I don't think it is the same thing,' Angela said. 'And also, if Brian is . . . able to say what happened, he'll never admit that he was trying to hurt me. It'll be my word against his.'

'She's right,' Helen said. 'He'd also argue that even if it's true that he was angry, what I did wasn't a proportional response. That I was deliberately trying to kill him.'

'But you weren't!' Sara said. 'We'll back you up. This is madness.'

'I was on the verge of leaving him,' Helen said. 'What if the police found that out? It would make them look twice at me.'

'Helen's right,' Angela said decisively. 'What we need to do is—'

They were never to discover what it was Angela thought they needed to do, because at that precise moment, the doorbell let out a loud chime that made them all jump.

'Who's that?' Helen whimpered.

Angela, who was nearest to the bay window which had a vantage point on the front path, poked a finger between the slats of the wooden Venetian blind and peered through. A familiar figure stood there dressed in chinos and a bright red jumper.

'It's Nigel!' She backed away from the window as if it had burned her.

'Thank God,' Sara said. 'He's probably returning the golf clubs he borrowed from Brian. I'll let him in.'

'No!' For a moment Helen thought it had come from her own mouth, because the word had been reverberating around in her head, but it was Angela who said it.

'What?' Sara stopped on her way to the door. 'What do you mean, no?'

'Please, I don't want Nigel to see,' Helen whispered, as if Nigel could hear her through the thick brick walls of the house.

'Helen's right,' Angela said. 'We need to decide what we're going to do and . . . say . . . before we involve anyone else.'

'What we're going to do?' Sara repeated. 'We're going to call an ambulance, aren't we?'

'Yes, of course,' Angela said. 'But isn't it a good idea to get our story straight first? For Helen's sake?'

Helen's knees buckled beneath her and she sank down into the armchair behind her. It was Brian's chair, the one she wasn't allowed to sit in, and even in the midst of this terror and chaos she experienced a pang of fear.

'Isn't that what you would prefer?' Angela asked her urgently. 'That we don't let Nigel in?'

Helen nodded, unable to speak.

The doorbell rang again.

'What is he still doing here?' Angela hissed. A minute or so passed before the tinny sound of the letterbox opening and closing rang through the hallway. Finally, they heard the latch of the garden gate and the sound of Nigel's car roaring into life and off down the road.

'What did he put through the door?' Helen said.

'I'll have a look.' Angela hurried out. Sara and Helen stared at each other – anything was preferable to seeing the twisted shape of Brian on the floor.

'He dropped a note through saying he came by to drop the clubs off but as there was no answer he'll take them home and try another time.'

'What do you mean by getting our story straight?' Sara said.

'Let's think,' Angela said. 'Helen was on the verge of escaping from this shitshow of a marriage. I can't bear it if this complicates things. Self-defence isn't going to be believable – she was about to leave her husband and she hit him with a heavy, blunt instrument. We've got to think about how that looks.'

'So if it wasn't self-defence,' Helen said. 'It was . . . ?'

'An accident,' Angela said with some force. 'Wasn't it, Helen?'

Helen looked at her vacantly.

'I don't know about—' Sara began.

'Yes, that's right,' Angela butted in, answering her own question. 'If we explain exactly how it happened, that it was self-defence, that implies that he was violent towards us, and we don't necessarily want them to know that. It just makes it more suspicious. They'll think Helen did it deliberately.'

'But what are you proposing we say?' asked Sara with a note of hysteria.

'For now, let's say we found him like this. The golf trophy hit him on the left side of his head, and he's fallen on the hearth on the same side, so it could well be that he fell, and it was the hearth that did the damage. We can clean up the trophy and put it back. Hasn't he been unsteady on his feet recently, Helen?'

'No, not—'

'Let's say he has, shall we?'

'You want us to lie?' Sara said, appalled.

'What's the alternative?' Angela snapped. 'Look at Helen.' They both turned to her. She wilted under their scrutiny. 'How long's she going to last if she gets arrested, or sent to prison? You know what her life has been up 'til now, and we're partly to blame for not seeing what was going on. Do you want that on your conscience? Just when she was about to escape?'

'No,' Sara said uneasily.

'What if he wakes up?' Helen had finally found her voice. 'What if he's not . . . you know?' She couldn't say the words, the idea that she might have actually killed Brian being too big a concept to face.

'Quite,' Sara said. 'What then?'

'We'll cross that bridge when – if – we come to it,' Angela said decisively. 'If he does wake up, it's likely he won't have any memory of what happened. And if he does, well, we'll deal with it then. So are we agreed? We'd been out for coffee . . . no, they'll want to know where . . . how about a walk in the woods, the Southborough woods, we didn't see anyone, and we all came back here, intending to have lunch? And we found Brian like this. Does that sound OK, Helen?'

Helen felt as if she was floating above her body. The idea that she was in a position to make any kind of decision was faintly ludicrous. Angela, forceful at the best of times, had gone into overdrive and it was easy to be swept along in her wake.

'Oh no, hang on,' Angela was saying now. 'That won't work. If there's ever any reason for them to suspect foul play—'

Helen gave a whimper.

'I'm sure they won't,' she said hastily, 'but in case they ever check CCTV and whatnot – do you know if your house is covered by CCTV?'

'It doesn't show the house itself,' Helen said, trying to collect herself. 'Moira next door complained about it when she got burgled. But there's a camera at the end of the street that would have captured anyone coming here.'

'So they'll be able to see that Brian came home around three, and that we were already here, and then by the time we call the ambulance it'll be . . . what,' she checked her watch, 'ten past, quarter past, something like that. So what would fit those timings?'

'We could say we were having coffee in the garden?' Helen suggested. 'It is a lovely day. Although, Moira might remember that we weren't, if she's ever asked. It's like living next door to the Gestapo.'

'I think that could work,' Angela said. 'Around three o'clock, we made coffee and took it into the garden. Fifteen or twenty minutes later, you went in to see what had happened to him and found him here on the floor, having had a fall.'

'Fifteen or *twenty*?' Sara said. 'You said ten or quarter past.'

'Do you think . . . maybe . . . we *should* go and have a quick coffee in the garden, now, before we call the ambulance?' Helen suggested. 'Then if anyone ever asks Moira, she'll confirm it.'

Sara was caught between fear and admiration for this new version of Helen. 'Seriously? Do neither of you think we should tell the truth?'

'Hand on heart, do you think that's the best thing for Helen?' Angela asked.

'But what would I tell Nigel? What are you going to say to Greg?'

'I'll say exactly what we say to the police, what we say to everyone, and you'll have to do the same. We can't involve anyone else, it's too risky.'

'You'll lie to Greg?'

'That's no problem, he's so busy with his quoits or whatever it is this week I doubt he notices if I'm there or not. You'll have to do the same with Nigel. Are you prepared to do that? We can't call the ambulance until we know what our plan is.'

Sara looked helplessly at Brian. The pool of blood that had leached into the carpet around his head was bigger than it had been a moment ago.

'Helen?' she said. 'Are you sure this is what you want to do?'

Helen thought of all the years she had spent in a prison of Brian's making, convinced by his protestation that his jealousy was merely a measure of his overwhelming love for her. There had been a moment that first night, before they were married, when he had got so angry about her being late home, that she had wondered if she was making a mistake. She had spoken to her mother about it, one week before the wedding. Her mother had told her not to be so silly. She said all men were like that, and that now Helen was getting married she couldn't think only of herself. Brian's wellbeing ought to be as important to her as her own. That was what marriage was, her mother had said, and in any case they couldn't possibly cancel the wedding now, they would lose so much money, and her sister was coming all the way from Edinburgh, and had she double-checked when the florist was delivering the bouquet? So she had squashed down the question, and never allowed it to rear its head again. She had always been adaptable, so she shaped herself around Brian, softening her edges to fit into his contours until she no longer knew what shape she had been to start with. Until Brian raised his fist to Angela, Helen had thought that today was going to be the start of a new life for her, that being in her mid-fifties didn't preclude her from pursuing the life she wanted, instead of accepting what she'd been given. How stupid that had been. She should have known it wouldn't, couldn't be that easy for her. But was she ready to give up on the idea altogether?

'Yes,' she said, with a strength that been absent since she had heard the crunch of metal on bone and watched as Brian toppled to the ground. 'Poor Brian, so unsteady on his feet. Now, coffee in the garden – do you mind instant?'

Chapter 19

A few moments later, the three friends arranged themselves self-consciously around the glass-topped garden table on the neat, weed-free patio. The rest of the garden consisted of a ruthlessly mown square of lawn. Brian wasn't a fan of flowerbeds or growing your own vegetables. Helen had never interrogated why this was, but she was beginning to understand that he wouldn't countenance anything he couldn't entirely control.

'Afternoon!' Moira called from the other side of the fence where she was weeding a chaotic raised bed stuffed with frilly lettuces and pale green spears of asparagus. She was dressed in a sky-blue boiler suit, her wispy, silvery hair caught up in a spotted bandana. 'What a lovely day.'

'Hello, Moira!' Helen said. 'Hang on, Angela, don't put your mug down yet, I need to get a coaster – oh.' She broke off. The only person who cared whether the glass-topped table got a ring on it from a coffee mug was lying on the lounge floor, blood pouring from his head. 'Perhaps it doesn't matter,' she said.

'I'd say that's certainly the least of your worries,' Sara said grimly.

'We need to act normal,' Angela whispered. 'Would you normally talk to her, exchange pleasantries?'

'It doesn't exactly look normal if we're muttering away to each other,' Sara said, whispering nonetheless.

'Your lettuces are looking wonderful, Moira,' Helen said stag-ily. 'How do you do it?'

'Don't overdo it,' Angela murmured.

'Thank you!' Moira said. 'It's mostly a question of keeping them well-watered, and of course protecting them from the dreaded slugs!'

'Oh golly,' Helen said. 'Any tips?' Golly? Who said golly these days?

'I like to take a three-pronged approach,' Moira said, apparently undeterred by Helen deploying the vocabulary of a 1950s schoolgirl, 'using a combination of physical barriers, repellents and trapping methods. I can take you through what I've found most effective for each, if you like?'

'Maybe some other time,' Helen said, her mouth dry. 'I've got friends here. We're just having a coffee in the garden.'

'Yes, I can see that,' Moira said, slightly puzzled. 'Well, any time.' She attacked the soil with renewed vigour.

'This coffee is delicious!' Angela said loudly. The other two peered into their mugs dubiously. In her confusion, Helen had spooned too much coffee powder in and omitted to add milk, so what they were pretend-sipping might as well have been liquid mud. 'We're going to have to put on a show!' she added under her breath.

'A show?' Sara said, leaning forward. 'Yes, isn't it? Where did you get it?' she almost shouted.

'When Helen goes in and "finds" Brian, she's going to have to come out all shocked and crying, as if she's really just found him.'

'It's Columbian! Waitrose own, would you believe?' Helen already sounded mildly hysterical, so perhaps the upcoming performance wouldn't be too much of a stretch. 'Oh God,' she said to the other two. 'I don't know if I can.'

'You can, Helen,' Angela said firmly. 'Let's give it a few more minutes, then say you're going in to see how Brian is.' She raised her voice again. 'I wonder if it's going to rain tonight?'

'I do hope so,' Moira said, as if she was at the table. 'We could do with some after the dry spell we've been having.'

'What about those new roadworks on the A26?' Angela ploughed on, gesturing under the table for one of the other two to join in. Sara stared at her blankly. Helen looked as if she might pass out.

'Such a pain,' Moira agreed. 'What are they doing there?'

'Gas works, I think,' Angela managed.

'Oh good heavens, not again. Still, better than being gassed to death, I suppose.'

Angela agreed that indeed, it did seem the better option.

'Have you seen these new plans for traffic calming in the St John's area?' Moira went on. 'That's going to make every-thing even worse. If I want to pop to the industrial estate for a bag of compost, I'll have to go all round the houses. You should come to the public meeting – the more objections the better.'

Angela said she would bear it in mind. It was a low point in the already mind-numbing conversation, so she raised her eyebrows at Helen, jerking her head towards the house. Helen took the hint and stood.

'I'll just go and see if Brian's alright,' she declaimed in the manner of a narrator in a primary school nativity play, chosen for the role due to her loud, clear voice and ability to remember her lines.

Angela and Sara waited in silence. Angela wondered what Helen was doing inside. Would she be continuing with this pantomime, as if performing for an imaginary audience inside the house? Or standing just inside the back door and counting to twenty? She got the answer when Helen came running out after a minute or so, with blood on her hands and a streak of it smeared vivid scarlet across her cheek.

'Brian's fallen!' she said, with a realistic air of panic. Angela was rather impressed.

'Is he OK?' she asked.

'No, he's bleeding, unconscious – I think he's hit his head – we need to call an ambulance.'

Sara fumbled for her phone and dialled 999.

'Shall I come round?' Moira shot up from the vegetable bed and came over to the fence, eager to play a part in this drama. 'I'm a registered first aider.'

'No!' Angela's voice was rather louder than she had intended. 'No,' she repeated more quietly. 'I'm a first aider too. I'll go. We'll update you when we know what's what.'

The three women hurried into the house, Sara instructing the emergency services on the phone as they went.

'Well done,' Angela said to Helen once the three of them were safely inside. 'The show's over.'

'Is it?' Sara said, hanging up the phone. Privately, she feared it had only just begun.

Chapter 20

Angela and Sara drove from Helen's house to the hospital in a loaded silence. Parking was the usual stress-inducing nightmare, but once they had found a space they hurried into A&E. Angela was about to text Helen, who had gone ahead in the ambulance with Brian, when Sara poked her in the arm and pointed to where Helen sat, staring into space, on a moulded plastic chair that was bolted to the ground.

'This is like the seventh circle of hell,' Angela muttered.

On Helen's left, a harried woman tried to quiet a fractious baby, her toddler pulling urgently on her arm asking for snacks. On her right was an elderly woman, her scalp pink beneath sparse, white hair, her skin deeply lined, clinging for dear life to a cardboard sick bowl shaped like a pork pie hat.

Helen didn't notice her friends until they were right in front of her. She stood up, having seemingly aged in the fifteen minutes since they last saw her. She was deathly pale, mascara smudged and bleeding into the lines around her eyes.

'Any news?' Angela asked, aware that usually when one asks that question, one is hoping for good news. She wasn't quite ready to examine what she was hoping for.

'No. I don't know what's going on. They told me to wait out here while they do some tests.'

'Did he . . . wake up at all in the ambulance?' Angela asked.

'No, not at all.'

'That's good,' Angela said.

'Good?' Sara asked. 'Jesus Christ, Angela. I'm still not sure about this.'

'We need to hold our nerve,' Angela hissed, looking around fearfully, although everyone in the vicinity was more worried about their own health than what three middle-aged women were talking about. 'We've made the decision now, Sara. We can't go back. We haven't done anything so very bad. We called the ambulance didn't we? It's out of our hands now. We need to hold it together for Helen's sake.'

'But what about—' Sara began.

'Come on,' Angela interrupted. 'Let's see if we can find anything out.'

As they headed towards the reception desk, a red-haired young man in blue scrubs came out of the double doors at the other end of the waiting room.

'That's him!' Helen said, waving at him.

He smiled and beckoned her over.

'Come through and we'll have a chat,' he said to Helen.

'These are my friends, is it OK if they come too?'

'Of course,' he said, holding the door open into a small room with low sofas and a coffee table. It reminded Angela of the bad news room she'd been ushered into to receive her diagnosis of breast cancer twelve years earlier. She'd known the moment they took her in there. Good news is given in the consultant's examining room, almost before you've taken off your coat. *Everything looks fine, Ms Masterson.* Bad news needs soft furnishings and natural light and the tissues that sit on the coffee table, waiting to be plucked out and shredded into pieces by nervous fingers. Greg had gripped her hand tightly throughout. She'd been dreading the moment they were left alone, when they would have to acknowledge between them the unvarnished, monstrous truth of what they'd been told. She knew he was going to be devastated, and although she understood that, she couldn't in that moment deal with his own distress as well as her own. The relief had been tremendous when instead of the histrionics she'd feared, he'd been calm and reassuring. *This is the boat we're in,* he'd said. *There's a plan in place and we'll take it one step at a time. Everything will be OK.* It was exactly what she'd needed to hear at the time.

'Is he awake? Helen asked.

A

'I'm afraid not,' the doctor said. 'He's gone up for a CT scan and we'll know more when we get the results of that. He took quite a whack to the head when he fell, so if the scan reveals any pooling of blood or fluid, we may need to operate. After that, it's likely we'll take him to Intensive Care and place him into an induced coma to prevent further damage to the brain. Can I ask – how did it happen?'

Angela felt Sara go very still beside her. Her instincts screamed at her to jump in, speak for Helen in case she gave the game away, but would that be more suspicious?

'My friends and I were in the garden,' Helen said clearly. 'It was a lovely day. When Brian didn't come out to join us, I went in to check on him and found him on the floor. There was . . . a lot of blood . . . sorry,' she faltered.

'Take your time,' the doctor said, kindly. 'Had Brian fallen before? Was he unsteady on his feet?'

'It's all my fault,' Helen said in a small voice.

Angela braced herself. This was no time for a confession. They all needed to hold their nerve. 'No, Helen,' she said forcefully. 'Don't be silly, you weren't there.'

'What do you mean?' Sara said. Angela had a horrible feeling she hoped Helen was going to tell the truth.

'I told him to go to the GP, over and over again,' Helen said, looking dead into the kind eyes of the A&E doctor. Angela sat up straighter. 'The first time he said he'd tripped over some shopping bags that I'd left lying around, although I know I hadn't. Then he blamed his shoelaces. The third time he couldn't make something up because I saw it with my own eyes. He was carrying a cup of tea and he missed his footing. Hot tea every-where. He could have been badly burned.'

'It's a familiar story,' the doctor said sympathetically.

'I begged him to seek help, but he was too proud. He hated . . . hates thinking of himself as an older person. I should have tried harder.'

'It's not your fault,' the doctor said. 'We see it a lot, with men particularly. They're reluctant to admit they need help.' He stood up. 'It's unfortunate but he's in the best place now. I'll come and see you when we've got the results of his scan. In the meantime, try not to worry too much.'

When he'd gone, the women remained silent for a short while, as if checking he wasn't going to pop back in.

'Bloody hell, Helen.' It was Sara who broke the silence. 'You were frighteningly convincing.'

'I thought it might help if I added some detail.'

'That was a stroke of genius,' Angela said. 'Well done.'

'What if he wakes up, though?' Sara said. 'He's going to say you're lying.'

Helen looked from Sara to Angela and back again, eerily calm.

'We'll just have to hope he doesn't wake up, then,' she said.

Chapter 21

'How's Helen holding up?'

Nigel handed Sara a glass of wine and she took a grateful gulp. Of course she was capable of buying and pouring her own wine, but how delightful it was to have it served with a side order of love, care and attention. She felt disloyal admitting it, but James had never made her feel cherished in the way Nigel did. He had always been so busy working, and the boys had still been living at home, so she had been taken up with the minutiae of life with teenagers – lifts and homework supervision and the endless, endless meals. They had still loved each other, but at times they had felt more like partners in a team than lovers. There never seemed to be time for the small acts of care that Nigel lavished on her daily.

'Pretty well, all things considered.' Sara chose her words carefully. In fact, Helen was coping frighteningly well and had taken to lying to the doctors like a duck to water, but she mustn't say that to Nigel. Angela had impressed upon her the need to keep the truth of what had happened between the three women. She'd agreed but she wasn't happy about being forced into lying to Nigel.

'It's lucky you and Angela were there – if she'd been alone it would have been even worse. Hang on, what time did you say you came in and found him?'

'About twenty past three.' It had been nearer three o'clock, but they needed to stick to their story that they had called the ambulance without delay.

'He must have been in there when I called round earlier, that was shortly after three. I hope he couldn't hear me, but wasn't able to call out. How horrible. You must have been in the garden.'

'Yes, we were. I mean, I suppose we must have been.' Almost too late, Sara remembered she wasn't meant to know Nigel had been there at all. She feared she was going to struggle with maintaining this lie long term. 'You were there?' she added quickly. 'At Helen and Brian's? We wouldn't have heard the doorbell out in the garden – that is, if you rang the doorbell, I guess you did, but . . .'

'I popped round to return those golf clubs I'd borrowed, but there was no answer.' Nigel didn't seem to register her discombobulation. 'I didn't want to leave them round the front, so I brought them back with me. Don't worry – I've put them back in your shed for now, I knew you wouldn't want them cluttering up the place.'

'That hardly seems to matter now.' She placed the wine glass on the table with a shaking hand. 'I don't feel too good, my heart's going like the clappers.'

'It's shock.' Nigel took her hands in his. 'Breathe slowly, in through the nose, out through the mouth. That's it.'

She did as he said for a minute or two until her pulse returned to something approaching normal.

'Thanks,' she said. 'I think I went straight into emergency mode earlier, dealing with all the practical stuff. It's only hitting me now.'

'You did everything you could,' Nigel said.

She nodded her agreement, although it couldn't be further from the truth. What if Brian died? Did that make her and Angela accessories to murder? Was that a thing or did it only exist in golden age detective novels?

'I got some stuff in to make dinner – do you like meatballs?' he asked.

'Yes, lovely.'

'I'll get going on that – you sit there and drink your wine. Let me look after you.'

As Nigel mixed mince, breadcrumbs and a beaten egg, adding a pinch of herbs here and some seasoning there, Sara wrestled with her conscience. What was the lesser of these two evils? In the eyes of the law, it was clear. They should have told the truth about what happened. But if they had, Helen might be sitting in a police cell right now. There were mitigating circumstances – coercive control was a crime punishable by law, and there was a chance that could have worked in her favour eventually, but the plain truth of it was that if Brian died, Helen could be up on a murder charge. Was that what she wanted for her friend, just as she was on the cusp of a new life?

Keeping quiet was legally wrong, but was it morally wrong? There was a chance they were going to get found out anyway – particularly if Brian woke up – in which case Angela and Sara would be in hot water with the police. If Sara took it upon herself to disregard Angela and throw Helen under the bus by confessing now, presumably that would go in Sara's favour – but would she always wonder if she was doing it to save herself? Because that was the one advantage, other than, well, that it was the truth. Owning up now meant consigning Helen, and possibly Angela too, to an uncertain fate, whilst saving her own skin.

It would mean the end of the friendship, but on top of that, she wasn't sure she'd be able to live with herself.

'What do you think of this?' Nigel held out a wooden spoon coated with the homemade tomato sauce he had bubbling away on the hob. 'More seasoning?'

'It's delicious,' she said. 'Absolutely perfect. Like you.'

He grinned and kissed her forehead. 'Let's eat.'

Nigel served up two steaming plates of pasta and meatballs and refilled both their wine glasses.

'I'd like to go and see Brian if that's possible,' he said, sitting down opposite her. 'I know I haven't known him long, but I enjoyed our chats at the golf club and it might give Helen a break.'

'I don't think you can at the moment – he's in an induced coma and they've moved him up to Intensive Care. I think it's only Helen that's allowed in.'

'We could go and have a coffee with her in the café at the hospital, then. Might be nice for her to have a change of scene and some company.'

'That's such a lovely idea.' Sara's eyes prickled with tears. Nigel was such a decent man. She wished she could confide in him. Perhaps he would understand? 'We could go tomorrow afternoon. I said I'd go and see Mum in the care home in the morning – not that she'll remember.'

'Why don't I come with you to the home?' he said. 'I'd love to meet your mum.'

'Oh, you don't have to do that. She's got dementia. The home's nice, as far as these things go, but it's still a dementia care facility, with all that entails – one of the residents regularly accuses me of having murdered her son, and it always smells of boiled cabbage no matter what they've had for dinner. I wouldn't put you through it.'

'It's fine, I'd like to come. Just let me know what time.'

'Thank you.' The tears that had been threatening spilled down her cheeks. James had rarely come with her to see Mum. Her dementia wasn't even that bad when James was alive – you could have a decent conversation with her most days – but still he refused to come. It would make such a difference having someone else there to help fill the silences. It was so hard to think of things to say, to ask – Mum had no idea what she'd done or even what she'd had for her last meal. Sometimes Sara suspected her mother didn't know who she, Sara, was at all, but was pretending in a heartbreaking attempt to save face.

Nigel's phone began to trill and he picked it up.

'It's Isabel on FaceTime. I'll call her back later.'

'Don't be silly, answer it. I'll say hello quickly and then leave you to it.'

Sara had 'met' Isabel several times on video calls, and was looking forward to meeting her in person when she came over for a holiday in a few weeks' time.

'Hi, darling!' Nigel said. Sara leant over his shoulder and waved at the screen.

'Hi, dad.' Isabel was subdued, not the ebullient young woman Sara had spoken to previously.

'Everything alright?' Nigel asked.

'No,' she said tightly. 'There's something I need to talk to you about.'

Chapter 22

'I'm afraid we need to keep Brian in the induced coma for the time being,' Mr Tarapore, Brian's consultant neurosurgeon, said from behind his desk. The light bounced off his shiny, bald head and his shirtsleeves were rolled up, revealing muscular forearms.

The moulded plastic chair dug into the back of Helen's legs. She shifted position.

'Oh. Right.' Icy fingers of fear clutched at her every time she thought of Brian coming out of the coma. She'd barely slept, turning the possibilities over and over in her mind. What would Brian remember of that day? Dared she hope that the answer to that question would be nothing? If she was brutally honest, what she really hoped was that he wouldn't wake up at all. She didn't know if that was a normal response in these circumstances, or whether her marriage to Brian had hardened her, like a piece of tempered glass.

'You know that Brian has suffered what we call a Traumatic Brain Injury?'

'Yes. He hit his head on the hearth when he fell.' The lie fell so easily from her mouth now it might as well have been the truth.

'Mm. Yes. So this has caused his brain to swell, affecting blood flow around the brain. We've been keeping a very close eye on

Brian, and unfortunately his latest scan shows that there is a pooling of fluid on his brain.'

'What does that mean?'

'It means we'll have to operate.'

'Brain surgery?'

'Yes. We'll implant a thin tube called a shunt into his brain that will drain away the excess fluid. Whilst we're in there, we'll make a hole in the floor of Brian's brain to allow any trapped fluid to escape.'

'That sounds . . . difficult.' The phrase *It's not brain surgery* popped into her head and she suppressed the urge to laugh.

'It's a delicate procedure, yes, but I do it all the time.' Mr Tarapore might have been aiming for reassurance but in fact sounded slightly peeved. 'There are risks, as there are with all surgery, but we'll take you through those before we proceed. Do you have any questions?'

'I don't think so.' What would a genuine, concerned wife ask in these circumstances? She would have liked to ask what the chances were of Brian making a full recovery, but she was worried about her voice giving away her hope that they were extremely low.

'I do have one question for you, Mrs Greenwood,' Mr Tarapore said hesitantly.

'Yes?' She gathered up her coat and handbag and perched on the edge of the chair, her mind already back in the ICU, soundtracked by the rhythmic hum of the ventilator as it filled and emptied Brian's lungs.

'It's about the nature of Brian's injury.'

Helen felt as if all the breath had left her body in a single whoosh, like the noise her phone made when she sent an email.

'There is an injury to his skull consistent with him having hit his head on the hearthstone, as you said.'

'Yes, he fell. I told the doctor in A&E, he's been very unsteady on his feet lately. Me and my friends were in the garden.' She was aware she was babbling but didn't have any control over what came out of her mouth. 'He hit his head when he fell.'

'On his latest scan I noticed another injury, on the same side of his head. This one is different in nature, and distinct from the one caused by the hearth. Is there something else that Brian could have caught his head against on the way down?' His voice was level, his expression bland. Helen couldn't tell if there was an accusatory undertone, or if that was a product of her guilty conscience.

'Well, there's a . . .' Her mind raced. What was there? 'Along the edge of the fireplace itself, there's a sort of . . . I don't know what you call it, like a little fence? It's not a real fire, it's one of those ones with the pretend coals. We've been meaning to replace it, but I worry that the smoke from a real fire makes everything dirty, and now it's meant to be bad for the environment, so . . . he could have knocked into that. It's got sharp spikes on each of the little fence posts.'

'A little fence,' Mr Tarapore repeated, scribbling away on Brian's notes.

'Yes. A sort of guard, to prevent sparks from flying out. Not that there are any sparks, of course, because it's not a real fire, but it's made to look like one. At least I think that's what it is.'

He paused, as if considering probing further, but then seemed to change his mind, putting the lid back on his pen and popping it into the breast pocket of his shirt.

'I see. I'll let you know when we're going to do the surgery and someone will take you through the whole thing. Are you going to be in ICU this afternoon?'

'Yes.' Was he implying she might abscond? She was second guessing his every remark now. 'Some friends are coming in shortly to have a coffee with me, but I'll only be gone for half an hour or so.'

'Very well. I'll be in touch later.' ✓

Helen made her way through the rabbit warren of corridors back to the coffee shop near the main entrance to the hospital. She passed patients and visitors on their way to and from appointments or wards, the patients walking slowly or on crutches, in various states of distress and elation, the visitors dreading or perhaps looking forward to their brief sojourn on the ward. Some of them had clearly just received life-changing news, but today she noticed nothing, thinking only of discussing this latest, somewhat worrying line of questioning with her friends.

She searched the café for them, her heart sinking when she saw not only Sara and Angela, but Nigel too, ensconced at a corner table. How were they supposed to discuss anything with him there? Bloody Sara. He leapt up and gave her a warm hug. ✓

'What can I get you to drink? We've already bought up half the cake cabinet – we weren't sure what you'd like.' On the table in front of them was a plate containing a random selection of muffins, cupcakes and flapjacks.

'I'll have a cup of tea please – English Breakfast.'

'Lovely. Be right back.'

Helen sat down in the free seat. ✓

'Now you're both here, there's something I need to tell you,' Sara said.

'In a minute,' Helen said, her eyes flicking to Nigel at the counter. 'The consultant's asking questions.'

'What kind of questions?' Angela said urgently.

'He said there's another injury on Brian's skull – not just the one from the hearth. It must be from the . . .'

Sara paled, her own news temporarily forgotten. 'Did he think it was suspicious?'

'I don't know! I was so flustered, I started gabbing on about the fireplace and how it could have been from the fireguard thing.'

'Did he believe you?' Sara said. 'Of course he didn't!' she went on, not waiting for an answer. 'Why would he have asked you if he didn't suspect you had a hand in it?'

'I don't know!' Helen said. 'I suppose it's natural that he asked me. Isn't it?'

'We've got to be so careful,' Sara said. 'I keep thinking what if Brian wakes up? We need to have a plan. It's all very well, Angela, you saying we'll cross that bridge if we come to it, but we need to be prepared.'

'I agree we need a plan,' Angela said. 'Let me think about it.'

'There's no immediate danger of him waking up.' Helen leant forward, her head bowed towards the other two. 'They're keeping him in the induced coma for the foreseeable – he's got to have surgery to remove fluid from his brain.'

'Surgery, did you say?' Nigel placed a steaming cardboard cup in front of her, making her start. 'Are you talking about Isabel?'

'No, I haven't had a chance to tell them yet,' Sara said.

'I've just come from a meeting with Brian's consultant,' Helen said. 'There's fluid pooling in his brain, so they want to operate as soon as possible. They'll be keeping him in the coma until they know how the surgery has gone.'

'That's good,' Angela said absentmindedly. Nigel frowned. 'I mean, he's in good hands, that's the main thing. What haven't you had a chance to tell us?' she asked Sara.

'Nigel's had . . . *we've* had some bad news about his daughter, Isabel. I think I told you she lives in the US?'

'Oh dear,' Angela said. 'What is it?'

'She's . . .' He took a breath and composed himself. 'She's been diagnosed with breast cancer.'

'I'm so sorry to hear that,' Helen said.

'Me too,' Angela said. 'I don't know if Sara's told you I went through it myself twelve years ago. The treatments are amazing now though – things have moved on even since I went through it. There's so much research that's been done.'

'That's what I've been saying,' Sara said. 'And it seems as though they've caught it early, doesn't it?'

'Yes, yes it does. It's just . . . when it's your child, and there's nothing you can do to protect her . . .' Nigel pressed his lips together. 'She'll be fine, I know she will.'

'Are you going to go out and see her?' Angela asked.

'Yes. She said not to, but I don't think she meant it. My ex-wife will be going too, but we'll try and arrange to go at different times. We don't have the greatest relationship, so that's the last thing Isabel needs, having to referee our slanging matches.'

'Will you go too?' Helen asked Sara.

'Not this time – Isabel needs her dad's undivided attention. I'll go another time, when she's finished her treatment.'

'Absolutely,' Nigel said. 'The main thing is that she gets the best possible treatment – like Brian is, I'm sure. Listen, I don't want to derail everything with my problems. How are you coping, Helen?'

'You know . . . I'm getting through.' Helen was rather ashamed in the face of Nigel's real grief and worry, when her main concern, if she was brutally honest, was whether she was going to get away with what she had done to Brian.

'Is there anything we can do to help?' Nigel said. 'Anything we can bring in for you, or Brian?'

'No, please don't worry. I can't sleep here, so I'm at home every night.'

'And is that OK for you?' he asked. 'Being back at the scene of the . . .'

Helen thought for a terrifying second he was going to say *crime*.

'. . . accident,' he finished. 'Because – well, I don't want to overstep, it's Sara's house after all, but I'm she wouldn't mind if you stayed with us for a while?'

'Not at all,' Sara said. 'And it's your house now too, Nigel.'

'That's very kind,' Helen said, 'but I'm happy at home. Can we talk about something else? I'm sick to the back teeth of talk of surgery and brains and injuries.'

Nigel looked taken aback.

'What I mean is, I need distraction,' she qualified, reminding herself she was meant to be playing the part of the distraught, loving wife whose husband was so sadly in a coma, not the violent criminal who had put him there and was hoping he would never wake up. On a rare holiday abroad, she and Brian had taken a tour of the Arc de Triomphe in Paris. The guide had described how the weight of the structure itself, the downward force, counteracted any sideways pressure it might experience. Essentially, the more pressure you heaped upon it, the stronger it became. She ought to be grateful to Brian for keeping her down for all those years. He had made her stronger than he would ever have believed possible.

Chapter 23

It had been raining for hours, one of those dank, gloomy days where it never gets fully light. Sara pulled up the hood of her coat before she got out of the car, but the minute she stepped out onto the drive, it blew down. She scurried round to the boot to retrieve two bulging shopping bags – she'd popped in for milk on the way home from seeing Helen at the hospital, but when did anyone in the history of the world come out with only the item they had gone in for? Angela hadn't been able to come with her today, being too busy with work. The surgery had been successful in that they'd managed to drain the fluid, but Brian was still in a critical condition and there were no immediate plans to bring him out of the coma. Without Angela's bullishness, Sara and Helen had spent their time together fretting about what to do if and when they did.

She battled through the driving rain to the front door. In an attempt to keep the bags away from the wet, muddy ground, she tried to get her key into the front door without putting them down, but one of them slipped down over her wrist, biting into her flesh. She regretted that 2kg bag of Maris Pipers. Just as she managed to slot the key into the lock, the door opened from the inside to reveal Nigel wearing her apron, a pink floral affair spattered with the remnants of meals past, a tea towel slung raffishly over one shoulder.

'Oh my darling, you're soaked! Quick, come in. Here, give me those.'

He relieved her of the shopping bags and helped her out of her coat.

'Take your shoes off,' he said. 'I'll get your slippers.' She followed his instructions obediently, relishing this relinquishing of the responsibility for everything that had been the mainstay of her life for the last five years. Nigel came down with her cosiest jumper and fluffy slippers.

'Put those on and come through.'

In the kitchen, he'd turned the main light off, leaving only the side lamps, and had lit several candles that flickered invitingly on the laid table, complete with champagne flutes. Delicious smells wafted from the oven.

'Wow. This is lovely. I can't tell you how nice it is to come home to all this, instead of a cold, silent house.'

'My pleasure.' He enveloped her in a hug and she leant against his chest.

'What's all this in aid of?'

'I wanted to thank you for your support since we found out about Isabel. I know I've been worried and probably a bit distant—'

'I wouldn't have expected anything else!' Sara put in.

'It's also a farewell dinner.'

'Farewell?'

'I'm going to fly out to Boston tomorrow for a week or so. My ex has been there all week but she's got to come back to the UK for work, so I'm going to take the opportunity to spend some time with Isabel.'

'That's great.' Sara was embarrassed at how abandoned she felt. She'd spent years on her own. It was pathetic to feel so dismayed about the prospect of a week without him. 'She'll be so happy to see you. How's she doing?'

Sara took a seat at the table. Nigel poured them both a glass of fizz and sat down opposite her.

'She's being incredibly strong,' he said. 'I'm so proud of her. She's got some appointments this week, so hopefully she'll have a treatment plan soon, which I think will make her feel better.'

'Definitely,' Sara agreed. Even though James's prognosis had been bad, it had been a burden lifted when his treatment plan had been agreed, the sense that somebody was in charge of his care. It had replaced the feeling she'd had previously that he was hurtling alone and unheeded towards certain death.

Nigel must have gone rooting far back in the kitchen cupboards because he'd dug out some jewelled, hand-painted ramekins that Sara had brought back from a long-ago holiday in Crete, and filled them with fat, shiny olives and smoked, salted almonds.

'I warn you, I could get used to this,' she said, popping an almond into her mouth. 'I can't remember the last time anyone cooked me dinner in my own house before you came along.'

'What about the boys?'

'Ha! No chance! That's the one thing I never missed after they left home – that constant cry of *what's for dinner?*'

'Well tonight, what's for dinner is boeuf bourguignon, creamy mash and tenderstem broccoli. Sound alright to you?'

'It sounds divine.' She took a sip of ice-cold champagne, the bubbles pricking pleasantly on her tongue.

Nigel was caring and attentive whilst they ate, asking about Brian's progress and how Helen was coping, but he was naturally distracted by thoughts of Isabel and his upcoming trip. Once he had cleared the cheesecake plates (*I'm going to get fearfully fat if you carry on like this*, Sara had said. *Get as fat as you like, my darling*, Nigel had replied) he sat back down opposite her.

'Shall we watch another episode of that drama?' she said. 'I could do with taking my mind off everything, and I'm sure you could too.'

'In a minute. There was something I wanted to ask you first.'

Her heart leapt. Every time Nigel broached any kind of serious topic she had the horrible feeling he had guessed there was more to Brian's accident than met the eye.

'Right, here's the thing,' he said, and then stopped, running a hand through his hair.

'What? Nigel, what is it? You're scaring me!'

'I hope you agree that things have been going well between us,' he said.

'You know I do – I couldn't be happier.'

'Me too.'

'So what's the problem?'

'There's no problem,' he said. 'Quite the reverse.'

That was a relief. He hadn't guessed the truth about Brian.

'What is it, then?'

'Phew. This is harder than I thought. I think I'll just have to come out with it. I wasn't going to, so soon, but all this stuff with Brian and Helen, and now Isabel – it makes you realise how short life is, doesn't it? Sara, I'm happier with you than I've ever been with anyone in my life – and don't worry, I don't expect you to say the same, I understand that if James hadn't died, you'd still be with him. It's not like being divorced, where you've fallen out of love, or everything's gone wrong. I totally get that.'

'It's OK.' She laid her hand on his. 'I don't want to get into comparisons but I've certainly never been happier.'

'I feel as if I can be myself with you,' he said. 'That you see and accept me for who I am. I've always felt in past relationships that my partner was in love with their idea of me, and it wasn't who I was at all. But it's so different with you.'

'I feel exactly the same.'

'I'm glad to hear that, because . . . because . . . I hope you don't think this is too soon, but I was wondering if you'd . . . well, if you'd, you know, agree to marry me?'

'Oh.' She put her hand across her mouth.

'You think I'm mad, don't you? Sorry, forget I said anything. Wipe it from your mind. Let's watch some telly.'

'No! I don't want to wipe it from my mind.'

'You don't?' he said, perking up.

'No. It's just—' What was it? It wasn't the timing that held her back. She'd never been so sure about anything or anyone in her life. Her hesitation was purely due to the huge lie she was engaged in about what had happened to Brian. Was it fair to agree to marry Nigel when she was keeping, and would have to continue to keep, this massive secret from him? What sort of a basis for a marriage was that?

'If you need some time to think about it, that's fine,' he said, watching her anxiously. 'And if you're not ready, that's also fine. I don't want to put any pressure on you but I also don't want there to be any misunderstanding about how I feel about you. So . . . I wanted to give you this – and please take it, whatever your answer is.'

He reached into his pocket and drew out a small, square, moth-eaten red velvet box. He opened it and held it out to her. A diamond winked at her from an antique gold ring.

'It belonged to my mother,' Nigel said.

'It's beautiful,' Sara said. She took it out and held it up to the light. 'I love it.'

'Try it on,' Nigel said.

She slipped it onto the fourth finger of her left hand.

'It's a perfect fit.' It was disconcerting to have a ring back on that finger. She had continued to wear her wedding and engagement rings for several years after James died, only taking them off when she started dating, thinking they'd make potential suitors uncomfortable.

'It could have been made for you,' Nigel said, taking her hand and kissing it. 'Would you . . . would you like to keep it on that finger?'

She looked into his dear, hopeful face, and thought about how extraordinary it was that she had found him, how easily she could have missed him if she hadn't gone to the speed dating event. She thought about Brian, and how different Nigel was to him. She thought of James too, and how finding happiness with someone else felt like a way to honour his memory and the happiness she had shared with him. She pushed Helen's situation to the far reaches of her mind and gave the only possible answer.

'Yes.'

Chapter 24

Angela scanned the tables in the hospital coffee shop. Helen was in the far corner with Sara, who despite the tropical temperature of the hospital was wrapped up in a cashmere cardigan, its long sleeves pulled down low over her wrists. They were deep in conversation. Angela hoped it didn't mean bad news. And by bad news she meant she hoped Brian hadn't come out of the coma, ready to spill the beans. She was fairly certain Helen wanted the same thing, although she wasn't sure what Sara was hoping for.

She got a coffee first – if Brian had woken up, she would need to keep her brain sharp – and went over to join them.

'Ladies,' she said, sliding onto the bench next to Helen. 'Sorry I'm late, work is a nightmare. What news?'

'Still nothing,' Helen said. 'He's stable but the damage to his brain is such that the best thing for him is to keep him in the coma for now. He might have to have another operation too.'

'Great,' Angela said.

Sara winced.

'Well, it is, isn't it?' Angela said. 'For now, while we're deciding what to do.'

'Are we?' Sara said. 'You just keep saying we'll worry about it if it happens.'

'I don't know what else we can do,' Angela said. 'There's no way to predict what he'll remember even if he does wake up. We'll have to respond dynamically. The best case scenario is he has no memory of that day at all – which I'd say is quite likely, isn't it, following a brain injury? Have the doctors said anything about that, Helen?'

'No, and before you say anything, I can't ask. The consultant's already suspicious of me, going on about this second head injury. If I start asking what Brian's likely to remember, I might as well go straight to jail without passing go.'

'Have they mentioned it again?' Sara asked.

'No, but he's looking at me in a funny way.'

'I'm sure he's much too busy for that, Helen,' Angela said. She had the feeling that she was the one holding this unruly mess together. If she didn't keep a tight grip on it, before she knew it Sara would be spilling the truth to Nigel and Helen would be slipping up under questioning. 'If Brian does know what happened, our response will have to depend on what state he's in. Let's face it, he's taken a mighty blow to the head. Who's to say how lucid he'll be? He may have sustained some fairly serious brain damage.'

'Let's hope so, eh?' Sara said sarcastically.

'Sorry, but what are you hoping for?' Angela snapped. 'That he wakes up, makes a full recovery and points the finger of blame squarely at Helen, and by association at you and I? That Helen gets arrested and has to stand trial and instead of escaping from the prison of her marriage, swaps it instead for an actual prison?'

'No. Yes. I don't know.' She put her face in her hands and her left sleeve rode up, revealing the sparkling diamond.

'That's not . . .' Angela said, astonished. 'Is it?'

'Oh. Yes.' Sara reddened. 'I wasn't going to mention it yet – not with all this going on with Brian. Sorry, Helen.'

'Don't be silly, it's lovely to hear some good news!' said Helen warmly. 'Congratulations.'

'Good news?' Angela didn't attempt to conceal her alarm.

'Yes. Nigel asked me to marry him last night. This was his mother's engagement ring.'

'It's gorgeous,' said Helen. 'Isn't it, Angela?'

Angela threw the ring a cursory glance. 'But you hardly know him! Moving in together is one thing, but marriage?'

'Life's too short – I mean look at what's happened to Brian.' There was a pause where they all remembered that what had happened to Brian was that Helen had whacked him over the head with a golfing trophy, but Sara was not to be deterred. 'I don't want to let happiness pass me by. I want to grab it with both hands.'

'That's all very well, and I understand the sentiment, the desire,' Angela said. 'But what's the rush? Apart from anything else, marriage is a legal contract. How are you going to arrange things financially? James left you pretty well off, Sara. You need to be careful.'

'I appreciate your concern,' Sara said stiffly, in a way that indicated that she did not appreciate it one little bit. 'But you don't have to worry, of course Nigel is going to contribute financially. As I've told you about a million times, he's very well off himself. If anything, he should be worried about me marrying him for his money. He's not some freeloader. Honestly, Angela, you don't need to worry.'

'Even so,' Angela said, 'will you please get some legal advice before you commit to anything? To protect both of you?' She couldn't care less about protecting Nigel, but she thought that might make it more palatable for Sara.

'We were going to do that anyway,' Sara said. 'We both have children, and we don't want them to be disadvantaged in terms of inheritance. And if it makes you feel any better, we're not in any rush to tie the knot. He's got enough on his plate with what's going on with Isabel, for a start. We just wanted to demonstrate our commitment to each other. Let's talk about something else – how are you holding up, Helen? You look exhausted.'

'Mostly I'm bored, to be honest, sitting by his bed for hours on end.'

'Could you not go home?' Angela said. 'They'd ring you if there was any news, wouldn't they?'

'They would. I just worry it looks bad if I'm not there,' said Helen. 'Like, a real devoted wife wouldn't want to leave his side? I've been reading a bit, but it's hard to concentrate. I was wondering about teaching myself to knit, or crochet or something.'

'God, things must be bad,' Angela said. 'You could help me out with some work stuff if you're really stuck? I'm snowed under since Saskia left, but I haven't had time to recruit someone to replace her.'

'What sort of thing? Would I be able to do it? I haven't done any paid work for years.'

'It's all pretty simple stuff, just time consuming. I'm happy to pay for you to do a quick online course to update your tech skills if that helps. You'd be doing me a huge favour – and I'd pay you, obviously. You could do it from the hospital. Have you got a laptop you could use? If not I can find you one at the office.'

'I could use Brian's – although I don't know the password.'

'Is it a Mac? If so it should have fingerprint ID,' Angela said.

'You could hold his finger against it to open it initially and then reset the password.'

'Angela!' Sara said.

'What? I'm just being practical.' Angela was beginning to get a touch fed up with Sara's holier-than-thou attitude. She was in this as deep as the other two. The time to insist on telling the truth about what happened to Brian had well and truly passed.

'I know, but it feels a bit gruesome,' she said. 'Don't feel you have to, Helen.'

'She doesn't need you to protect her,' Angela said. 'She's capable of making up her own mind.'

'Yes, I am,' Helen said, 'and please don't talk about me as if I'm not here. It is a Mac, so I'll try that.'

'Sorry, sorry,' Angela said. 'Of course it's up to you.'

'I'd like to do it, if you think I can. I need something to occupy me, and whatever happens it'll be useful for me to earn some money. I know what you mean about the laptop, Sara, but it's OK. It'll be handy for me to get into it – Brian's always dealt with all the house stuff, there might be information in there that I'm going to need about bills and things. I'll bring it in tomorrow and see if I can get it open, and we can go from there. Right, I'd better get back up there and resume my position.'

Helen was gathering up her things when her phone began to ring with a withheld number.

'That's probably the ward. What now?'

She snatched it up and answered breathlessly.

'Hello? Yes, this is Helen Greenwood.'

The person on the other end spoke for a while. Helen's face tightened as she offered the occasional 'Yes' and 'I see'. Finally she agreed she would see them tomorrow and hung up.

'What's up?' Sara said as Helen laid her phone gingerly on the table as if it was in danger of exploding. 'Is it Brian? Has something happened?'

'No. That was the police. The hospital have been in touch with them regarding their concerns about the second head injury. They want to talk to me about it tomorrow. This is it. It's over. They know what happened. What am I going to do?'

Chapter 25

Helen had offered to come in to the police station but the officer had insisted on coming to the house. Helen had a horrible feeling it was because she wanted to check out the scene of Brian's fall. She checked around the living room for incriminating evidence. She'd done her best with the blood-stained carpet (not that it was incriminating, she reminded herself – they knew he'd fallen and hit his head) but the stain would never come out. The golf trophy was back in its place on the mantelpiece. She'd considered hiding it away, but worried that if the police ever got to the stage of searching the house and found it hidden, that would look much more suspicious. Instead, she had put on some disposable latex gloves, a remnant from the start of the covid pandemic, and scrubbed every inch of it with neat bleach. No accusatory blood or fibres could have survived that, surely.

Needing to fill the time before the police arrived, she went into the kitchen and opened Brian's laptop. She had taken it to the hospital that morning, held Brian's finger onto the key necessary to open it and then changed the password. Angela hadn't allocated her any work yet, but she'd given her the various logins she needed to access the Kiss, Marry, Avoid systems. She skimmed through a couple of spreadsheets. One of them listed the agency's clients and any dates they'd been on with a column for dater feedback. Sara's name caught her eye. For her date with Ben, her comment had been 'Bitter divorced guy, misogynist' and against Steve's name 'Nice guy, data conspiracy nut'. While she was on the laptop, she decided to have a nose around and see what Brian was up to when he was tapping away. There were a couple of spreadsheets on the desktop. She opened the one labelled household expenditure and wasn't surprised to find that Brian had kept a detailed record of every penny she had spent. Some of the transactions, mostly things like the very occasional coffee or sandwich she had out, were highlighted in yellow, which was manifestly a personal code to which he didn't provide the key. She guessed it indicated unnecessary transactions, or possibly even ones that represented 'evidence' that she was having an affair.

The other spreadsheet was labelled Travel. She studied it, unsure for a moment what she was looking at, but gradually it dawned on her. It was Brian's record of the mileage data from the car cross-referenced with every single journey she had made, or at least had told him about. There was a new tab for every month, with any discrepancy between mileage and journeys taken highlighted in red. Even though she had suspected he kept tabs on where she went in the car, seeing it in black and white was a punch to the gut.

Closing that down, she saw an unfamiliar icon on the desktop called APS Digital. She clicked on it and the programme opened. There were two options or folders to choose from – Live Feed and Auto Downloaded. She clicked on Live Feed, which offered a suite of further options, each one named for a room in the house. Kitchen, Living Room, Hallway, Landing, Bedroom 1, Bedroom 2, Bedroom 3, Bathroom, Shower Room. She clicked on one at random. A new window opened up, but it was black and blank, with the error message 'No Live Feed Available'. She went through the other rooms, but they were all the same.

Baffled, she went back a step and clicked on Auto Downloaded. This had the same folders, organised by room. She opened Kitchen, and saw that it contained multiple documents, or to be specific, videos. They were organised by date, the most recent one being the day of Brian's injury. With a sense of foreboding, she clicked on it and watched as her past self came into the kitchen in her dressing gown and made two cups of tea. The on-screen clock told her it was 7 a.m. The camera must have been motion-activated because once she had gone out with the tea, it stopped recording, and then sprang to life again as she and Brian appeared. She bustled around the kitchen, boiling his eggs for the prescribed five and a half minutes. She fought the urge to vomit, hardly able to believe her eyes. It was so audacious, such a violent invasion of her privacy that her brain could scarcely comprehend it. Brian had placed hidden cameras in their home. Every time she thought she had been alone, he had been watching her every move. How long had he been doing it?

With mounting horror, she fast forwarded through the day until the time Angela and Sara had arrived to help her escape. She watched herself come into the kitchen with her friends, her suitcase in the corner. Watched as they took the bags out to the car and then left the room for a final sweep of the sitting room. She had an impotent urge to reach into the screen and tell herself to run, that she hadn't forgotten anything, that she should run as fast as she could away from there. She paused the video and leaned back in the chair, her palms sweaty. She had known that Brian liked to keep abreast of where she was and what she was doing, and the expenditure and travel spreadsheets had come as no real surprise, but this was on another level. It was obscene. She tried to think of anything she might have done that he would have seen that would be particularly humiliating, but he must have been watching her like this for years. There was too much to be able to think of specific events, and anyway, it was all humiliating.

He'd obviously had the cameras set up to automatically download their recordings, but presumably the batteries would only last a day or so and without Brian to replenish them, they would have stopped recording since he'd been in the hospital. With a sick feeling deep in her stomach, she clicked on the Sitting Room camera footage for the same day and skipped through until she saw herself and her two friends come in from the kitchen. When it got to the part where Brian came home, she kept her eyes trained on her own face, transfixed by the fear on it, the way she looked nowhere but at Brian, her terror when he drew out her passport. Knowing what was coming, she felt a sick apprehension as the events unfolded. She watched as Brian raised his fist to Angela and then as she herself lifted the golf trophy, an avenging angel in jersey and linen. At the exact moment she brought it smashing down on his head, the doorbell rang. It must be the police. They were early. She pressed pause. It was time to put on the performance of her life.

She stood and tucked her hair behind her ears. It was longer than it had been in years, the roots a soft grey that blended into the ash-blonde highlights below. She'd missed the monthly trim and root touch-up that maintained it in its customary neat bob. She'd suggested growing it out to Brian once, but he had been against it, saying long hair on older women was witchy and frightfully aging. She took a deep breath and opened the front door.

'Do come in,' she said, aiming for the nonchalant tone of a woman with nothing to hide.

'Thanks. I'm DS Paskell.'

She was a woman of about Helen's age, dressed in a dove-grey trouser suit and thick-soled brogues.

'Would you like to come through to the kitchen?'

'Thanks.'

DS Paskell followed her down the hall.

'Please, sit down. Can I get you a cup of tea or coffee?'

'No thanks.' The detective sat down at the dining table, placing her large handbag on the floor beside her. With a thrill of pure terror, Helen realised she had left the laptop open. How could she have been so monumentally stupid? The video was still paused on Helen with the bloodstained golf trophy in her hand, Brian's body clearly visible, prostrate on the floor in front of her.

'Isn't it a beautiful day?' Helen said wildly, gesturing out of the window where drizzle fell from a slate-grey sky which only the most glass-half-full type could describe as beautiful. DS Paskell looked out, bemused, and Helen smoothly closed the lid of the laptop. 'I mean, what a horrible day,' she said, taking the seat opposite the detective. 'Sorry, I'm all over the place at the moment.'

'That's understandable. This shouldn't take too long. As I explained on the phone, Brian's consultant at the hospital has been in touch with some concerns about the nature of Brian's head injury. I'd like it if you could talk me through what happened the day of the accident?'

'My friends Angela and Sara had come over for a coffee.'

'What time was that?'

'Around 2.45.'

'And Brian came home unexpectedly, I think?'

'That's right, he wasn't feeling well, so he'd left work early.'

'What was wrong, specifically?'

'Sorry?' Helen wasn't sure what she was driving at.

'You said he wasn't feeling well – was it stomach problems, or a cold, or . . . ?'

'Oh, I see! It was . . . er . . . a headache.' Helen had a sudden vision of the bloodied mess of Brian's head as he fell to the floor and had to stifle an unseemly giggle. If he hadn't had a headache before she hit him with his own golf trophy, he sure as hell did afterwards.

'What time did he arrive back?'

'It was just before three o'clock.'

'I see. What happened next?'

Helen swallowed. What would an innocent woman say here?

'Sorry, what's going on here? Are you . . . am I in some kind of trouble? We called the ambulance as soon as we found him.'

'At the moment I'm just after a general picture of what happened that day. Nothing to worry about. So what happened?'

'We decided to take our coffee out into the garden. It was a lovely day. I was expecting Brian to join us, so when he didn't—'

'I thought you said he was feeling unwell? Why were you expecting him to join you?'

'Well . . . what I meant to say is, after fifteen minutes or so I went in to check on him, to see if he was feeling better and wanted to come out and join us. And that's when I found him on the floor.'

'What time was that?'

'It was around quarter past three. We called an ambulance straight away.'

'Could I see where Brian fell?' the detective asked. 'To get a better idea of how it happened.'

Helen had been right, she had known it. They suspected her of having done something to Brian. She clenched her fists, trying to stop her hands shaking.

'Of course. Come with me.'

She led DS Paskell into the living room.

'So you found Brian lying here?' She pointed at the hearth. 'His head where the stain is?'

'Yes,' Helen croaked, trying to sound as if she was stifling a sob. 'Poor Brian. He'd been unsteady on his feet for a while. I was always telling him to be careful. I wish he'd listened to me.'

'How old is Brian, Mrs Greenwood?'

'He's just turned sixty.'

'That's quite young to be getting unsteady and falling.'

'Yes, I know.' She looked the detective in the eye. 'That's precisely why I was worried – that there was something physically wrong with him. I tried to get him to go to the doctor, but you know what men can be like.'

'Mr Tarapore tells me that Brian has two distinct injuries to his skull. One consistent with hitting the hearth and another, on the same side of his head, more consistent with some kind of blunt instrument.'

'Yes, he did mention that. He must have hit his head on something else as he fell. As I say, I wasn't here.'

'Do you have any idea how that could have happened?'

'I don't know. I can't bear to think about it.' The tearful voice was back. She must be careful not to overdo it. This wasn't an amateur dramatics performance.

'We're going to get the forensics team to have a look, to be on the safe side.'

The safe side of what? Helen didn't dare to ask.

'How were things between you and Brian?' Paskell went on. 'Had you been arguing at all?'

'Arguing? No, not in the slightest.' She was able to say that with conviction. She and Brian had never argued – it simply hadn't been worth her while.

'Alright, Mrs Greenwood. I'll be in touch when the forensics team have reported back.' She picked up her bag, looking down at the floor as something caught her eye. Helen followed her gaze and her heart jumped when she saw a flash of orange, the edge of the foolscap folder peeking out from under the sofa. Angela had dropped it when Brian threatened her, and in the ensuing scuffle it must have got kicked under the sofa. How could she have missed it? If Brian was around it never would have happened. Without him, she had got into the luxurious habit of not cleaning under things.

'What's this?' the detective asked.

'It's some household filing. I wondered where that had got to.' Helen held out her hand for it.

'May I?' she asked, lifting the flap.

'Yes, I suppose so,' Helen said in strained tones.

She took out the photocopied sheets and leafed through them.

'Some household filing, you said? Looks like bank statements, pension information, mortgage documents.'

'Yes, that's right. I thought it would be useful to keep all the important information in one place.'

'I see.' She placed the papers back in the file. 'Are you happy for me to take this with me?'

'I suppose so.' Helen wanted to ask why, but she wasn't prepared to hear the answer. If Paskell came out and said she suspected Helen had had a hand in Brian's injury, Helen would need to be ready with a reply, and she wasn't.

She saw the detective out, closed the door behind her and leant against it, her knees weak. Had she struck the right note?

Did DS Paskell see a distressed wife, longing for her husband to make a full recovery, or a cold-blooded murderer lying through her teeth? She needed to speak to Angela. Even though Brian hadn't woken up – yet – it seemed they had come to Angela's fabled bridge, and it was time to figure out how they were going to cross it.

Chapter 26

Joy swelled within Sara when the taxi pulled up outside the house. Nigel had insisted that she didn't need to collect him from the airport, knowing she was no fan of motorway driving. She found she couldn't wait until he got into the house, opening the front door, running down the path and flinging herself into his arms with no care for the beady eyes of her neighbours. He engulfed her in a tight embrace and she buried her face in his neck.

'I missed you so much,' they both said at the same time, and laughed.

'Cup of tea?' she asked.

'You read my mind. I haven't had a decent cuppa in a week.'

'How's Isabel?' Sara asked, once they were settled at the table with tea and biscuits.

'She's doing amazingly, all things considered. She has her moments, but she's being so strong.'

'And how are you? I know I went through it with James, but I can't imagine the pain of seeing your child in that situation.' Her recollection of the early days of James's diagnosis was fuzzy, as if her brain was softening it to protect her from the misery, the way TV documentaries blur people's faces to protect their identity. His last weeks, however, were pin sharp in her mind. It had taken a long time for them to be superseded by memories of happier times.

'It's tough,' he said. 'All your life, all you want to do is protect them, keep them safe from harm, but there's nothing you can do, I . . .' He broke off, fighting back tears.

'You being there will have helped. Knowing she has support will help, I promise. It's not a small thing.'

'It feels small. I feel helpless. Sorry, I know you've been through this with James. I hope it's not bringing back too many painful memories.'

'It's fine.' She felt a deep pulse of love for him at this sign of his care for her – that he could think of her even during this terrible time for him. 'I want to do anything I can to support you. How was the appointment with the oncologist?'

'Good. He's very well-respected in the field. They have caught it early, which is positive, but the tests have shown that it's a pretty aggressive, fast-growing variety.'

'Catching it early is a real plus point. I think I read somewhere that it's the biggest predictor of a good outcome. So what's the plan for her treatment?'

'First an op – she's considering going for a double mastec-tomy with reconstruction as with the particular type she has, it's covered by her healthcare plan.'

'That makes sense. I think I'd feel the same. And after that? Will she have to have chemo?'

'Yes, definitely.'

'The poor thing. I'll speak to Angela – she had chemo twelve years ago when she went through the same thing, she might have some tips for getting through it.' Sara had driven Angela to every appointment that Greg wasn't around for, taken Angela wig shopping, checked in on her daily and taken her out for gentle walks and coffees when she felt up to it. James had had chemo too, although his had been palliative and he wasn't here to ask. She wouldn't remind Nigel of that now.

'Thanks,' he said. 'The oncologist also mentioned immuno-therapy – I know you've said before that you wish James had been able to have it.'

'Yes. In my darker moments I berate myself for not pushing harder for it, but to be honest it wasn't being widely used then. Is it a common treatment for Isabel's cancer?'

'No, that's the problem. The doctor says he has seen some encouraging results using immunotherapy in combination with chemotherapy for patients with her particular diagnosis, but because it's not considered a standard treatment, her healthcare plan won't cover it.'

'But she could pay for it herself?'

'Yes. Well, realistically, I could pay for it – she wouldn't be able to afford it.'

'How much are we talking?' Sara asked.

'Around £150,000 all in.'

'Whew! I'm glad I don't live in the States. Would she consider coming back here to be treated? She'd be eligible to be treated on the NHS, wouldn't she?'

'She doesn't want to – all her friends are there, her boyfriend's there – and I don't mean to throw shade on the NHS, but she's under a very well-regarded consultant at one of the best hospi-tals in the state. Plus I doubt she'd get immunotherapy on the NHS either.'

'Fair enough, although I can't fault the care James had on the NHS. So you'll help her out with the treatment cost?'

'Yes. The issue is a lot of my money is tied up in bonds and things which I can't access with any degree of urgency. Once the house is sold, it'll be no problem. I'll have to speak to the bank. They might be able to offer a bridging loan until the house sale goes through.'

'Don't bother with that – I can lend you the money.' The words were out before she'd had a chance to think about them, but then she didn't need to. There was no question that she wouldn't help him out with this. She had absolutely no doubt that he would do the same for her if the situation was reversed.

'That's incredibly kind, but I couldn't possibly ask you to do that, my darling.'

'Don't be silly. I know I haven't properly met Isabel yet, but she's your family, so she's family to me too.'

'That's a lovely thing to say, and I feel the same about your boys, but it's too much to ask.'

'It's really not,' she said. 'I wouldn't be able to live with myself if I knew I was able to help, but didn't and . . . well, if the unimaginable happened.' A flash of pain at the thought of it crossed Nigel's face. 'Please,' she said. 'We're a team. Let me help you.'

'Well, if you're really sure, that would be amazing. But can you lay your hands on that kind of money at such short notice?'

'Yes, that's no problem. To be honest, I've always felt guilty at how well off James left me. I'd be delighted to feel that his money was doing some good in the world. I think he would be too.'

'It would be amazing to get the ball rolling on her treatment,' he said. 'Just to be absolutely clear, I'm going to pay you back the minute Claricoates is sold.'

'I know you are. Don't worry about it. The most important thing is that Isabel gets the right treatment.'

'You are amazing,' he said, leaning across the table to give her a kiss. 'How's everything here? Any update on Brian?'

'No, there's been no change.'

There might come a day when she would have to tell Nigel that the police suspected Brian's death wasn't an accident, and that if they were not precisely investigating Helen, certainly considered her a person of interest. But today was not that day.

'How's Helen doing?'

'She's . . . managing.' In fact, Sara had been almost frightened of Helen the last few times she'd seen her. When she told Sara and Angela about the video footage she'd discovered, whilst they'd been outraged, disgusted, she'd been dispassionate, cold, hard-edged. Sara supposed she was doing what she needed to survive.

Tea turned into wine and dinner, and Sara allowed herself to relax into the pleasure of Nigel's company. Later, as she drifted off to sleep, his arms wrapped tightly around her, she shut down the voices that bombarded her with questions – would Isabel be alright, was Helen going to be arrested for her attack on Brian, and if so to what extent would Sara be implicated? Instead, she allowed the wine-fuzziness of her head and the warmth of Nigel's body against hers to lull her into a dreamless sleep. Everything was going to be fine.

Chapter 27

'Is Helen coming?' Sara asked.

'She said she was, but maybe she's got held up at the hospital,' Angela said.

They were back in their usual haunt, The Daily Grind on the high street. Sara could almost pretend that none of this had happened, that their most pressing concern was whether to treat themselves to one of the café's famous brownies or stick to a skinny latte.

'We need to talk about what she's going to tell the police.'

'It's been a week now since that detective came and she hasn't heard anything – they could've abandoned the whole idea,' Angela said hopefully.

'I doubt it,' Sara said. 'What about the folder with all those documents?'

'That doesn't prove anything. It's exactly what Helen said it was – household filing.'

'But the detective was obviously suspicious or she wouldn't have asked to take it away.'

'She can be as suspicious as she likes but she'll need evidence to take things further, and those papers are evidence of nothing,' said Angela with all the confidence of a woman who had watched countless episodes of *Law and Order*.

'What about the video footage? I still can't believe Brian had all those cameras in the house. He really is a piece of work.'

'Helen's deleted the program. There's no trace of it now on the laptop.'

'There's always a trace with these things though, isn't there? If they get a computer expert to look at it.'

'Yes, but they'd have to know what they were looking for, wouldn't they? She's removed all the cameras themselves as well. It took her ages to work out where they all were – they were tiny little things, and he'd been so clever about where he hid them.'

'And the head injury?' Sara said.

'That could easily have happened as he fell. I don't think they've got a leg to stand on. And I reckon the longer they keep Brian in the coma, the less chance there is he'll remember what happened if he wakes up. There are all sorts of side effects from long term sedation – memory loss in particular. He'll be in a terrible way.'

'No need to sound so pleased about it.' Sara felt as though she was the only one of them that had any grip on reality.

'I'm not pleased about any of it. I just feel like it's the least I can do. I was at a pretty low ebb when I met you and Helen. You were the first mum friend I made who I didn't feel was silently judging me for not being one of those natural mothers, and Helen was such a brilliant support with Lizzie, even though it must have been hard for her, when she was so desperate to have her own children. You were both amazing when I went through my cancer treatment too. I honestly don't know if I would have got through any of that without you. I'm glad of a chance to pay it back finally.'

'How are you finding it keeping it from Greg?'

'I don't see much of him at home to be honest, but when I do it's not great having to lie to him, but it's necessary. I'm sure it's the same for you with Nigel.'

'It was alright while he was in Boston, but it's so hard now he's back.' Perhaps it was different for Angela, deep in her long relationship. Maybe she had kept other things from Greg over the years, but for Sara it was torture.

'You have to keep it from him, Sara. I know you're all loved up but you can't tell him.'

'I'm not going to. But I'm not happy about it.'

'How's his daughter?'

'She's OK – well, as OK as you can be in that situation. She's got some good friends out there, and a boyfriend who's been on the scene for a while, so she has a support network.'

'That'll make a real difference. Like I said, I would never have got through it without you and Helen – and Greg, of course. What's the treatment plan?'

'An operation first, then chemo plus immunotherapy.'

'Wow! She's getting the five-star treatment. I didn't know immunotherapy was offered for breast cancer.'

'That's the problem, it's not covered by her healthcare plan, but her consultant says he's seen some really encouraging results with it so Nigel's going to pay for it himself.'

'I bet that's not cheap.'

'It's not. A hundred and fifty grand.'

'Blimey!' Angela's eyebrows shot up. 'Can he afford that?'

'Easily. The problem is a lot of his money is tied up in bonds and things, so he can't access it quickly. But once the sale of his house goes through, he'll have many times that.'

'Which estate agent has he got it on with?' Angela asked. 'I had a nose the other day and I couldn't find it online.'

'No, you wouldn't have. That's not how it works with these very expensive houses. He's using this high-end, premium estate agent for people who don't want their houses splashed all over the internet. They've got all these high-net-worth clients and it's all done personally, like the old days.'

'I see,' Angela said doubtfully. 'But I see massive houses on Rightmove all the time.'

'Yes, not everyone uses these high-end ones, but Nigel said you tend to end up getting a better price if you do.'

'Has he had much interest in the house?' Angela asked.

'Some. It's a question of finding the right buyer for a house like that.'

'So what about this money for the treatment?' Jesus. Angela was like a dog with a bone.

'If necessary, I can tide him over.' Sara wasn't sure why she was making it sound as if there was only a small chance she'd be lending Nigel the money, when in fact he had accepted her offer. Angela had been so spiky about them moving in together, and then the engagement. Sara didn't have the energy for another battle.

'Really? What do you—' Angela didn't get to finish because at that moment, Helen burst into the café, ashen-faced and wild-eyed.

'Are you alright?' Sara asked.

'Not really.' She sat down without taking off her coat. 'Brian's taken a turn for the worse. Mr Tarapore says it's touch and go.'

'Oh dear,' Sara said sympathetically, although she was surprised at her friend's distress. She had begun to suspect that Brian's death was the outcome Helen was hoping for.

'Is that . . . necessarily a bad thing?' Angela was of the same mind and wasn't afraid to voice it.

'It's not that,' Helen said impatiently. 'I had a call from DS Paskell. She wants me to go in for a formal interview. She said I wasn't being arrested but I didn't seem to have any choice in the matter.'

'If they're not arresting you, that means they don't have enough evidence.' *Law and Order* expert Angela was back.

'Not yet,' Helen said, 'but she said she wants to talk to me about the forensic evidence, so they've clearly found something. And if Brian does . . . well, if he doesn't make it, and they suspect foul play, that's going to make this a murder investigation. They're going to be looking for suspects. And who else could it have been but me?'

Chapter 28

'Are you sure you don't want me to come?' Sara said as Nigel swiped his car keys from the kitchen worktop.

'No. It'll be incredibly boring for you, and it's all stuff I need to sort through myself – you'd have to ask me every time whether I wanted to keep it. It's quicker to do it on my own. You stay here and relax.'

The estate agents had arranged a viewing of Claricoates, so he was going over to do a clear out and make sure the place was presentable.

'In that case, I'll spend the afternoon making a delicious dinner.'

'Marvellous,' he said. 'See you later.'

The front door slammed behind him and Sara opened the fridge. What could she make with radishes, mozzarella and some elderly spinach? As she checked the expiry date on an open jar of mustard – if it was within this decade she was going to risk it – a phone trilled from the next room. It wasn't hers, which was in her back pocket. Nigel must have forgotten to take his. She ran into the living room, where the ringtone emanated from behind one of the sofa cushions. She located it and saw that it was Isabel calling. She took the split second decision that she'd better answer it in case it was an emergency. She swiped right and raised the phone to her ear. She was about to speak. The words were on the tip of her tongue – *it's Sara, your dad left his phone at home* – but Isabel didn't wait and began to speak herself.

'Col, can you pick up some milk on your way over? We're nearly out.'

'Isabel?' Sara said, confused. 'It's Sara.'

'Oh!' If Sara was confused, Isabel sounded even more so – shocked, in fact.

'Your dad's out, he forgot to take his phone. I thought I'd better answer in case . . .' she trailed off.

'Sorry, I've rung the wrong number!' Isabel said. 'I meant to ring my friend Col, he's on his way over and I'm out of milk. What an idiot!'

Music was playing in the background at Isabel's end and an ambulance siren sounded faintly in the distance. Sara had the distinct feeling that something wasn't right if only she was able to identify it.

'How are you doing?' she asked.

'I'm good. I mean, trying to stay positive as best I can,' Isabel said. 'I'd better go, I want to catch my friend before he arrives. Tell Dad I said hi.'

'Will do.' Sara put the phone down, her chest tight. She started to make a list for the supermarket, trying to keep some new and unwelcome thoughts away but they continued to batter down the doors of her mind. In the end she gave up and examined them. What was making her so uncomfortable? Was it the tone of Isabel's voice when she answered, the casual friendliness that had turned to defensive shock when she realised she was speaking to Sara? Perhaps, but there was something else too. It took her a few minutes but eventually she got it. The siren in the background had sounded like an ambulance siren in the UK. But

Isabel was in Boston – surely their sirens sounded different? They did in the movies. She didn't want to think too hard about the implications of Isabel being in the UK, but nonetheless found her fingers typing in US ambulance sirens to YouTube, which brought up various videos aimed, she supposed, at people who really liked listening to sirens. She played a couple. The US ambulances were higher pitched, screechier, less the traditional nee-naw nee-naw of the British ones. But who's to say what ambulances they had in Boston? And why was she even entertaining these thoughts?

If she was able to ring Isabel herself, she'd be able to see whether it was a US number – and wouldn't the ringing tone sound different? She remembered calling hotels in other countries to book rooms before the days when everything was done online, the steady beep of the ringing tone. Was that the same in the US? It was immaterial because Nigel had never given her Isabel's number, and she didn't know the code to unlock Nigel's phone.

This was ridiculous. How was this doubt creeping into her mind, based on a misdial and a siren? It was Angela's fault, with her dire warnings about protecting herself. She knew if she could see Nigel, everything would be OK. He would be able to silence these imaginings with a word, a touch. She would go to Claricoates, take him his phone and help him with the sort out. There must be something she could do, some cleaning or tidying.

In the car on the way over, she listened to the radio, the DJ's inane chatter drowning out the questions that flooded her mind. In the driveway, there was no sign of Nigel's BMW, but the sleek, red Jaguar she had heard about on her first visit was parked near the front door. Perhaps he'd put the other car in the garage for some reason. The front door was ajar and she poked her head in, feeling like an unwanted guest. The parquet floor was shining and the hall smelled of beeswax. Fresh flowers sat on the low table near the bottom of the staircase that led upstairs. In a nearby room, a hoover hummed.

'Hello!' she called.

Nobody answered. The hoover continued to run. Sara followed the sound into the room on the right, Nigel's study. A young woman in a white vest and tracksuit bottoms with earbuds in was pushing the hoover back and forth across the plush, grey carpet.

'Hello!' Sara said more loudly.

The young woman started. She switched off the hoover and whatever she was listening to on her phone.

'You gave me a fright,' she said. 'Can I help you?'

'I'm looking for Nigel. Is . . . is he here?'

'Yes, he is actually, although we weren't expecting him today. Just arrived from London. Would you like me to get him for you?'

'Yes please, if you don't mind.'

It was a relief to hear that he was here, but why did the cleaner think he'd come from London? She must be mistaken. The room was much as it had been when she was here last time. He must have started elsewhere in the house with the clearing out.

A tall, athletic man with blond hair swept into the room. He was wearing well-cut jeans, expensive-looking brown boots and a chunky polo-necked jumper. Everything about him screamed wealth. He even smelled expensive.

'Are you selling something?' he asked peremptorily. 'Because if you are, I don't want it.'

'No. I'm looking for Nigel Peters.'

'You found him.' He spread his arms wide, as if taking a bow.

Her brow furrowed in confusion. 'No, I mean the Nigel Peters who lives here.'

'Yes. I am he,' the man said, speaking slowly as if to someone with limited knowledge of the English language. It was probably how he spoke to anyone he met abroad, whether they could speak English or not.

'No, you . . . sorry, what do you . . .' Sara trailed off, unable to find the words, not knowing what questions she ought to be asking. What the hell was going on here?

'If you're not going to tell me what you're doing here, I'll have to ask you to leave,' he said. 'So are you?'

'I . . . No . . .' Her face burned. 'I must have made a mistake. I'm so sorry.'

She almost ran from the room on shaking legs. She didn't know what was going on, but she had an overwhelming urge to get herself away, where she could think. Was Nigel not who he said he was? In which case, who was he?

She was fumbling for her car keys when she heard the sound of feet on gravel behind her. Turning, she saw the cleaner coming out carrying two large, full bin bags. Nigel (her Nigel) must have something to do with the house. He had keys, he knew where everything was. Had she somehow misunderstood what he had told her? Was it at all possible there was a simple, innocent explanation?

'Excuse me,' she said to the cleaner. 'Sorry if this sounds like a stupid question, but that man in there, the one I just spoke to, he's Nigel Peters, the owner of the house?'

'Yes.' The cleaner looked at her strangely.

'So . . . so . . .' Sara extricated her phone from her pocket and opened the photo app. Her sweaty fingers slid across the screen as she brought up a photo of Nigel. She'd taken it surreptitiously in the garden the other evening as he sipped on a glass of rosé and enjoyed the sunset. She knew he hated having his photo taken, but she wasn't going to do anything with this one except look at it herself, relishing the pleasure he took in the pink and orange hues of the evening sky. 'Do you know who this is?'

The cleaner leaned in closer.

'That's Colin.'

Sara's stomach gave a sick lurch. *Col, can you pick up some milk?*

'Colin,' she repeated dully. If Nigel was Colin, then who was Isabel?

'Yes,' the cleaner replied patiently. 'Colin Sanderson. He works here. He looks after the house when Nigel's in London or away, which is most of the time. He's got a flat in the converted stable building and Nigel lets him drive the BMW. Quite a cushy little number.'

Somehow, Sara got into the car. Something red peeked out from beneath the passenger seat – Nigel's jumper. He must have left it there last time they'd been out. She lifted it to her nose and inhaled the scent of him – partly his deodorant and aftershave, but mostly the indefinable scent of him, a sharp stab to the heart.

It was a minor miracle that she didn't crash, because all the way home the tears were coming so thick and fast she could barely see the road. She felt hollow, as if her insides had been scooped out. She still didn't fully understand what was going on, what Nigel had done, but what she did know was that he had been lying to her since the day they met. How could she have been so blind, so easily fooled? Was she that desperate to be loved? Was it her fault? Was the universe punishing her for those treacherous thoughts that crept into her head when Nigel was being particularly lovely, about how if James hadn't died, she would never have met him. She'd never quite allowed herself to consider the question of what she would do if she was offered the chance to change the past so that James didn't die, but she had come shamefully close.

With no memory of how she had done it, she made it in one piece back to her house. What she'd begun to think of again as *our house*. Hers and Nigel's. If she'd hoped to have a pocket of time to gather her thoughts before confronting him, those hopes were dashed when she saw the BMW parked on the drive. He was back.

Chapter 29

'I'm in the kitchen!' Nigel called as Sara came in the front door. 'Where have you been?'

Slowly she hung her coat on the peg, wondering why she was bothering. She might as well just drop it on the floor. What did anything matter anymore?

'I forgot my—' He broke off as she came into the kitchen and he saw her tearstained face. 'What's the matter?' His tone conveyed the care and concern for her wellbeing she had grown so used to from him, but she detected an underlying note of panic.

'I went to your house,' she said dully. 'You left your phone here.'

'I know – that's why I came back. Have you – have you got it?'

She held it out.

'Isabel called.'

'Is she OK?'

Part of her wanted to hurl all her accusations at him, force him to acknowledge his lies, but there was another part of her that urged caution, advised her not to lay all her cards on the table until she had seen his.

'I'm sorry you went all that way. I turned round as soon as I realised I didn't have my phone. We must have crossed paths.'

Sara wished to God they never had.

He moved towards her, arms outstretched. There was nothing she wanted more than to melt into his embrace as she would have done before today, to turn back the clock and not answer the phone, not go to the house, never find out about his lies.

'I went to your house,' she repeated.

'Yes, I'm sorry I missed you. Like I said, we must have passed each other on the road.'

For a wild second, she considered not saying anything. How hard would it be to pretend to herself that she had never heard Isabel saying *Col*, never heard a British ambulance blaring in the background, never met the real Nigel Peters, never heard the cleaner saying *that's Colin*, as if it was the most obvious thing in the world? Almost as soon as she'd had the thought she knew it would never work. What kind of a relationship would that be? There was no way round or through this without confronting him.

'I wish I'd never met you,' she said despairingly.

'Don't say that, my darling,' he said nervously. 'What's going on?'

'I met Nigel Peters,' she said, looking him dead in the eye. 'The real one.'

Sara had never seen anyone blanch in real life. She had thought it was one of those things that only happened in books, but she watched as the colour literally drained from his face.

'I . . . no . . . what do you mean? I'm Nigel,' he spluttered.

'No,' she said. 'Stop lying. It's over. You're Colin Sanderson. The cleaner told me. I showed her your picture.'

'The cleaner? What cleaner?' he said. 'Why would you believe some random woman over me? You must have misunderstood. I'll sort it out. Please don't throw this away – I love you, Sara.'

He seemed genuinely distressed, and despite everything Sara felt a pang of doubt. Could he really have been lying to her for the past four months? Or was it possible that there was an innocent explanation?

'I met the real owner of the house. Nigel Peters,' she repeated. 'I showed the cleaner your picture and she said your name is Colin Sanderson, and that you work for Nigel looking after the house when he's away.'

'That's ridiculous!' he said, fumbling in his pocket for his wallet and pulling out his driving licence. 'Look – Nigel Peters.'

If she hadn't brought up two teenagers in recent times she might have been convinced, but both her boys had had fake driving licences when they were seventeen so they could get served in the pub. A boy in their year had had a lucrative little business procuring them for people.

'What about your passport?' she said.

'My passport?' If he could have gone any paler, she had the feeling he would have done.

'Yes. You only got back from Boston yesterday, it must be here. Can I see it?'

'I'm not sure I can lay my hands on it right now, I've been sorting through all my stuff. Sara, please don't do this. I love you. Don't throw it all away.'

'I haven't done anything! You're the one who's thrown it all away! You must have been delighted when you met me – I thought we'd fallen in love but I was just a meal ticket for you and your . . . well, who is she? Isabel?'

'She's my daughter,' he repeated, but his conviction was fading.

'She called you Col,' Sara said. She felt sick at his deceit, wanted to scream at him to leave but she needed answers. 'When I answered your phone, she said, "Col, can you pick up some milk?" She came up with some story about how she was expecting a friend called Col, but now that I know your real name, it's all making a horrible kind of sense. Tell me who she is.'

'It doesn't matter about Isabel,' he said. 'I want to talk about you – about us. You've got it all wrong – I can explain everything.'

'It doesn't matter? About a woman who's supposedly your daughter, who's got cancer? But she's not your daughter, is she? And she doesn't have cancer, and you're not Nigel Peters. It's over. Stop lying.'

Nigel groped for something to say, but nothing came and eventually he sank down in a dining chair, deflated, as if someone had let all the air out of him.

'How dare you use that against me?' Sara said, a wave of rage surging through her, overriding the sorrow that had engulfed her since she left Claricoates. 'My husband died of cancer. I nursed him through the last unbearable, pain-filled months of his life. I watched as he wasted away before my eyes. I held his hand in the hospice as he drew his last breath and you have the *nerve* to use that, knowing I'd be sympathetic to a cancer diagnosis – knowing, even, that I felt guilty about not pushing for James to have immunotherapy. I can't begin to comprehend all the lies you must have told me, but this one is the worst.'

But as the words left her lips, she knew they weren't true. Lying about Isabel to defraud Sara and pretending to be someone he wasn't were bad enough, but the worst thing was knowing that every touch, every kiss had been a pretence. The fact that he had never truly seen Sara, or known her, or loved her, dwarfed all the other lies. She began to weep again, the anger that had made a brief appearance subsumed once more by overwhelming sadness.

'I need you to leave,' she said. 'Get your stuff and get out. I never want to see you again.'

She slid the diamond ring from her fourth finger and held it out to him.

'You'd better take this, too. I suppose it didn't really belong to your mother? Where is it from really, Argos?'

Nigel took the ring, opened his mouth to say something but then thought better of it, and walked slowly from the room. As she listened to him packing up his things upstairs, she cursed herself for being so foolish as to seek happiness in her fifties. It was the same for Helen, who had been on the brink of a new life only to have it snatched away, and who was now potentially facing criminal charges. Should they both have put up and shut up, accepted their lot? Angela's dating agency peddled the line that it was never too late to find love, but perhaps that was a myth. Her mother's generation wouldn't have expected to find it at this age. Had Helen's mother, Sheila, been right all along when she said looking for love in midlife was both risible and degrading? Should Sara have been content with the memories of her twenty-five-year happy marriage, instead of greedily seeking more? Was this her punishment? Sara didn't know, but there was one thing of which she was absolutely certain – she would never enter into another relationship again.

Chapter 30

Angela muted the Teams call. 'Greg! There's someone at the door!' she called at the top of her voice.

This was the problem with working from home – there was no way to control external events, and what's more, other people thought you were at their beck and call for household tasks or personal admin. She unmuted herself and tuned back in to what Colleen, one of her most successful matchmakers, was saying.

'John Silverton Introductions are offering a compelling discount at the moment. We ought to think about doing something similar, otherwise they're going to cream off all the new daters coming into the local market.'

'Good idea.' Greg obviously hadn't heard either her or the doorbell because it rang again, longer this time.

'I'm sorry Colleen, there's someone at the door. Do you mind if I run and see who it is?'

'No problem, go.'

Angela hurried out of her office into the hall and yanked open the door, ready to tell whoever was there that no, she didn't need new windows, or her gutters cleared, or to find Jesus. The words died on her lips when she saw Sara, her arms wrapped around herself as if to keep out the cold despite the warmth of the day, her eyeballs threaded with red.

'What's the matter? Is it Helen? Has she been arrested?' They were waiting to hear from Helen, whose interview with the police was that day.

'No, it's nothing to do with that.'

'What is it? Are you alright?'

'Not really.'

'Come in, come in. Hang on, I've got someone on a Teams call – let me go and wrap it up.'

She ushered Sara through to the kitchen and hurried back to her laptop, explaining to Colleen that a personal matter had come up and she'd call her back later.

In the kitchen, she found Sara standing by the patio doors staring out woodenly into the garden where Greg was putting up a bird feeder, having got very excited at spotting a bearded tit earlier that morning.

'Sit down. I'll make you a cup of tea.'

'I don't want anything.'

'At least come and sit down.'

Angela guided her into a chair at the kitchen table and took the seat opposite.

'What's all this about?'

'Please don't say I told you so,' Sara said.

'I won't, I promise.' Angela's heart sank. 'Has this got something to do with Nigel?'

Sara nodded. Her hands twisted around and around each other, her fourth finger conspicuously bare.

'Have you broken up?' Angela asked cautiously.

'Yes, but it's not just that. He was . . . he wanted to . . . oh, I can't say it, it's so embarrassing.'

'Sara, if he's done something to you, it's not your fault. It's down to him. What's happened?'

'He's been lying to me all along.'

'Lying to you about what?'

'Everything,' she said despairingly. 'Who he is, what he does, his daughter, his . . . feelings, his love for me. He was faking the whole thing.'

'What? Why?' Angela cursed herself inwardly for not trying harder to protect Sara. Not only had she introduced Sara to Nigel via the agency, her intuition had told her something wasn't right. Why hadn't she listened to it? She had always thought of herself as someone who was fiercely loyal to her friends, but first she had let Helen down and now Sara.

'For money.' Her voice was barely more than a whisper.

'Not the . . . for his daughter? The money for the immunotherapy?'

'She's not his daughter. She's his . . . well, I don't know to be perfectly honest. Accomplice, I guess. And I suppose, girlfriend? I don't know. There were things I couldn't bear to ask.'

'So there's no daughter, no cancer?' Angela asked.

'No, they made the whole thing up. She doesn't live in America. I only found out because he left his phone at home today and she called him. I had a funny feeling something wasn't right, so I went to Claricoates – that's where he'd told me he was going, to sort through his stuff, but he must have been going to see Isabel . . .'

She wavered, took a breath and started again.

'He wasn't there. But Nigel Peters was.'

'You mean . . . that's not even his real name? Sara, I'm so sorry. I mean, we do all sorts of ID checks – he must have had some pretty convincing fake documentation. So how did he have access to the house?'

'Nigel – well, his name is Colin, apparently, but I can't stop thinking of him as Nigel – works for the real Nigel Peters. He works in the City – doing the job that my Nigel told me he does. He was the one I found when I googled Nigel, although he's hardly got an online presence, I guess for security reasons. He has a flat in London but keeps Claricoates for occasional week-ends, although he's hardly ever actually there. Nigel – my Nigel – is a sort of house-sitter, housekeeper type thing. He's meant to live in a flat in the grounds but he has keys to the house, and to all the fancy cars.'

'Did you tell the real Nigel what was going on?'

'No, I was too shocked. I just made my excuses and left.'

'What did your Nigel say, when you confronted him? You did confront him, didn't you?'

'At first he tried to deny it, kept saying he loved me, that I'd misunderstood.' There had been a part of Sara that had thought if she believed that hard enough, she could make it true; that there could have been some fantastical chain of events that meant Nigel hadn't lied and cheated and tried to defraud her. 'He had the gall to suggest that it was me who was throwing our relationship away, when he's been lying to me since the day we met. He saw a vulnerable, wealthy widow and a money-making opportunity for him and . . . whoever Isabel really is.'

'Would he have gone through with marrying you?'

'I doubt it. It would have been too hard to keep up the decep-tion, for one thing. It was all a way of reeling me in, making me believe he really loved me. As soon as I'd handed over the money, he'd have been off.

'Has he gone? Please tell me he has.'

'Yes, I made him pack up all his stuff. It didn't take long. I questioned when he first moved in why he had brought so little with him, but he'd said a lot of his stuff was still at the house, and he'd wait until he had a chance to sort through it before bringing the rest of it over. Now I realise he was travelling light so that when he'd got my £150,000, he'd be able to flit off.'

'You are going to tell the police, aren't you?'

'Tell them what? That my fiancé is a liar and a cheat? They're not going to be interested in that. I doubt there's anything they could do. I didn't give him the money in the end, thank goodness, but how could I ever prove what he's done? He'll just deny everything.'

'You can't let him get away with it.' Angela burned with righteous indignation.

'I'm too ashamed,' Sara said quietly. 'I don't want anyone to know about it. How could I have been so gullible? You hear these stories about women who get conned, and you think how could they not have seen what was going on? But he was so convincing. I had no reason not to trust him.'

'This is absolutely not your shame,' Angela said. 'He's the one that should be ashamed.'

'I know, but everyone will think I've been stupid. I know they will.'

'Hello, Sara!' Greg came breezing in from the garden. 'How are you?'

'Read the room, Greg,' Angela said.

'Oh, sorry.' Greg stopped and took a closer look at Sara's tear-stained face. 'What's up?'

'Can you leave us alone?' Angela said. 'She may not want to talk to you about it.'

'No, it's fine,' Sara said. 'I don't mind Greg knowing. Nigel and I have broken up,' she said to Greg. 'He wasn't . . . what he seemed to be, put it that way.'

'I'm sorry to hear that,' Greg said. 'I hope Angela hasn't been saying she told you so.'

'No, I haven't! Honestly, Greg.'

'She hasn't,' Sara said. 'You've been great. I'm only sorry I didn't listen to you before.'

'Sorry, Angela,' Greg said. 'I'll leave you to it – I'm on my way out to soap carving. Let me know if you see the bearded tit again, won't you?'

When he'd gone, Angela directed her attention back on Sara. 'Did you pack up all his stuff? No chance he'll be coming back for anything, trying to wheedle his way back in?'

'Pretty much. There may have been some toiletries and things, but I doubt he'd be back for those. There was one thing . . . You're going to say I'm being stupid.'

'I won't! You are not stupid and the shame is all his – and mine, for not seeing what was going on under my nose. He's the one that should be paying for this, not you.'

'He'd left his red jumper in my car. I was going to throw it away, but I couldn't do it. He loves that jumper, and it still smells of him. I've got it with me in my bag. How stupid is that?' She opened her tote bag, revealing a flash of scarlet.

'It's not stupid, but you need to get rid of it, it won't be helping.' Her phone rang. 'It's Helen. I'd better answer it.'

'Don't tell her about all this now – she's got enough on her plate.'

'Alright. Hi, Helen.'

Sara watched, chewing her lip, as Angela listened to Helen,

giving the occasional *mm-hmm* and saying things like 'don't panic' and 'it's going to be OK'.

'What's happened?' Sara asked when Angela had hung up, having told Helen to come straight round.

'It doesn't sound great, to be honest. Brian's not good, the hospital have said it's touch and go whether he'll survive. She said the police went really hard on her – she's convinced they're on the verge of arresting her. She's coming over now to talk about it.'

'What a mess,' Sara said. 'What are we going to do?'

'That's what I'm thinking about,' Angela said slowly. 'I may have had an idea.'

'What idea?'

'I'll tell you when Helen gets here,' she said. 'But in the meantime, I've changed my mind about that red jumper. Hang onto it for now.'

Chapter 31

'It was awful,' Helen said, the three of them now gathered around the kitchen table. 'I felt like a criminal.'

Sara decided not to point out that that was effectively what she was.

'But they didn't arrest you,' Angela said. 'That's got to be a good sign.'

'She said they were waiting for the report from the forensic team. They're examining Brian's X-rays right now. They'll be able to tell he didn't fall, I know it. The doctor was already suspicious enough to call the police. I can't go to prison, I just can't.'

'It might be that they know the evidence won't be compelling enough, so they were trying to get you to confess,' Angela said. 'You didn't, did you?'

'No, but I did get in a bit of a fluster.'

'Don't worry about that − you're a woman of a certain age, they'd be expecting you to get flustered even if you were innocent. Anyway, I may have a plan.'

'A plan for what?' Helen looked from one to the other. 'Are you alright, Sara? You look upset.'

'I don't want to go into it too much,' Sara said. 'Your problem is more pressing. But basically Nigel and I are over.'

'Oh no! What happened?'

'I found that he's been lying to me all along. He's not who he said he was, he doesn't have a daughter with cancer. He was scamming me, basically.'

'What? That's terrible, Sara. I'm so sorry.'

'Thanks,' Sara said. It was kind of Helen to show such concern considering what she was going through. 'But back to your problem.'

'That's the thing,' Angela said. 'The solution I'm thinking of solves both problems – kills two birds with one stone, as it were.'

'I don't have a problem to solve, as such,' Sara said. 'I just need time to get over the crushing humiliation. Luckily I hadn't got to the stage of transferring the money – and before you ask again, no, I'm not going to the police.'

'Aren't you angry, though?' Angela said. 'You should be fuming. Forget all this crying and mooning about with his jumper – you should be spitting feathers. How dare he do this to you? I'm talking about revenge.'

'Revenge?' Sara said. 'I don't know – I think I'd rather forget it ever happened and move on. What do you mean about killing two birds with one stone?'

'Nigel was there the day of Brian's . . . accident, wasn't he?'

'Yes, he rang the doorbell,' Sara said.

'I think – and this is what gave me the idea – he was wearing that red jumper, wasn't he?'

'I don't know,' Sara said. 'I can't even remember what I was wearing.'

'He was definitely wearing a red jumper. Does he have another?'

'No, I don't think so.'

'And what was he doing there? Dropping something off?'

'He was bringing back some golf clubs he'd borrowed.' It was painful to think of those days before she found out the truth about Nigel, when she had thought herself so completely loved.

'That's ideal,' Angela said. 'He didn't leave them outside?'

'No, he brought them back home. They're in my shed.'

'Perfect.'

'Perfect for what?' Sara said. 'Why are you being so cryptic?'

'Just hear me out. It sounds left field, but I'm wondering if we can make it look as though Nigel attacked Brian.'

'Frame him?' Sara said, aghast. 'That's ludicrous. Isn't it, Helen?'

'I don't know,' Helen said slowly. 'I'm willing to consider anything that keeps me out of prison. It sounds as if Nigel's the one who ought to be there anyway. I doubt you're the first person he's done this to – there'll be a string of women like you, all too ashamed to go to the police.'

'Exactly!' Angela said. 'I keep telling her that the shame should be all his. Look what he's done to you, Sara – he spent all that time gaining your trust, your love, and all along he was lying to you. He only wanted your money. I mean, thank God you found out before it was too late, but imagine if you'd given him that money. Other women probably have – I'd be willing to bet he's been doing this for years. And if we do nothing, he'll continue to get away with it. But if we can make it seem as though he attacked Brian, Helen will be safe and he'll be appropriately punished.'

'For something he didn't do,' Sara said. It wasn't easy to go, in the space of a day, from thinking of Nigel as her beloved fiancé, a man with whom she had been able to be entirely herself, to seeing him as a cold-hearted predator who had specifically targeted her vulnerability.

'But he's not innocent, is he?' Angela said. 'What do you think, Helen?'

'I wouldn't dismiss it out of hand. I've spent so many years trapped in my marriage, I can't bear the thought of losing my freedom another way. But it has to be up to you two – I'm the only one culpable for what happened to Brian. I could confess, keep you both out of it – you could walk away. But if we decide to pursue this Nigel idea, you're both implicated. It's much more of a risk for you two than it is for me.'

'We've already lied about what happened,' Angela said. 'May as well be hung for a sheep as for a lamb. And getting you off the hook whilst simultaneously dropping Nigel in it does have a pleasing symmetry, don't you think?'

'You'll have to lie to Greg, though,' Sara said.

'Let me worry about that. I doubt he'll even notice anything's up. It's time to get angry, Sara. I know it's horrible to think of, but he didn't care about you at all. He lied to you and cheated on you and tried to steal from you. He's not the man you thought he was. Now, that's no reflection on you – he was excellent at it – he had us all fooled. I'm furious with myself for not seeing it. But it's time to show him the same care and consideration that he showed you – and save our friend in the process. What do you say?'

What could she say? From what Helen had told them, it wouldn't be long before the police arrested her on suspicion of the attack on Brian – or indeed for his murder. 'Alright. I'm in.'

'I truly believe this means the best – or the most appropriate – outcome for everybody,' Angela said. 'Now – the evidence. There's the golf clubs, and it's great we have the jumper he was wearing that day. We can definitely use that. I was thinking: the trophy Helen . . . er . . . used that day, it's shaped like the head of a golf club, isn't it?'

'Yes,' Helen said.

'So if they can tell – and I have no idea how accurate these things are – but if they are able to tell that the injury to Brian's head was caused by something shaped like the head of a golf club, what's more likely than the head of an actual golf club?'

'But there wouldn't be any forensic evidence to support that,' Sara said.

'There would if we put a drop of Brian's blood on one of the clubs – you said yourself they're still in your shed.'

'But we can't . . . how would we . . . ?' Sara felt as if she was on a wild horse careering down a mountain path with no idea how to make it stop. She looked to Helen for support, only to see her nodding eagerly.

'I could get some of Brian's blood next time I'm in the hospital – we only need a drop, right? I'm sure I can manage that. They're always taking his blood, so I might be able to swipe some, and if the worst comes to the worst, I'll cut his finger and use that.'

'But the nurses will notice, they'll want to know how he got cut,' Sara said.

'Good point,' Helen said thoughtfully. 'I know, I could take a glass bottle of water in with me and "accidentally" drop it. Who's to say a shard of glass wouldn't find its way into his bed?'

'Bloody hell, Helen,' Sara said. She was like the embodiment of that inspirational meme, *A woman is like a teabag, you can't tell how strong she is until you put her in hot water.* Helen was extra-strength builders' tea, muddy no matter how much hot water you added.

'I'm just being practical,' Helen said.

'So we'll put some on the golf clubs,' Angela said, 'and some on the red jumper. That should be sufficient in terms of forensics.'

'I think we're missing a significant piece of the puzzle here,' Sara said, metaphorically pulling on the reins. 'Why would Nigel have wanted to hurt Brian?'

'Hmm, good question,' Angela said.

'What if we said Sara and Brian were having an affair?' Helen suggested. 'And Nigel had found out?'

'No!' Sara said, appalled.

'Why not?' Angela said. 'It'd be poetic justice – he'd been cheating on you, after all. And it's the only thing that would make any sense – a crime of passion!'

'You've been reading too many Agatha Christies,' Sara said.

'Not at all,' Angela retorted. 'You see it on the news all the time. These type of murders, where someone ordinary has done it, it's always to do with either money or sex.'

'But why wouldn't I have told the police this in the first place?' said Helen. 'It's clear they think I had something to do with it. It would have been the ideal way to get myself off the hook.'

'You didn't know!' Angela said. 'Sara and Brian would have been keeping it from you. Sara could come forward and say that Nigel found out about the affair on the day of Brian's accident, and that she's just found the clubs and the jumper hidden in the shed, and is now worried Nigel attacked Brian.'

'They'll want to talk to Nigel, though,' Sara said, sick at the thought of having to face him, 'and he'll say we're making it up.'

'That's precisely what he would say if it were true,' Angela said. 'But we've got golf clubs with his finger prints and Brian's blood on, we've got Brian's blood on his jumper – the jumper he was wearing on the day he came to Brian's house. They'll be able to see him on the CCTV driving to your house and then driving away a few minutes later.'

'But was he at the house long enough to have done it?' Sara asked.

'Yes,' Helen said eagerly. 'He rang the bell a couple of times. Then he wrote that note and put it through. Easily time to come in, give Brian a swift whack on the head, and leave.'

'What happened to the note?' Sara asked. 'Have the police seen it? Because they'll know Nigel didn't come in if they have.'

'Oh, well . . . I pocketed it, that day,' Helen admitted.

'What? But we didn't know about Nigel then!' Sara said. 'Surely you weren't planning . . .'

'Of course not,' Helen said. 'I just had . . . I don't know, I suppose you'd call it an instinct. And thank goodness I did.'

'And where were we meant to be when Nigel was coming in and attacking Brian?' Sara said. 'If there's CCTV or other police camera footage of Nigel arriving and leaving, there's also footage of Angela and I arriving and not leaving. They'll know we were in the house.'

'We stick to our original story,' Angela said. 'We were in the garden. Nigel didn't know we were there. We didn't hear him come in.'

'I don't know about this at all,' Sara said.

'Did Nigel think about how you'd feel when you found out he'd been lying to you?' Angela said.

'What if Brian wakes up, though? Even if he's disorientated and can't remember the day of the attack, he'll know we weren't having an affair.'

'I think that's very unlikely,' Helen said. 'They've been preparing me for the worst for a few days now. The nurses have implied it's only a matter of time before we have to *take some hard decisions*.'

'So, we're doing this?' Angela asked. 'Because once we've gone down this road, there's no turning back. And we all have to be on board and singing from the same hymn sheet, otherwise we're just throwing each other under the bus.'

'I'm in,' Helen said. 'And I'll never forget that you've done this for me. I'm so grateful. If you agree, of course, Sara,' she added quickly.

Sara thought about all the times Nigel had told her he loved her. All the meals he had cooked and the drinks he had poured and the times he had rubbed her feet after a long day. About how he had told her no one had ever got him the way she did, and how she had felt truly seen for the first time in her life, and how that had all been a lie. About how, as a result, she'd never be able to trust a man again, and would have to somehow make her peace with spending the rest of her days alone. She took a deep breath.

'I'm in.'

Chapter 32

Mr Tarapore may have implicated Helen in a possible attempted-murder investigation, but nonetheless he remained professional.

'I'm afraid Brian needs to have another operation,' he said across Brian's inert body, speaking loudly to be heard above the wheezing of the ventilator. She wondered if it was true that coma patients could hear what was being said around them.

'His latest scans show that he is suffering from a chronic subdural haematoma. That means old liquefied blood is pooling between the outermost membrane and the underlying brain. This can sometimes happen a few weeks after the initial injury. This will be putting pressure on the brain, so the plan is to perform a surgery called burr hole drainage, where we drill small holes into the skull to permit drainage of this blood.'

Helen winced at the mention of drilling holes in Brian's skull.

'I know it sounds serious, and it is, but as I've said to you before, I've performed this surgery hundreds of times.'

Helen didn't ask how many of those times there had been a successful outcome. She didn't want her treacherous voice to give away that she hoped the answer would be not very many.

'I'm afraid if the operation isn't successful,' Mr Tarapore continued, avoiding her eye, 'there are some difficult conversations to be had around withdrawal of treatment.'

She wished these medical professionals wouldn't talk in riddles. It was as if they thought they were doing worried relatives a favour by shielding them from the truth. When her father was dying, Helen had no idea how close he was to the end, because none of the staff involved in his care had the courage to come out and say it. They must have thought she wasn't strong enough to face it – but she, along with the Floozy from the Haberdashery Shop, with whom he'd had a very happy second marriage, had had to face it regardless once her father was gone.

'You mean . . . there may be nothing more you can do for him?' She put it as delicately as she could, as he seemed to be having trouble with the concept.

'Indeed,' he agreed gratefully. 'In some cases, continuing to treat someone in a coma is no longer of any benefit to them. We always make these decisions with the patient's best interests at heart. We may have to consider whether Brian is likely to ever regain a meaningful quality of life. However, let's not go there yet. We should have a slot for him in theatre tomorrow, and I'll know more after that. In the meantime . . .'

'Yes?' Had the police questioned Mr Tarapore about her?

'We'll keep you posted,' he said, sweeping out of the room. They definitely had. What had he been going to say? *In the meantime, don't hit him on the head again?* She had no intention of doing that, although in fairness she had been thinking about how she could extract a sample of his blood in order to implicate an innocent man in his murder.

'Hello!' Rosa, a friendly but somewhat chaotic healthcare assistant in her mid-forties, poked her head in. 'I've come to take some bloods now the lord and master's gone.' As ever, Rosa's hair was falling out of its ponytail and there were a couple of worrying stains in shades of rust and tan down the front of her tunic. She always had the faint air of someone who was running late, or who had turned up at the wrong place on the wrong day.

Helen stood up and moved away from the bed towards the window to give her room for her ministrations. Her handbag was heavy with the glass water bottle she had brought in case she needed to cut Brian's finger.

'Hello, Brian!' Rosa said cheerily. 'Just going to take some blood for testing before your surgery tomorrow.' Helen half hoped Brian could hear – he'd be furious at someone of such low status (in his warped opinion) calling him by his first name. A dental nurse had once felt his wrath for the same thing. Helen had pretended to have left something behind in the room so she could go back and apologise to her for his rudeness.

Rosa hooked up her syringe to Brian's cannula and drew several small vials of blood. She screwed the top on each one, laying them onto a chrome trolley at her side. Helen eyed them hungrily. One of those would be ideal for the purpose. Did she dare? It would be much easier than the whole performance of breaking the bottle.

'I'm going to go down and get a coffee,' she said to Rosa, evenly.

'No worries. I'll be here for a bit – got to do his obs once I've finished with the bloods.'

Were there cameras in here? Surely resources wouldn't stretch to that?

'Just one more, sweetie,' Rosa said, bending over Brian's hand. If Brian would be angry at her using his first name, he'd be apoplectic at that endearment.

Rosa was absorbed in her task, with her back to the trolley. It was now or never. Without giving herself time to overthink it and change her mind, Helen walked across the room, swiped one of the vials of blood from the trolley and slipped it into her pocket. She walked down the corridor to the lifts, her heart pounding, feeling as though everyone she passed had X-ray vision and could see what she had done. In the café, she took her coffee to a table and drank it slowly, wanting to make sure Rosa was gone by the time she went back up to ITU. She felt an unexpected little throb of pride in herself every time her fingers touched the small cylinder. Brian would never have dreamed she would be capable of such a thing. She almost sent a photo to Angela and Sara, before realising that would be a very bad idea indeed should there ever be a police investigation against her.

Burying the vial deep in her handbag, she made her way back up to the ward. As she walked past the nurses' station, behind the pane of glass she could see Rosa being berated by her supervisor, a terrifying woman with an air of Nurse Ratched about her. Rosa looked close to tears. Guilt nibbled at the boundaries of Helen's consciousness. What if Rosa lost her job over this? Surely not – it would be a case of a warning or somesuch, wouldn't it? She looked away and continued on her path back to Brian's room to resume her role as his devoted wife. It was too late to try and save Rosa. The die was cast and she had gone much too far down this particular road to turn back now.

Chapter 33

'Are you sure you're happy to do this?' Angela asked Helen for the millionth time, wiping a smudge off one of the champagne glasses set out on the trestle table. 'Your mind must be on the meeting with Mr Tarapore tomorrow morning.'

'It's fine – I need the distraction.'

Angela was holding one of the regular get-togethers she organised for her daters in a local hotel's function room. There were always more women than men, and it wasn't billed as an opportunity to meet potential dates (although that did happen sometimes) but more of a social gathering. The women appreciated the chance to meet other older single women. When most of your friends were married, it became a bit tiresome being the only singleton, always being asked to wheel out your dating disasters for the amusement of your smugly coupled-up pals.

'I mainly need you to keep glasses topped up and take round the canapés. I'll be keeping an eye out for anyone who needs help mingling, but if you do see someone standing alone, could you introduce them to someone – either someone else who's on their own, or bring them into one of the groups? Doesn't matter if it's men or women.'

'No problem. It'll be nice to have something else to focus on other than this Brian business.'

It was an interesting way of putting it. Angela did wonder if Sara was right to be a tiny bit frightened of the way Helen was coping with all this, although she had been immensely impressed by Helen's blood-gathering escapade. It was rather extraordinary how she'd grown in confidence since Brian's effective departure from her daily life. Brian had had his second round of surgery yesterday and Mr Tarapore had asked Helen to come in tomorrow to discuss next steps.

'Hi, Angela!' Leila came sailing into the room, always the first to arrive. She was gorgeous as ever in a deliberately oversized, wide-leg, teal trouser suit and cream silk blouse.

'Leila, hello!' They kissed on the cheek. 'You remember my friend Helen – she's working with me at the agency now.'

'Of course, how are you?'

'Very well, thanks,' Helen said, having intuited that the real answer – *oh, bit worried I'm going to be arrested for my husband's murder but planning to frame someone else for it* – wasn't called for. 'How are you?'

'The usual. Working, going out, bit of dating here and there.'

'Anyone special?' Angela asked. 'Did anything come of the men you met at our last speed dating event?'

'Funny you should say that, actually. There was one guy I met there – Nigel, d'you remember him?'

Angela felt Helen tense beside her, but remained centred on Leila.

'I remember him.'

'After we met at your event, we'd arranged to go out but then he cancelled – said he'd met someone else that he wanted to pursue a relationship with – all very honourable. Most men would have carried on dating us both.'

'Mm-hmm.' Honourable was the last word to describe the man who called himself Nigel Peters, but Angela waited to see where Leila was going with this.

'Then I got a match this week from John Silverton Introductions – sorry, I know he's your competitor, but a girl's got to keep her options open.'

'I understand,' Angela said. 'What happened?'

'Who should it be but Nigel? He said it hadn't worked out after all with this other woman – he's had an absolute nightmare, in fact – and was I still interested in meeting up?'

'And were you?' Angela asked. Jesus Christ, it had only been a week since Sara chucked him out and he was already back on the dating scene, scenting out fresh prey.

'Yes, why not? He seems a nice man, and I'm not exactly inundated with them. I met up with him last night.'

'Leila, I need to talk to you about this,' Angela said. 'Please don't think this is anything to do with any professional jealousy – I absolutely accept that you are going to use all the tools at your disposal when it comes to meeting a partner.'

Three women came in, chatting and laughing. Angela recognised them – they'd met and bonded at her last social event. Maybe she should pivot to providing a service matching women with platonic female friends.

'Helen – could you get those ladies a drink? Thanks.'

She drew Leila aside as Helen poured drinks for the new arrivals.

'What's up?' Leila said.

'I have to warn you about Nigel Peters,' Angela said. 'The woman he was dating is a friend of mine – Sara, you met her at the hospice fundraising event.'

'Yes, I know who she is.'

'The reason things didn't work out between them is that she found out he was lying to her about who he was, and planning to defraud her. He told her he had a daughter in America who needed cancer treatment that wasn't covered by her healthcare plan. She was on the verge of giving him an enormous amount of money.'

Leila shifted uncomfortably. 'The thing is, Angela, he said something similar about her.'

'What?' Her voice was loud enough that the three women looked over in alarm.

'Sorry!' Angela said, giving them a wave. 'Just catching up on the . . . er . . . gossip. Lovely to see you all!' She turned back to Leila. 'What did he say about Sara?'

'He said she was pressuring him to change his will and life insurance in favour of her, instead of his daughter.'

'That's a complete lie!'

'He showed me texts and emails from her, Angela.'

'From what email and number? Show me! He must have been faking them.'

'I don't have them on my phone, obviously. He showed me on his. And there was something else, but it's a bit delicate . . . I know she's a good friend of yours.'

'Just tell me,' Angela said, with a horrible sense of foreboding.

'He had the feeling she was up to something, so he checked her search history on her computer when she left it open one day. She'd been googling poisonous plants, especially ones where the symptoms mimic real illnesses. He was worried she was going to try and . . . harm him. He confronted her and she disappeared – he hasn't seen her since.'

'This is ludicrous! He was the one trying to scam her, Leila. You have to believe me.'

'To be honest, Angela, that's exactly what he said she was saying. In fact, he's quite worried that she's spreading these rumours about him.'

'Would you meet up with Sara? If you spoke to her, you'd be able to see that she's telling the truth.'

'I don't think so.' Leila edged away from Angela. 'Don't worry, I can look after myself. He's not the only man I'm seeing, and I'm the last person who'd get scammed.'

That was debatable – Angela thought she was precisely the sort of person to get scammed, just as she had been the sort of person to fall for a compulsive gambler and a man with a secret wife and children.

'That's what Sara thought,' she said. 'Nobody thinks they'd fall for it, but he's clever. He'll make you feel like you're the most special woman in the world, like you're the only one who's ever understood him, and vice versa. It's hard to resist. I imagine you're a wealthy woman, Leila, and I'm not being funny but you don't have the best track record when it comes to spotting red flags.'

'How dare you!' Leila said. 'Is that what you've thought about me all along? Poor old Leila, she's so stupid, wouldn't be able to spot a red flag if it was waving in her face?'

'Not at all. I'm just trying to stop what happened to my friend from happening to you. If you won't believe me, please just . . . be vigilant.'

'I always am,' she said stiffly. 'There's someone I want to say hello to over there – if you'll excuse me.'

Angela watched her go, anxiety gnawing at her. More people, mainly women, had arrived while she was talking to Leila and the room swelled with noise as they swapped dating horror stories for each other's amusement. Helen moved easily among the guests, pouring sparkling wine and introducing anyone standing alone to one of the little groups that had formed. She was a different woman to the mouse who had scurried around Brian on a futile mission to meet his every need. Whereas Sara, although Angela knew she would be OK in the long run, was currently a shadow of her former self. She couldn't bear for Nigel to dim Leila's shine in the same way. She went out to the corridor and ducked into a nearby unused function room to call John Silverton.

'Angela!' he said. 'To what do I owe this pleasure?'

'I wanted to have a confidential word with you about one of your clients.'

'Which one would that be?'

'Name of Nigel Peters.'

'Aha. I thought you might say that.'

Had Nigel spun John the same line Leila had fallen for?

'I don't know what he's told you, and I'm not asking you to break any confidences, but John, your business is built on trust. Your USP is you're a personalised dating agency that espouses old-fashioned values in a world where everyone else is swiping left and right. Nigel Peters dated a friend of mine and she recently found out he was lying to her about who he was and trying to defraud her. Is that the sort of man you want on your books?'

'I'm afraid Nigel warned me to expect your call,' John said. 'His story is that it was your friend who was trying to defraud him – and possibly worse. He showed me some pretty incontrovertible evidence. I would argue that it's you who is being unprofessional here. I think it's unwise to take on friends as clients – the boundaries get blurred and you're always going to have a blind spot where they're concerned.'

'What was this evidence?'

'Come on, I can't tell you that, Angela.'

'Whatever it was must have been fake.'

'You say he tried to defraud your friend – did she go to the police?'

'She was too ashamed! That's what he's done to her. She's done nothing wrong but somehow she feels it was her fault.'

'Maybe she's not as innocent as you think?' John said. 'Look, Angela, unless there's a police investigation, which there obviously isn't, this is all gossip and hearsay, and I don't conduct my business based on gossip and hearsay. I suggest that if you don't want your business to fail, you do the same. Have a good evening.'

Angela stood alone, her face burning. The condescending twit. Helen poked her head through the door.

'Are you coming, Angela? The fizz is running low, are we offering any more?'

'I'll come and sort it out. But Helen – let's not waste any more time. The likelihood is Brian's never going to come round, and if he does he'll be highly confused. Let's prepare everything tonight – the golf clubs, the jumper – and tomorrow I'll meet you after the consultation with Mr Tarapore and we'll go straight to the police with our evidence.'

'Are you sure?' Helen asked.

'Absolutely. I can't bear the thought of another woman suffering like Sara has. Nigel is going to get what's coming to him.'

Chapter 34

'How much do you think we should put on the golf club?' Helen held the vial of Brian's blood up to the light. 'There's not much in there.'

'It only needs to be a trace,' Angela said. 'We want to make it seem like he's tried to wipe it off. Then we'll put the rest on the jumper. You could say you found it hidden at the back of a cupboard, Sara.'

'Alright,' she agreed absently. The other two were approaching the framing of Nigel with something frighteningly close to glee. Sara just felt sick at heart. Sick at what Nigel had done to her, and terrified at the prospect of this wholesale lying to the police they were about to embark on. Finding out that Nigel was dating Leila had plunged her further into despair. How could she have been so stupid as to not see what was in front of her nose?

'Which cupboard?' Angela asked.

'What?'

'Which cupboard? You can't just say a cupboard, the police will want specifics.'

'I could say I found it hidden in the shed? With the golf clubs?'

'Good idea,' Helen chimed in. 'You need to have a reason to be suspicious of the golf clubs, otherwise the police won't examine them. You should say it was all hidden away together.'

'Excellent,' Angela said. 'So you'll go to them, say you've found the hidden items and that the day Brian was injured, Nigel had found out about your affair with him.'

'Is there really no other story we could come up with?' Sara said. 'It feels so weird and unnatural. I don't know if I'll be able to pull it off.'

'You'll be fine,' Angela said. 'If you're awkward about it, that'll seem natural – of course you'd feel odd about confessing to an affair with your friend's husband. That's a point actually – you two can't be seen together in public. Helen wouldn't want to be friends with you after that. You should probably say that you've only just told Helen as well, on the day you tell the police – that Nigel didn't tell her. In case someone at the hospital says you've been seen together there.'

'This is all so complicated,' Sara said. 'What if I get something wrong?'

'Don't worry – just keep it simple,' Angela said. 'You were having an affair with Brian, Nigel found out on the day Brian fell. He went to the house to confront Brian, not realising that we were there in the garden. You could say he was very distracted that evening, that you knew something was up.'

'How long am I meant to have been having this affair?'

'Hmm, good point,' Angela said. 'Maybe it'd be simpler if you said you only slept with him once.'

'And why didn't Nigel leave me when he first found out?' Sara asked.

'You were trying to work on things,' Helen suggested. 'You begged him to stay? But in the end, he couldn't cope with the knowledge of what you'd done, so he left. That's why you're no longer together.'

'This all sounds so melodramatic, like a soap opera.'

'These things do happen, though. I'm sure they will have seen it all before,' Angela said.

'It's all very well for you two – I'm the one that's got to do most of the lying,' Sara said.

'I do appreciate it, Sara,' Helen said. 'I'll never forget that you did this for me.'

'It's alright. I'll never be able to trust anyone again anyway, so what does it matter if everyone thinks I was bonking your husband? Let's get this bit over with. Hand me the golf club. Which one is the 9-iron?'

'Wait!' Angela said. 'Don't touch them!'

'What?' Sara said, bewildered.

'Fingerprints!' Angela said. 'Do they still test things for finger-prints, or is that a bit *Murder She Wrote*?'

'I don't know,' Helen said. 'Let's wear gloves, to be on the safe side.'

'But I've already touched the golf club bag!' Sara said with a twinge of alarm. 'My fingerprints will be all over it!'

'Hang on, you're taking the clubs in and saying you've found blood on one of them, aren't you?' Angela said. 'So your prints would be on it. It's just Helen and I who shouldn't touch them.'

'This is what I mean!' Sara said. 'If I'm panicking like this now, how will I be when the police interview me? I know, I know,' she held up a hand to pre-empt Angela's reply. 'Everything will be OK. Right, give me the blood.'

Helen passed it over and Sara unscrewed the cap and tipped a few drops onto the head of the 9-iron.

'Here, wipe it off with this,' Helen handed her a piece of kitchen towel.

'What do you think?' Sara held up the club to the others, the blood now just a faint smear.

'I think that's ideal,' Angela said. 'Not so much that it's an obvious fake, but enough so that you might have noticed it. That can go back in the bag. Right, now the jumper.'

Sara took Nigel's red sweater out of her bag, resisting the compulsion to bury her nose in it and breathe in the last vestige of his scent.

'Whereabouts should I put the blood? How is it meant to have got on there?' she said.

'On the sleeve?' Helen suggested. 'He could have . . . um, I don't know . . . knelt down to check if Brian was breathing?'

'The sleeve it is,' Sara tipped the remainder of the blood onto the cuff.

'Now shove it back into the golf bag – as if he'd hidden it in there, that's it,' Angela said.

'Look at the time. I need to go to the hospital, I'm seeing Mr Tarapore at eleven thirty,' Helen said.

'We'll come with you for moral support,' Angela said.

'I thought I wasn't supposed to be seen in public with her?' Sara said.

'She hasn't told you yet,' Angela said. 'This can be your last hurrah.'

The three women were silent in the car on the way to the hospital, and as they waited for Helen to be called in for the appointment. Angela tried to make desultory conversation with Sara once Helen had gone in, but neither of them could concentrate. Sara leafed through a pamphlet on the One Life Service. It was a guide to living a healthier life, full of such revolutionary suggestions as giving up smoking, eating more vegetables and walking instead of taking the car. According to the leaflet, the maximum recommended units of alcohol for a woman was fourteen per week. It said that was equivalent to six glasses of wine, but that couldn't be right, could it?

'She's been a long time, hasn't she?' Sara said, putting down the leaflet after what felt like hours but had only been around ten minutes.

'Not really,' Angela said. 'Oh look, here she comes now.'

Helen emerged from the consulting room, deathly pale, and lowered herself into the next chair.

'What is it?' Sara asked. 'Is he . . . are they going to turn the life support off?'

'No.' Her voice was little more than a strangled croak. 'The operation was a success. They're bringing him out of the coma. There's a long way to go, but Mr Tarapore is confident he's going to recover. Brian's back.'

Chapter 35

Helen walked down the hospital corridor towards Brian's new room, her legs barely able to carry her. Over the last week, the doctors had been gradually reducing the medication that had been keeping him in the coma. The first time he had opened his eyes had been a horrible shock, even though she'd been told to expect it. She'd got used to this new version of Brian – inert, whey-faced, chest rising and falling in time with the ventilator. Preferred it, if she was honest. He hadn't spoken yet but his eyes had met hers in recognition and he had found her hand where it rested near his on the bed and given it a faint squeeze. They'd called this morning to tell her he was now breathing unaided, which meant they'd been able to move him down a level of care from ITU to the High Dependency Unit.

She hadn't heard from the police since getting the news that the medical team were bringing Brian back to himself. She got the sense that they were waiting to see what Brian's memory of the event was – if he remembered it at all. If he had a pinpoint recall of what happened, that would do their job for them – they could arrest her without the need for any further investigation on their part. Sara had hidden the bloodied golf club and jumper away in her shed until they knew what Brian could recollect of that day, and his life generally before the head injury. They couldn't risk implicating Nigel until they knew how much Brian remembered.

Helen was concerned to see Rosa taking Brian's blood pressure when she entered the room – she'd imagined Rosa worked exclusively in ITU and had been looking forward to being away from her accusatory gaze. Helen was sure she suspected that she had taken the vial of blood, although what she thought Helen was going to do with it was anyone's guess.

'Morning,' Rosa said, in a somewhat guarded fashion. 'I'm just finishing up here and I'll be out of your way. He's doing well this morning, aren't you, Brian?' She raised her voice as if he was hard of hearing, which Helen supposed he might be now. Mr Tarapore had given her dire warnings about how changed Brian could be as a result of the lengthy induced coma. Over the past week, as Brian had become more aware of his surroundings, he had been confused and agitated. On a few occasions he had spoken, but he was delirious and what he said made no sense. Mr Tarapore had warned of longer-term issues such as disorientation, amnesia, difficulties with comprehension and speech, seizures and depression. However he had also said that Brian could make a more or less full recovery in time. She wasn't exactly sure what she was hoping for.

Brian smiled thankfully up at Rosa and put his hand out to her. She gave it a quick squeeze, then vacated her place at his side. Helen settled herself into the blue, moulded plastic chair.

'Hello, Brian,' she said stiffly. She'd found it incredibly difficult when he was in the coma speaking to him as if he could hear her. It felt so unnatural when you weren't getting any response.

'Hello,' he croaked, turning his head towards her.

'Oh! You're . . . you can speak!' With that, the last shred of hope she'd been clinging to, that she was going to finally escape Brian and live a life of freedom, slithered from her grasp.

'Yes.' He licked his cracked lips.

She took his hand. The weeks where he had been in a coma took on the golden hue of a halcyon time, despite the threat of arrest that had hung over her. She hadn't appreciated then what a huge weight had been lifted from her shoulders in Brian's absence from her life, but she was acutely aware of it now as it settled back upon her like an iron cloak. She felt as if she were watching herself from the outside, a character in a play acting the part of a devoted wife.

'It's good to see you,' he said. 'You look nice.'

It had been many years since he'd said anything like that to her. She questioned for a second if he knew who she was – had he taken her for an extra-friendly healthcare assistant? Or could Brian's personality have been changed for the better as a result of the coma? Mr Tarapore hadn't mentioned that as a possible side effect.

'How are you feeling?' she asked.

'Tired. The doctor explained what happened, how long I've been in here.'

'Yes. It's been about a month since the . . .'

'Accident?' Brian whispered into the space she had left.

'Yes. Yes, the accident. Do you . . . do you remember anything about that day?' She might as well find out what she was up against.

'Not much. The doctor said I fell and hit my head.'

Helen couldn't tell if he was staring at her meaningfully or if he was simply too tired to move his head.

'That's right.'

'He said you found me.'

'Yes.'

'That must have been frightening.' He was speaking slower now, with more obvious effort. 'Were you on your own?'

'No. I was with Angela and Sara, my friends. Do you remember them?'

'Of course I do.'

With that, any hope Helen had that they could go on with their story that Brian and Sara were having an affair, leading Nigel to attack Brian in a jealous rage, dissipated. If Brian could already remember Sara, there was no way he'd believe he'd been having an affair with her, no matter how muddled his memories of the day were. They would never be able to make it stick. It would just make her look guiltier – as would continuing with her original plan of leaving him. The iron cloak grew heavier still. All she could hope now was that Brian had no memories of the day itself, including that she had planned to leave him. She would unpack her cases and pretend that door had never opened. Maybe when he was better – whatever 'better' looked like for him – she could work up the necessary courage to try again.

'Were they there?' he said.

'Angela and Sara? Yes, they were with me when I found you.' Was this going to be the rest of her life? Repeating things she'd just told him?

'Were you there when I fell?' he muttered, his eyelids drooping.

'No,' she managed, feeling as though her heart was clamped in a vice. 'Do you think you're getting things confused, thinking of a different day?'

She thought Brian was sinking into sleep but then his body began to twitch and stiffen, mildly at first but becoming more violent. A terrifying gurgling sound emanated from his mouth.

She pressed Brian's buzzer but no one came, so she ran to the corridor and shouted for help. A nurse appeared and immediately took charge of the situation.

'Don't worry,' she said calmly. 'I know it looks bad but he's just having a seizure. It's not uncommon after what he's been through. It'll pass.'

Helen watched as Brian's convulsing body gradually stilled. His eyes opened and locked straight on to hers. As she stared at his familiar yet irrevocably changed features, she was immobilised by the realisation that her life now was caring for Brian. The sweet freedom she had tasted so briefly was over.

Chapter 36

'He seems to have accepted the story that he fell,' Helen said as she and Angela made their way through the maze of corridors that led to Brian's room. Another week on, and he'd been moved again, to a normal ward this time. He was doing so well that he no longer required the services of the HDU. 'But every now and then I catch him looking at me, almost out of the corner of his eye, and I think he *knows*.'

'But he'd say, wouldn't he?' Angela said. 'What would he gain from keeping quiet?'

'He'll be enjoying torturing me, making me wonder if he knows or not,' Helen said, as if it were the most obvious thing in the world.

'Oh, Helen.' The most heartbreaking thing about it was her matter-of-fact delivery. Angela cursed herself for not having been able to see what Brian was doing over the years. Or worse, had she chosen not to see? 'I understand that you feel you can't abandon him now, but when he's better, you must leave him.'

'I'll never be able to leave him now,' she said flatly.

'We'll see about that,' Angela said. 'But whatever happens, you'll have me and Sara. Things will be different now that we know what your relationship is really like. We'll be there to support you, whatever you choose. I know Sara's still reeling from Nigel's betrayal, but she's strong, she'll be OK.'

'You don't think she'll slip up and tell the truth, do you?' Helen said.

'No, I'm sure she won't,' Angela said. Helen had become almost frighteningly single-minded in her desire to conceal the truth of what she had done.

'I want to know what you think,' Helen went on. 'Whether you think he knows, and if he does, whether he's planning to tell the police. I can't bear this uncertainty.'

'If you can't tell, I doubt I'll be able to,' Angela said.

'We'll find out soon anyway. Mr Tarapore said the police have been in touch and they want to come and interview him. He said he thinks Brian's up to it now, so they could be coming any day. Here's his room. See what you think.'

Brian looked small and frail in the hospital bed, hooked up to various drips and contraptions.

'Hello! Look who I've brought to see you! It's Angela!' Helen said brightly.

Angela didn't think Brian, even on top form, would have been that bothered about seeing her, and especially not when he was so ill, but she followed Helen's cheery lead.

'You're looking well, Brian. Lovely to see you.'

'Hello, Angela.' He pressed a button on the remote control attached to the bed and it groaned into action, raising him up from a half-lying to a seated position like Frankenstein's monster coming to life.

'You remember Angela, don't you?' Helen asked.

'I haven't completely lost my mind, although you wouldn't know it from the way you treat me.'

'Sorry. I know, you're doing amazingly. Mr Tarapore said there could be all sorts of . . . cognitive issues,' Helen explained to Angela, 'but he's really pleased with how Brian's doing so far.'

'Did I hear my name?'

Mr Tarapore swept into the room on his daily ward round.

'I was just telling my friend that you're pleased with how Brian is doing,' Helen said.

'Yes, yes, we are. However, I wanted to talk to you about the seizures.'

'Right. The nurses told me he's had another one since the one he had when I was here last week.'

'Post-traumatic epilepsy is very common after head injury, but the good news is there are some excellent drugs available. I'm going to prescribe something that will massively reduce the chance of seizures in the future. You need to make sure he keeps taking it when he comes home.'

The smile Helen had pasted on for the consultant dimmed at the mention of Brian returning home. It faded further at what he said next.

'He's doing so well I've said the police can come and talk to him – they'll be here later today. Any other concerns?'

'No, I don't think so,' Helen said weakly. He swept from the room.

'Helen, why don't you go and get us all a proper coffee from the café downstairs?' Brian said. 'I'm sick of the pale brown water they call coffee that comes round on the trolley.'

'Really?' Helen said. 'I've only just got here, and Angela . . .'

'I'm sure Angela can manage,' he said. 'I'm hardly in a position to cause her any harm. I can barely lift my arm from the bed.'

'I didn't think you were going to harm her, I would never—'

'For heaven's sake, it was a joke,' he snapped. 'Just go and get the damn coffee.'

Helen left, close to tears, leaving Angela struggling to contain her anger. If she'd hoped that his near-death experience had changed Brian for the better, she was sorely disappointed. He was worse than ever. They had to find a way to get Helen away from him.

'It's funny,' he said conversationally. 'It's all a bit muddled but I'm sure I saw you and Sara before the accident. Were you at the house not long before I . . . fell?'

Thoughts scurried frantically around in Angela's brain.

'Yes, that's right,' she said cautiously. 'We were there when you fell, but we were in the garden.'

'That's right, Helen did say.' A fleck of spittle formed at one corner of his mouth. 'How was I, when you came around that day?' he asked. 'My memory is very hazy.'

'You'd left work early because you didn't feel well,' she said stiffly. 'You had a headache, you felt faint,' she improvised. 'Presumably that's why you fell.'

'Presumably,' he agreed. 'It's funny though, I keep getting flashbacks to things from that day that . . . well, they can't possibly be real.'

'It must be a side effect of the coma. Didn't they say you could suffer with amnesia, hallucinations, all sorts?'

'Yes, I suppose it must be. Because what I'm seeing in these flashbacks, it can't be true.'

'What are you seeing?' she asked with trepidation.

'Never you mind,' he said. 'No harm in having a little secret, is there, Angela?'

Chapter 37

Helen carried the three lattes back from the coffee shop in a cardboard cup tray, concentrating intently on not joggling them. Brian hated it when a bit of coffee escaped through the little hole in the plastic lid. She tried to balance moving slowly enough so that the liquid wouldn't spill, but not so slowly that the coffee began to cool. If it got even vaguely lukewarm, Brian would declare it undrinkable. She tried not to think about how close she had come to not having to make these kinds of accommodations on a daily basis. Despite all the stress and worry about whether her attack on Brian would be discovered, she had relished the ease of a life where, if your coffee was cooler than you'd like it, instead of starting World War Three you thought *never mind* and drank it anyway.

She'd nearly made it back to the room when Angela came charging down the corridor towards her, her face set.

'What is it? Why aren't you in with Brian?'

'He knows,' Angela murmured. 'Brian knows.'

'What? Did he say so?'

'Not in so many words, but he definitely knows. He said he remembers seeing me and Sara at the house with you that day, that he's been having flashbacks.'

'What did you say?'

'I stuck to our story – that we were in the garden and you went in and found him on the floor. But I don't think he bought it.'

'Is he going to tell the police?'

'Why wouldn't he?' Angela said.

'Is there any way we can salvage the plan to frame Nigel?' Helen asked desperately.

'I don't think so – it'll never work now Brian's awake and has memories of that day, and what was going on in his life before.'

'I can't talk about this now,' Helen said. 'I need to get him this coffee before it gets too cold – here, you may as well take yours. I'll call you later.'

Angela left and Helen took the remaining two cups into Brian's room.

'Here you go. I hope it's still hot enough.'

Brian took a sip, and winced.

'Sorry. I could go and get you another one, ask them to make it extra hot?'

'Why on earth didn't you do that in the first place?'

'You're right, I should have done. I'll go back.'

'Don't be ridiculous. I'll have to drink it cold. Might as well have had the mud they bring round on the trolley.'

'Sorry,' she said again. She had put her old meekness back on like a winter coat that had been put away during the warmer weather.

'Visitor for you!' Rosa poked her head through the door.

'Who is it?' Helen asked, but the question was answered when DS Paskell walked in.

'Hello again,' she said to Helen. 'Good morning, Brian. I'm Detective Sergeant Paskell. I'd like to ask you a few questions about the day of your injury, if you're feeling up to it?'

'Oh, I don't know. He's still a bit confused,' Helen said.

'You don't have to answer for me,' he said. 'I'm happy to talk to the officer. Do come and sit down, please.'

'Here, you can have my chair.' Helen sprang up, almost knocking the chair over. 'Should I . . . shall I stay, or . . .'

'Probably best if you leave us to it,' the detective said, taking a seat.

'If it's alright with you, detective, I'm happy for Helen to hear everything I've got to say. I'd like you to hear it, in fact,' he said, looking straight at Helen.

'That's entirely your call,' the detective said.

Helen stood behind DS Paskell. There was no other chair, not that she'd be capable of sitting down. Her body was tingling, adrenaline shooting through her veins. She clasped her hands tightly in front of her to keep them still.

'I'll try and keep it brief,' Paskell said. 'Can you remember anything about the day you acquired the injury?'

'Yes, I remember it very well.'

Helen gasped. Every time Brian had been asked this previously, his answer had involved the words *hazy* and *jumbled*.

'Can you talk me through the day?'

'I went to work as usual in the morning, but in the early afternoon, I felt unwell so decided to go home.'

'Do you know what time that was?'

'No, sorry. After lunch some time.'

'Did you see anyone when you got back to the house?'

'Yes.' His eyes flicked in Helen's direction. 'My wife was there with two of her friends, Angela and Sara.'

'You know these friends?'

'Yes, of course. They're my wife's best friends. Her very best friends. They'd do anything for her.' There was no mistaking the

267

emphasis he was putting on this. DS Paskell threw a look over her shoulder at Helen, who stood frozen in place.

'And what happened next?' she asked neutrally.

'Well . . .' He paused. Helen's knees threatened to give way beneath her. She felt as if she were hanging over a precipice, and any minute now she would find herself plunging, tumbling through the air and crashing into the rocks below.

'Helen and her friends went out into the garden,' he continued.

'Oh.' Helen couldn't help the little exhalation that escaped her lips. DS Paskell sat back in her chair.

'I still had this pounding headache, so I decided to go upstairs and get some painkillers from the bathroom cabinet. I stood up, walked around the coffee table and then I tripped on something – I'm not sure what it was, but I'd guess it was the rug we have by the hearth.'

'You tripped on the rug,' DS Paskell repeated, with a note of disbelief.

'That's right. There was a second of panic as I started to fall – and then nothing, until they brought me out of the coma two weeks ago.'

Helen was sure DS Paskell would be able to hear her heart thundering. What was Brian playing at?

'So you were alone in the room when you fell?' The detective sounded almost disappointed.

'Yes, completely alone.'

'Your wife did mention that you'd been unsteady on your feet in the months leading up to that day. Is that right?'

Brian raised his eyebrows just a touch.

'I'm afraid so, officer,' he said. 'You know us men, we don't like to admit to our failings and seek medical help. If I'd done so, I might not be in this state.'

'I see. Well, thanks for your assistance. We'll be back in touch if we need anything further.' She rose to her feet. She was almost out of the room, when she stopped and addressed Helen. 'Goodbye. I think you've been lucky there.'

'I'm sorry, what . . . ?'

'Brian's recovery, I mean,' she said blandly. 'He seems to be doing really well.' With that, she was gone, leaving the room thick with silence.

Brian was the first to break it.

'Come and sit down.'

Helen took a few, faltering steps across the room and collapsed into the chair next to him.

'What do you think of that?' he asked.

'I . . . I don't know.' Was there any chance he had misremembered the whole thing, and what he had told the police was what he genuinely believed had happened?

'A nice little story, wasn't it?' he said.

'Story?'

'Yes, Helen, a story. You can drop the act now. I wasn't lying when I said I remembered exactly what happened. You were planning to abandon me. After everything I've done for you. And when I had the temerity to be unhappy about that, you attacked me, and almost killed me. That's about the size of it, isn't it?'

'No . . . I . . .' Was that how it had been? Hadn't he been trying to hurt Angela?

'Lovely little detail about me being unsteady on my feet, Helen. Goodness me, you had it all planned out, didn't you?'

'No.' She was on firmer ground here. There had been no plan, other than the one which involved her leaving Brian. 'I never meant to hurt you.'

'That won't wash, I'm afraid. Even if my memory of that day isn't tip top, I don't need it to be. I've got a helpful visual reminder.'

Helen looked at him blankly.

'The cameras?' he said, faux-helpfully. 'I know you found them, because you made a risible attempt to delete the footage. Did you honestly think it wouldn't be automatically backed up? I can access it from any device. I shouldn't be surprised – you're not the most tech-savvy, after all. It was the first thing I looked at when you kindly brought my phone in for me the other day, all charged up and ready to go.'

Helen cursed herself. Why hadn't she thought of that? He was right, she was the least tech-savvy person around, mainly thanks to Brian's desire to keep her at home and away from the world of work. Why hadn't one of the others thought of it?

'Why didn't you tell the police?' she asked.

'I don't want you to go to prison, Helen. I don't want you to leave me.'

'Why not? You've got your evidence.' It was hard to break the habit of a lifetime and challenge him, but she tried to summon some of the strength it had taken to leave him in the first place, a strength that had been building steadily since the day she took a golf trophy to his head.

'Who would look after me? I'm going to need a lot of care when I get out of hospital. For the rest of my life. Who else is going to do it?'

Helen's existence – she could hardly call it a life – stretched out ahead of her with dull, painful certainty. She would never be able to leave now, with him holding the threat of going to the police with his video evidence over her head. Snatched moments with friends would be her only happiness.

'There are some conditions though,' he went on.

'Conditions?'

'Yes. Otherwise that video footage will find its way to DS Paskell. Firstly, you will never see Angela and Sara again. They're clearly a very bad influence on you. And secondly, you will only leave the house when I say so, for approved purposes. And don't think it'll be like before, when I was out at work all day and you got up to God knows what. I'll never be able to go back to work after this – I'm going to take medical retirement. I'll be at home all the time, Helen, and I want you where I can keep an eye on you.'

Chapter 38

'Have you heard anything from Helen?' Angela asked Sara, putting a cup of coffee down in front of her. Helen's usual place at Angela's kitchen table was conspicuously empty.

'No, not a word.' It had been two months since Brian's miraculous recovery and Helen's subsequent departure from their lives.

'Nor have I. He must have made her block us on her phone. I try every day, in case she gets a chance to remove the block, but it's the same automated message every time – not possible to connect my call.'

'I do the same with WhatsApp,' Sara said. 'I just want her to know we haven't forgotten her. I'm always hoping that second tick will appear, but it never does. I don't know what else we can do. I saw her the other day, you know. In town.'

'What? Did you speak to her? How was she?'

'I couldn't. She was with Brian. I was going to go over anyway, but then I saw the look on her face. She was pleading with me not to talk to her. So I didn't. I didn't want to make things even worse for her than they already are.'

'How did she look?' Angela asked.

'Drawn, exhausted. Defeated.' A different person altogether to the one who had emerged while Brian was in the coma, the one with wild hair and unpainted nails and a propensity for stealing vials of blood from underneath the noses of health professionals. 'What time is Leila coming?' she asked Angela.

'Any minute now. She doesn't know you're going to be here though.'

Once Brian had woken up and the women realised they had no choice but to ditch their plan to incriminate Nigel, they had decided to concentrate on getting Leila out of his clutches.

'I can't say I'm looking forward to seeing her smug face.' She knew it was misplaced, but Sara had never quite got over the animosity she had felt towards Leila ever since Nigel had sat down opposite her at the speed dating and smiled so broadly.

'She's not smug, she's deluded,' Angela said. 'She's just as taken in by Nigel as you were. You're the only one who has a chance of getting through to her.'

'I know. I'll do my best but I don't hold out much hope. Didn't you say she was the biggest ignorer of red flags going?'

The doorbell rang, but before Angela had a chance to answer it, Greg came clattering down the stairs and opened it.

'Leila!' they heard him say with delight. 'Lovely to see you – how are you?'

'I'm well, thanks. You?'

'Yes, marvellous. I'm just on my way out, but good to see you. Bye, Angela!' he shouted and trotted away down the road.

'Come through to the kitchen!' Angela called to Leila.

Leila came in smiling, but ground to an abrupt halt when she saw Sara.

'I didn't know she was going to be here.'

'I'm sorry if you feel ambushed, Leila,' Angela said.

'You shouldn't have ambushed me, in that case.'

'It's only because I'm so keen to make you see the truth,' Angela said. 'I thought if Sara could tell you about her experience . . .'

'I know all about her experience, thanks.'

'No, you know what Nigel's told you, it's not the same,' Angela said. 'Is it, Sara? He told her all sorts of lies, tried to defraud her . . .'

'I've heard this all before,' snapped Leila, 'and he hasn't asked me for a penny. If he tried so hard to defraud you, where's the proof?'

'She doesn't have any – luckily for her she found him out before she'd handed over any money,' Angela said.

'How convenient,' Leila said. 'Whereas I've seen some pretty compelling evidence that she was only after him for *his* money.'

'Ha!' Sara snorted. 'He's falsified it. You can't believe anything that comes out of that man's mouth.'

'Sara,' Angela said, with a note of warning. Getting angry would only put Leila's back up further, and she'd be even less inclined to believe them.

'Funnily enough, he says the same about you,' Leila said.

'Angela told me he showed you messages and emails from me.'

'Yes, he did,' Leila said, 'and pretty damning they were too.'

'I can assure you that none of those messages were from me. He'd obviously made a fake email address, and the phone messages could have been from any number saved under the name Sara. What was the number?'

'I don't know. That wouldn't prove anything anyway. Someone like you could have all sorts of different mobile phones and email addresses for . . . different purposes.'

'What do you mean, someone like me? Oh yes, I forgot, I was also planning to poison him, wasn't I?' Sara gave a mirthless laugh. 'That man is unbelievable. His name isn't even Nigel Peters. And that house? He doesn't live there. He works there.'

'You're not saying anything other than exactly what he told me you'd say,' Leila said. 'He said you'd try to claim that he isn't who he says he is, so he showed me his driving licence. He is Nigel Peters.'

'It's not hard to get a fake driving licence,' Angela said. 'It proves nothing.'

'It's a question of perspective,' Leila said. 'What's that saying? *If someone shows you who they are, believe them.* Nigel has shown me nothing but love, care, attention and generosity.'

'Oh, I'm sure he has,' Sara said. 'I know all about that.'

'I think I should go,' Leila said.

'No, don't do that!' Sara said. 'Why don't you stay here and tell us all about how wonderful Nigel is? How he's waiting for you when you get home with a glass of wine and a homecooked meal and sympathetic ear? That's how he gets you, Leila. It's nice. I get it. But it's not real.'

'It may not have been real for you, but it is for me. It's different.'

'Ha! Different? Did he say you're the only person who has ever seen him for who he is?' Sara said. 'That all his past partners were in love with their own idea of him, that it's so different with you?'

Leila blushed.

'That's hit home, hasn't it?' Sara said. 'He's obviously told you I'm crazy, and you can believe that if you like, but what if I'm telling the truth?'

'I appreciate you're trying to help,' Leila said stiffly, 'but I'm fine. I'll see myself out.'

'Well done,' Angela said sarcastically when she had gone, slamming the door behind her. 'I'm glad you didn't lose your cool.'

'Sorry. I said I wouldn't be able to get through to her, though.'

'I don't know what else we can do,' Angela said. She wished Greg was there to talk it out with. His solution-focussed attitude to all problems, when what she needed was a listening ear and a hug, was an occasional source of annoyance, but here she felt it might have been useful. She was on the verge of calling him at his origami class to ask if he could come home, when the doorbell rang. She wondered wearily as she went down the hall to answer it what was waiting for her on the other side of the door. She almost hoped for a Jehovah's Witness or a double-glazing salesman. It was neither of those things. Leila was standing there, looking sheepish.

'I got halfway down the road, and all the disasters I've had with men started flashing before me – all the red flags I missed. I'm sorry I didn't listen before. Tell me everything that happened with Sara and Nigel. I'm ready to hear it now.'

Chapter 39

Helen no longer had to find the razor blade, because now Brian was home from the hospital, he was directing and supervising her every move. At first, he'd allowed her to go to the supermarket on a weekly basis but after she mentioned that a helpful man had got a jar of mayonnaise down from the top shelf for her, they switched to an online grocery delivery. He had drawn up a cleaning schedule for her, with every moment of her day accounted for. Her hair had been returned to its old neat bob, all traces of witchery gone, any stray greys despatched by an appointment with a hairdresser that Brian had ordered almost as soon as he could speak. He'd suggested she book one – female, naturally – who would come to the house. Wouldn't that be more convenient for her? Her regular Pilates sessions had been replaced, again at Brian's suggestion, by online classes. He was still very frail. What if something were to happen to him while she was out? And she had a busy schedule to keep at home, what with the usual cleaning and cooking, plus the new responsibilities of caring for Brian and ensuring he took his regular cocktail of pills, including the anti-epilepsy medication.

The day before Brian's release from hospital, Helen had spent the day in a chokehold of sheer terror, cleaning and recleaning every surface in the house and moving every piece of furniture to hoover or mop beneath it. She dusted not only the obvious things

like cabinets and bookshelves but light fittings and bulbs, walls and ceilings, skirting boards and the tops of the doors, all the while trying to look at the house with Brian's eyes to work out what she was missing.

Although she had blocked Sara and Angela, she still found herself checking her phone for messages from them, as if somehow one might sneak through. Even if she hadn't blocked them, they had probably given up on her. They would never truly understand why she had gone back to Brian. It wasn't only his threat to reveal the truth about his injury to the police, although that was part of it. Once he had woken up, there was a part of her that knew she would never be able to escape him. It was impossible to put the hold he had over her into words, so she couldn't expect her friends to understand. They would have washed their hands of her by now, and even if they hadn't, there was nothing they could do to help her.

While she was more or less confined to the house, as Brian's health improved he was going out more and more. She welcomed the respite from his presence but it was limited by the fact that she now knew there were cameras filming her every move, Brian having replaced them all when he got out of hospital. Now that he no longer had to hide his surveillance, she grew used to texts or calls from him commenting on what she was doing.

He hadn't told her where he was going when he left the house at noon today, but he'd recently been spending a lot of time with Nigel, with whom he had struck up a surprising friendship, so she guessed it was a lunch with him. Before Brian's accident (she still found it easier to think of it as an accident), they had played golf together a couple of times, but she wouldn't have described them as friends. But once Brian was allowed visitors in the hospital, Nigel had been a regular. Brian had always struggled with friendships in the past – Helen knew Greg had never liked him, although he was far too polite to have ever said so, and he had never managed to forge any real friendships with the other men at the Freemasons or the Lions Club. Brian was too competitive, and too focussed on whether Helen was going to cheat on him with any male who came within her sphere. The man he really wanted as a friend, Patrick, chair of the Windell Golf Club, had always kept him firmly at arm's length, despite Brian's best efforts. But Nigel had slipped through the net, and now Brian wouldn't hear a word against him. He had successfully nominated Nigel for membership at the Windell, something he had never done for anyone else. Helen had tried to tell him what Nigel had done to Sara, but he hadn't been interested in hearing it. He said Nigel had told him everything he needed to know about that, and that it only gave him more reason to be glad that Helen and Sara were no longer in touch.

Her shoulders tensed as she heard Brian's key in the door. She donned her mental armour and went to the door to greet him, as was his request.

'Hello, darling.' She held out her hands and he thrust his coat and scarf into them. 'How was your lunch with Nigel?' she said, hanging them on the peg.

'What makes you think that's where I've been?' he said.

'I don't . . . I just thought, it's lunchtime. And you do often meet him for lunch. Have you not eaten? I can make you something.' She hurried through to the kitchen, Brian hot on her heels, and opened the fridge, surveying the contents. How could she be so stupid as to have eaten that last bowl of homemade soup herself? There were oatcakes in the cupboard, but was there any cheese? She still wasn't used to doing all the food shopping online. You had to be so much more organised when you weren't able to pop out for a top-up shop.

'No. I've eaten,' Brian said, leaning against the counter top.

'I thought you said . . .'

'I didn't say I hadn't had lunch. I asked why you assumed it was with Nigel.'

'Oh. Sorry.' She knew better than to ask who he had been with.

'Nigel was out with Leila looking at wedding venues.'

'They're getting married?' Helen couldn't hide her shock.

'Yes. What's wrong with that?'

'Nothing,' she said woodenly. 'Do give them my congratulations.' Angela was supposed to be Leila's friend. Why the hell hadn't she warned her about Nigel?

'Oh, I will. And congratulations are in order for me too.' Brian grinned smugly.

'Are they?' Helen said, confused.

'You still haven't asked me who I had lunch with.'

'Alright. Who did you have lunch with?'

'My new girlfriend.'

Helen felt as if she'd been struck dumb. It was so far from what she'd been expecting Brian to say. She opened her mouth, willing something to come out, but nothing did.

'Cat got your tongue?' Brian said jovially, enjoying himself.

'No,' she managed. 'I'm just a bit . . . nonplussed. How did you . . .'

'I met her in the hospital,' he said, smiling smugly. 'You might remember her – Rosa?'

'Rosa? The healthcare assistant?' Helen had an uncomfortable flashback to the vial of blood, Rosa's tears at the nurse's station.

'That's the one. Such a caring, sympathetic woman. She's horrified at how cold you are to me.'

'But you're . . .'

'Married to you? Well, yes, in theory.'

'No, you're actually married to me. It's not theoretical.' Helen's usual meekness deserted her.

'You've hardly made an effort in the bedroom department, have you?'

'I thought . . . since the coma, you wouldn't want to . . .'

'You thought wrong, then. I was waiting to see if you were ever going to resume your conjugal duties, but it seems not. Not that you were very enthusiastic in the first place.'

She had been, Helen thought, at the beginning of their marriage. But when they were trying to get pregnant, sex had become fraught with the weight of failed expectations, and eventually she had come to think of it as a chore. But she had never denied him – she thought of all the times she had lain back and gritted her teeth, made the right noises and told him how wonderful he was. If he had made any attempt to give her pleasure, she might have been a more willing partner.

'So . . . You're leaving me?'

Hope swelled wildly within her. She could see Angela's spare room in her mind's eye, the bed made up ready for her. She would let Brian have everything – the house, the car, all her possessions. She didn't care. Rosa was welcome to him. Maybe Angela could find some more work for her at the agency. She'd enjoyed it, and been good at it too. She would find a way to make it work.

'No need to look so happy,' Brian said.

'No no, I'm not . . .' She tried to force her mouth into a frown, her brow into a furrow.

'No, I mean there's really no reason for you to be happy,' Brian said. 'Do you think I'd let you walk away, get away with what you've done to me?'

The hope that had briefly flared within her was snuffed out.

'So you're going to continue to be married to me, but date other women, is that what you're saying?' Helen was surprised by how little she cared.

'That would suit you very well, wouldn't it?' he said thoughtfully.

Hardly, Helen thought. If you'd asked her on their wedding day what she hoped for from their autumn years, this would have been very low down the list.

'Helen, I don't need you anymore. Rosa comes from a family where traditional roles are valued. She's more than happy to do everything you do for me in the house, but she'll do what I want in the bedroom too. That means I have a choice now, about whether to tell the truth about the day you tried to kill me.'

She gripped the edge of the table to stop herself from collapsing.

'Are you going to show the footage to the police?'

'Oh Helen,' he said. 'I think I can do better than that.'

Chapter 40

Helen sat alone, chatter and laughter swelling up to the roof of the extremely swanky barn conversion in the grounds of Claricoates. The rafters twinkled with thousands of fairy lights and each circular, white linen-covered table was set with silver and sparkling crystal, a huge, spherical glass of pink roses in the centre.

Brian had been full of this engagement party for the past few weeks, revelling in his role as best man for Nigel and Leila. Helen had never told him the full truth about Nigel's attempted fraud on Sara, so he was under the impression (as was everyone there apart from Angela and Helen herself) that this was Nigel's house, his barn conversion – his life. She wondered where the real Nigel was.

The tables were filled with men she identified as members of the Freemasons or the local Lions Club, all wealthy local senior executives or business owners, for whom the cost of living crisis was merely an item on the news. Brian was acting as if it was his party, and was even planning to do a speech, as if this was the wedding day itself. Helen hugged her secret knowledge about this close to her, like a newborn baby. Ever since Brian had told her about Rosa, she had been poised for disaster, for Brian to reveal the footage of her hitting him with the trophy and the subsequent delay in calling the ambulance. She was fairly certain he planned to do it today, in front of all these people that he considered so important.

'Hello, Helen.' Patrick, the handsome and charismatic chair of the golf club, sat down next to her. 'How are you?'

'Good, thanks.' Normally she would have been aware of Brian's scrutiny, finding herself alone with another man, and fearful of the reprisals later, but today he was too busy playing the genial host and sucking up to his golf club cronies.

'I didn't know Brian and Nigel were such close friends, when Brian proposed Nigel for the Windell.'

'They weren't really,' Helen said, uncharacteristically frankly. 'They've only known each other four or five months even now.'

'And yet . . . he asked Brian to be his best man?'

'I know. I don't understand it either.'

'It's a bit awkward, but Nigel hasn't been paying his membership subs. The Treasurer has been trying to get hold of him. Do you know if he's having any . . . difficulties? We do like to be supportive if we can. Perhaps a payment plan, although having seen his house today, I can't imagine that's the issue?'

'I suspect you'll find there won't be a problem once Nigel has married Leila. She's a wealthy woman.' Helen was shocked at the words coming out of her mouth. She seemed to have lost all filter. Patrick looked shocked too, and made his excuses. Helen took a sip of her wine, anticipating the exposure coming her way if what she suspected about Brian's speech was true. Her breath caught as Angela walked in, elegant in a rust-coloured silk dress, accompanied by Greg, suave as ever in a dark grey suit and pale pink shirt. Tears sprang to her eyes at the sight of Angela's dear, familiar face. She had been hoping against hope that Leila would have invited her, although goodness knows how Leila had squared that with Nigel. It had been torture these last weeks, being unable to see her friends. At least after today, if what she suspected was correct, it would be over, one way or another. Angela looked tense, scanning the room. Her eyes stopped when they met Helen's. She whispered something in Greg's ear and made for the entrance hall. At the door she turned and beckoned Helen, who sprang to her feet and scurried from the room. In the hall, Angela peeped out from behind a heavy wooden door. Helen went through it into a bathroom, where Angela locked the door behind them and enveloped her in a huge hug.

'It's so good to see you. I've been so worried.'

Helen relaxed into her embrace, inhaling the familiar scent of Angela's perfume. 'He made me block you on my phone. What are you doing here? You can't support Leila marrying Nigel, surely?'

'It's complicated. I can't explain here, it's too—' She broke off as someone tried the bathroom door. 'Just a minute!' she called. 'I would have come regardless,' she went on, 'because I knew you'd be here. I've been dying to see you. Are you alright?'

'Yes and no. I can't explain now, there's no time.'

'When can we speak? Can you not get out at all?'

'Not rea—'

'Helen! Are you in there?' Brian called through the door. 'They're about to serve dinner.'

'Coming!' she trilled. 'I have to go,' she said to Angela.

'There must be something we can do. I can't bear for you to be living like this.'

'I don't think it'll be for much longer,' Helen said in a low voice. 'Things are going to change after today, one way or another.'

'What do you mean?'

'Helen!' he called again, more peremptorily this time. 'Come and sit down. What will people think? I put Patrick and his wife on our table!'

She gave Angela another brief hug and hurried outside, where Brian stood tapping his foot impatiently. She closed the door firmly behind her so he wouldn't see Angela.

'What were you doing in there?' he asked.

'Sorry,' she said.

'Come on, then.'

They traipsed back into the main room and over to their table, which consisted of Nigel and Leila, Patrick and his wife, Celia, and another golf club crony called Simon and his wife. Her name was Simone, and they were a ruddy, outdoorsy pair, who as well as having almost the same name, looked more like brother and sister than husband and wife. Everyone was already seated except Leila who was deep in conversation with Angela, the latter having returned from the bathroom.

The maître d', an immaculately groomed young man, tinged a glass.

'Ladies and Gentlemen, dinner is served!'

'Leila!' Nigel called across the room to her. She looked over – guiltily, Helen thought – said one last thing to Angela and came over to join them.

'There you are, darling!' Nigel kissed her as she sat down next to him. 'You've met Patrick and Celia, I think? And you know Helen and Brian.'

'Yes, hello, everyone.'

Leila was as gorgeous as ever, but Helen thought she could detect a hint of strain beneath her customary composure.

'And this is Simon and his wife, Simone.'

'Nice to meet you.'

This was the top table at her engagement party, yet Leila had never even met some of these people? Where were her own friends and family? And why was Angela supporting her in this doomed relationship with someone she knew to be a fraudster? She could only suppose that Leila was refusing to listen and that Angela didn't want to abandon her with no support, and wanted to be ready to pick up the pieces when things inevitably went wrong. Well, there was nothing Helen could do about that now. She had enough to worry about today.

Simone poured Helen and herself a glass of wine from the bottle on the table. Patrick was right, Nigel and Leila had spared no expense.

'Are you a dog person?' Simone enquired.

'I beg your pardon?' There was so much going on in Helen's head that she couldn't make sense of this question at all.

'Dogs? Do you have them?'

'Oh, I see. No, I don't have a dog.'

Simone's face fell.

'I love them, actually,' Helen said daringly, considering Brian was next to her on her other side, 'but Brian's not keen. He thinks they're too much of a tie.'

'They can be, but they give you so much. We've had our old lab Monty for coming up to ten years – he's like a member of the family, isn't he, Simon?'

'Absolutely.' Simon sloshed wine the same colour as his face into his glass. 'There's no loyalty like it.'

'A friend of mine runs a charity for rescue greyhounds,' Simone went on. 'They make the most gorgeous pets. If you ever change your mind, do let me know.'

A girlhood friend of Helen's had had a greyhound that had taken a real fancy to her. She couldn't recall the girl's name now but the dog had been called Freya. Every time she went to this girl's house, Freya would come and lay her head adoringly on Helen's lap, asking for nothing more than a pat on her soft coat or a stroke of her silken ears. The joy of having a dog was something else Brian had taken from her.

Waitressing staff in crisp, white shirts and black trousers streamed in and out of the swing doors to the entrance hall, going back and forth between the function room and the kitchen, placing a smoked mackerel salad in front of each guest. As a girl with a high, blonde ponytail and a salad in each hand swept in opening the door with her shoulder, Helen caught a glimpse of a woman hovering outside in the hall. She was wearing a beige cashmere shawl wrapped high around her shoulders and neck, almost covering her chin, and her eyes were hidden behind large sunglasses, but Helen recognised her straight away. It was Sara.

Chapter 41

Angela had seen Sara too, but she had been expecting her. She got up and hurried from the room.

'You look like Elizabeth Taylor in that get-up,' Angela said, giggling.

'That's exactly the vibe I was going for,' Sara said in delight. 'There was no way I was missing this. How does Nigel look?'

'Like the cat who got the cream – or the man who thinks he's got away with everything.'

'He reckoned without your watchword. It's like you said to me when I met Nigel: never put all your eggs in one basket.'

'Always have a backup plan,' Angela agreed. 'And whilst this isn't as dramatic as framing Nigel for the attack on Brian, it will cause him maximum humiliation.'

'And lose him his job and his home,' Sara reminded her. 'Is everything going to plan?'

'Yes, I've just had a text. He should be here any moment.'

Through the door they heard Brian calling for silence.

'I just want to say a few words, everyone,' he said. 'Firstly, a huge thanks to Nigel and Leila for putting on this wonderful engagement party, and a very warm welcome to all our friends, especially Patrick, chair of the Windell Golf Club, and his wife Celia, such a pleasure to have you here.'

'Could he have his nose any further up that golf club guy's arse?' Sara said.

'This is somewhat unconventional,' Brian went on, 'but as some of you know, I had an accident earlier this year, resulting in a very serious brain injury. At least, I thought at first it was an accident.'

Angela and Sara looked at each other, terrified. Was Brian about to reveal the truth of what they had done in the most public way imaginable, and before they had had the chance to reveal Nigel for the charlatan he was? This was not in their plan. At that moment, the maître d' spotted them through the small glass panel on the swing doors and popped his head out.

'Can I help you?' he said to Sara. 'This is a private function.'

Brian looked over and his eyes widened in recognition despite Sara's disguise.

'Come in, ladies,' he said. 'An uninvited guest, I see.'

Angela and Sara came into the room. Nigel stared at them in horror. Leila had convinced him that they should invite Angela, that she had smoothed things over and that Angela wouldn't make a scene at her friend's party, but Sara was a different matter altogether.

'I'm glad you're here actually,' Brian said, 'as this concerns you too.'

A murmur went up around the room and a few confused glances were thrown their way. Brian's laptop was open on the table in front of him, and for the first time, Angela noticed the large white screen on the wall behind the top table. Her stomach twisted into a tight knot and Sara went very still beside her.

'When I first woke up from the coma I'd been in for several weeks, I didn't know what had happened to me that day, but then it started coming back to me in fragments. I wasn't sure if my memories were accurate though – I'd had a traumatic brain injury, after all. Confusion, delirium and hallucinations are common after-effects of an induced coma.'

Angela noticed that Nigel was looking up at Brian, frowning slightly. He obviously had no clue of the bomb Brian was about to drop, but she feared she knew exactly what was coming. Leila was staring right at her, trying to understand whether this was all part of Angela's plan, and then seeing from her expression that it absolutely wasn't. Angela had to do something, she had to stop him. She looked at Helen sitting beside him, but instead of the terror she had expected to see, she was smiling. Angela couldn't read her – was she resigned to her fate, relieved the deceit was all over? Helen nodded at her as if to say, it's alright, stood and made her way over to her two friends. She stood in between them and put a hand into each of theirs.

'Don't worry,' she whispered.

'Then I remembered something,' Brian went on. 'And this was something I *was* sure of. Helen and I had installed cameras in our house for . . . er . . . security, so I was able to return to that footage to establish precisely what had happened on the day of my "accident".' He did exaggerated air quotes around the word. 'What I found was . . . interesting to say the least. The best way to explain is to let the footage speak for itself.'

He clicked on his laptop and the home screen was projected on the white board behind him. Angela glanced behind her and saw through the glass panel a tall, patrician blond man standing in the hall, a fierce expression on his face.

She pushed the door open and popped her head out.

'Nigel Peters?'

'Yes,' he said grimly. 'Bloody hell, look at all this.'

He stepped through the swing doors into the hall. Helen looked at him in confusion.

'This is the real Nigel, the owner of the house,' Angela said to her in a low voice.

'Right, this ends now,' he said, not troubling to keep his voice down. A few heads swivelled towards him, including the man Sara and Angela still struggled to think of as Colin. He looked utterly horrified.

'Can you wait a few minutes, please?' Helen said to him. 'I need my husband to show this video – I'll explain after.'

'No problem,' the real Nigel said. 'I'm happy to let Colin sweat for a few minutes, wondering what I'm going to do.'

The whole room, apart from Nigel who was caught up in his own private agony, watched as Brian double-clicked on a file labelled ENGAGEMENT PARTY SPEECH, and a grainy video began to play on the screen. At Helen and Brian's house, Brian came in through the front door in a suit and tie.

'Hello?' he called.

There was the sound of slow footsteps on the stairs and Helen came into view, a piece of paper in her hands.

In the hotel room, Brian paused the video.

'Sorry, technical difficulties, hang on.'

The air of confusion in the room deepened as he closed the video down and clicked again on ENGAGEMENT PARTY SPEECH.

'They do say that the definition of insanity is doing the same thing over and over again and expecting different results,' Helen murmured.

The video started again, at the point where he had closed it. This time, the audience watched as Brian spoke.

'Why weren't you in the hall to greet me?' he demanded.

Back in the barn, Brian reached down to stop the video, but Patrick, sitting next to him, picked up the laptop and moved it out of Brian's reach.

'I'd like to see this,' he said.

'I *knew* he didn't like Brian!' Helen whispered triumphantly.

The video continued to play. Brian half stood, stretching across Patrick to try and reach the laptop, but Patrick swatted him away and Brian sank into his chair, defeated.

The audience, agog now, having realised a Netflix-worthy drama was unfolding in front of them, watched as Helen confronted Brian with the proof of his vasectomy, wincing as he berated her for going through his private things. On the screen, Brian became increasingly furious until eventually he lost all control and punched Helen. The room took a sharp intake of breath as one. Calmly, Patrick closed the lid of the laptop. Brian looked broken.

You could have heard a pin drop as the real Nigel Peters walked up to the top table.

'Good afternoon, everyone. I'm sorry to interrupt your dinner, but I'm going to have to ask you all to leave.'

A flurry of murmuring went round the room.

'You know this man,' he pointed at Nigel, 'as Nigel Peters, the owner and resident of this property. He is no such thing.'

Nigel/Colin's face was now a deep puce. There was a brief second of silence while the room at large got to grips with this new development and then a hubbub broke out, with everyone frantically trying to find out if anyone on their table had a clue what was going on.

'I am Nigel Peters,' he went on, 'and this is my house. This man is my employee Colin Sanderson. I took him on a couple of years ago to look after the property when I was away, which is most of the time. It has recently come to my attention that he has been impersonating me for fraudulent gain – something in which I dare say the police will be very interested.'

'What about this?' Patrick's deep voice rose above the babbling around him. He pointed to the laptop, his disgust for Brian writ large.

'I don't know who this man is, if you can call him a man,' Nigel looked at Brian with towering contempt, 'but I imagine the police will be very interested in that too. In the meantime, Colin, you are fired, and evicted from the stables flat. I've had someone pack up your stuff – it's in the drive.'

Colin/Nigel rose to his feet, along with Brian. In silence, they threaded their way, heads down, between the tables filled with the great and the good of Tunbridge Wells. Freemasons, Lions and golf club members alike averted their eyes in apparent embarrassment, although it would provide an awful lot of dinner party conversation in the weeks to come.

Chapter 42

'It had to be champagne,' Leila said, popping the cork as the four women clustered around a table in the nearest pub to Nigel's house, a fancy gastropub with huge picture windows and chunky, solid oak furniture.

'I'm not quite ready to celebrate,' Helen said, tapping away at her phone. 'I've got a few last bits of admin to do to make sure Brian doesn't show the police the real footage of the day he had his . . . accident.' She looked uncertainly at Leila.

'Leila knows,' Angela said. 'We've been working together so closely on this Nigel thing since Leila saw the light about him, I thought full disclosure was better.'

'I'm absolutely on your side,' Leila said, pouring Helen a glass of fizz. 'After seeing that video today, I'd like to say no jury would convict you, but sadly they probably would. I totally get why you took things into your own hands. I'm just sorry you weren't able to make your original plan of framing Nigel work.'

'I want to know more about this video, though, Helen. How did all that come about?' Angela asked, with a note of admiration.

'Brian told me a while ago that he'd met someone else.'

'What?' the other three exclaimed in unison.

'I know, who'd want him, right?' Helen said. 'But apparently she does, or did. My first instinct was to be delighted – I thought it meant I could be free of him. But it didn't mean that at all – what it meant was he no longer had any reason to keep what I'd done to him a secret. The only reason he'd kept quiet up to that point was because he needed me to look after him.'

'How did you know he was planning to expose you today?' Leila asked.

'I couldn't be sure, but he kept hinting that he had a surprise for me, and that I should be ready for fireworks at the party. He kept saying how everyone would be there from the golf club, and the Lions Club, as if I cared about the opinions of any of those people.'

'He's the one who cares about them,' Sara said. 'Ha!'

'Quite,' Helen said. 'So one night, when he was asleep, I used his finger to open the laptop – he was out of it on sleeping tablets as usual – and I saw the file on the desktop labelled Engagement Party Speech. Of course it was the video of me . . . you know . . . on the day . . .'

'The day you tried to leave him after thirty-five years of coercive control,' Angela said. 'The day he attacked me and you stepped in to protect me. That day?'

'Yes,' Helen said gratefully. 'I had the idea of deleting the footage and replacing it with what you saw today, but there were a couple of problems with that – one, I had to do it as last minute as I could, otherwise there was a risk he'd open it again and see what I'd done and two, I didn't have the skills to actually do it. I was going to need some help.'

'Who could you possibly get to help you with that?' Sara asked.

'You'll see in a minute – he's coming to deal with this.' She took a tablet from her handbag. 'It's Brian's and it's linked to his laptop and to the camera app. I deleted everything off the laptop again last night while he was asleep but I know the camera app backs up automatically. I'm hoping to use the tablet to remove all trace of the footage. I then got my ... helper ... to log into the laptop remotely and switch the footage.'

'This is all very mysterious,' Angela said, smiling. 'What was your plan if Brian hadn't tried to show the footage today?'

'It was always going to be a risk,' Helen said. 'But I decided it was one worth taking. If it had all gone wrong, I was going to go to the police anyway and tell the truth. I couldn't take another day of him having that power over me.'

'Thank God it worked out,' Angela said fervently.

'Where's Greg, by the way?' Leila asked her.

'I sent him home to get Helen's room ready. You know you can stay as long as you like,' she said to Helen, 'and there's plenty of work for you to do at the agency as well. And I may as well tell you now: Greg knows the truth.'

'Angela!' Helen said. 'What were you thinking?'

'I couldn't keep it from him, it would have destroyed our relationship. He gets it, I promise. He'll never tell the truth about what happened to Brian.'

'How can you be so sure?' Helen said.

'I know him,' Angela replied simply. 'We've been together for almost thirty years. To be honest, the longer I run the agency, the more I realise how lucky I was to find him.'

'You certainly struck gold,' Leila said wistfully. 'Mind you, that Nigel – the real one, I mean – is a bit of a dish, isn't he? Would it be inappropriate if I asked him out?'

'Yes!' the other three women chorused.

'Spoilsports,' Leila said, topping up her champagne.

'While we wait, can you tell me what on earth has been going on with Nigel?' Helen said.

'When we found out that Leila was dating Nigel, we tried to warn her off,' Angela said.

'But I wasn't having any of it at first,' Leila chipped in. 'It's not so much that I ignore red flags, more like I stitch them together to make myself a dress. I simply didn't want to see it. But something Sara said that day struck a chord – it was about what he'd said to her, how she was the only person who had truly seen him. He'd said exactly the same thing to me.'

'Of course he had,' Sara said.

'I stormed off that day, but then I came back. I asked Angela to tell me everything, and . . . well, it was like the scales fell from my eyes. I couldn't believe how stupid I had been.'

'I know that feeling,' Sara said.

'Neither of you have got anything to feel stupid about,' Angela said. 'It happens all the time.'

'Why didn't you just leave him?' Helen asked. 'I know that sounds ironic, coming from me – you could ask me why I didn't leave Brian. But partly I was scared of him, and partly he'd made me believe that I was this terrible wife, that all the problems we had were my fault. But you could have walked away.'

'I could,' Leila said. 'But I wanted him to pay for what he'd done – to Sara and to me, and to the nameless other women who were too embarrassed to go to the police about it. So Angela, Sara and I came up with a plan. Angela got in touch with the real Nigel Peters and told him what had been going on. He was fuming – not only had Nigel been using his house, driving his cars and drinking his eye-wateringly expensive wine, he'd been impersonating him – using his name.'

'Is that a crime?' Helen asked.

'Identity theft in itself is a grey area,' Angela said. 'Unless the real Nigel can prove that Nigel – Colin – was using his identity to defraud him financially, there may not be much the police can do.'

'But it was very enjoyable seeing him lose his job and his home right in front of us,' Sara chipped in.

'And his dignity,' Leila said. 'That was why we arranged for the real Nigel to turn up at the party – we wanted our Nigel to feel as humiliated as Sara did when she found out he'd been lying to her. In the meantime, I had to keep pretending everything was OK between us as I didn't want to spook him. He was insistent on having this big engagement party at "his" house. Luckily, he booked and paid the deposit for the catering – I think he was playing the long game there, didn't want me to get suspicious if he asked me to pay. No doubt when it came to the final payment there would have been some reason he couldn't have paid it, but unfortunately for him, they'll now be pursuing him for the balance.'

'Did he ever tell you about his "daughter", Leila?' Helen asked curiously.

'He told me he had a daughter who lived in America, but he said that Sara had invented the cancer story to discredit him, and that it was Sara who was trying to defraud him. I have no doubt though that there would have been some sob story soon enough, something that he needed money for. He certainly wasn't genuinely in love with me.'

'Here he is!' Helen's face lit up as a man crossed the bar towards them. He was clad in black jeans, a Motörhead T-shirt and dark glasses. He had a baseball cap pulled low over his forehead, concealing the unhealthy pallor of one who rarely sees the light of day. He slid into the seat next to Helen.

'Ladies.'

Sara peered at him more closely. 'Steve? Is that you?'

'Who?' Leila asked, confused.

'Steve the Data Conspiracy Theorist!' Sara said. 'I went on a date with him – you remember, Angela?'

'How could I forget? He messages me weekly criticising the agency's data privacy practices.'

'I'm afraid you'll find there is no conspiracy,' Steve said pityingly. 'And I'm only trying to protect you and your clients,' he added to Angela.

'He's not just a conspiracy theorist – I mean, he's not a conspiracy theorist,' Helen amended hastily. 'He's a computer security wizard, and he's the one who's been helping me with the videos.'

'How did you find him?' Sara asked.

'You told me about him after the date, so I looked him up on the agency system – Angela gave me all the logins for the work I've been doing for her. When I told him my husband had been covertly filming me as a means of coercive control, he was happy to help.'

'Couldn't be more up my street, to be honest,' Steve said. 'I've deleted what I can remotely, but let me just check on the app on the tablet as well.'

Helen passed it to him.

He tutted and sighed as he opened APS Digital.

'This really is the go-to app for stupid people who have no idea how any of this stuff works. Dear oh dear.'

'Can you really make it all go away?' Helen said. 'Because my husband told me there was some kind of automatic back-up, so I'd never be able to fully delete it.'

'Certainly *you* would never be able to fully delete it. And in a sense he's right – I can do my best, but no data is ever truly irrecoverable. However, once I've finished, there's no way Brian or any layperson will be able to recover it. There is a chance it *may* be recoverable by a forensic data analyst – but if the … er … scene in question is ever recovered, the data analyst would also uncover the archive of the emotional and physical torture your husband put you through. I doubt he'd want that made public knowledge. So I think you're safe.'

Steve tapped away. The four women waited in awed silence, aware they were watching a master at work. Five minutes later, he passed the tablet back to Helen.

'All done.'

'And the laptop? Because Brian took that with him to the police station.'

'I've erased the entire account. If Brian tries to access it via the laptop – or any other device for that matter – it will be as if it never existed.'

'Wow,' Helen said, 'that's amazing. How can I ever thank you?'

'All I ask is that you stop giving your data away to the state.'

'Ah. Right. Will do,' Helen said uncertainly.

'And the same for the rest of you,' Steve said. With that, he settled the peak of his baseball cap even lower and walked away.

'Gosh, there's something rather attractive about a man being extremely competent at what he does, isn't there?' Leila said, looking after him appreciatively.

'For God's sake, Leila!' Angela said. 'Is there a course you can take in spotting red flags? I should set it up as another string to the agency's bow.'

'That's not a bad idea,' Leila replied, unoffended. 'Although I was thinking there is something else you could use the agency for.'

'Something else?' Angela said.

'Sara and I are not the only women who've fallen prey to these . . . vultures who seek out the most . . . I was going to say gullible, but that's wrong. The most *vulnerable* women, the ones they know they can exploit. A friend of mine recently found out her husband of twenty years has put himself up on Tinder. What if you could attract him to the agency, and then expose him, humiliate him as much as possible? He's a teacher, if you can believe it. There must be some mileage in that.'

'I love it!' Helen said. 'I'm going to be working at the agency anyway – this could be my specialist area!'

'Hang on a minute,' Angela said feebly, but as Leila filled her champagne glass to the brim, she sensed that this idea was only going to gather momentum and she might as well let herself be swept along. Every business needs a Unique Selling Point, after all, and it was rather poetic. Kiss, Marry, Avoid would finally be living up to its name. The decent men would get to kiss and marry, but Angela, Helen, Sara and Leila would do their utmost to ensure that women could avoid the bad apples, leaving them to rot in their barrels.

Chapter 43

Alone in the house he used to share with Helen, Brian boiled the kettle. He'd wanted to make himself a cup of tea but there were no teabags left in the jar on the counter top. He hadn't worked out where Helen kept the rest so he made instant coffee instead. There was a fine spray of crumbs on the worktop, and a dried, crusty orange stain on the front of the kitchen cabinet where his hand had slipped opening a tin of beans last night. His shirt was crumpled because he couldn't work out how to use the iron and he was fast running out of clean underpants. The drawer in the kitchen island that housed the bin was open, its contents spilling out. He had asked Moira next door when the general refuse collection was, but for some reason she wouldn't help him, telling him to check the council website. He hadn't got around to it yet.

He had hoped that Rosa, with her traditional values, would have taken pity on him, but that evil foursome of women had made sure that she heard about the video, and now she was shunning him, and she wasn't the only one. Patrick had emailed him to let him know that his membership at the Windell Golf Club had been revoked, and the heads of both the Freemasons and the Lions Club had indicated that he was no longer welcome. No longer able to work, and with all his hobbies and friends (such as they were) stolen from him, he spent his days gazing mindlessly at the television and plotting his revenge on Helen and her band of harpies.

He had just picked up his coffee to take it into the living room, where it would join several of its abandoned, half-drunk brothers and a selection of greasy plates, when he felt a familiar wave rising in his stomach, the prelude to one of the seizures with which he had been suffering since his head injury. The medication he was on hadn't been controlling them as well as the consultant would have liked, and they had been talking about trying him on a different anti-seizure drug. Lights flashed in his eyes and his body began to jerk and twitch. Blackness descended upon him as he lost consciousness and went crashing to the ground. If he'd simply fallen to the floor, all might have been well, but as he went down, he caught his head with a terrific crack on the overflowing bin drawer, open due to his lack of knowledge about the local refuse collection schedule.

If anyone had been around to come to his aid, he could yet have been saved, but there was no one. Nobody came to help him, and even if they had known what was going on, there was no one who would have cared as his life slowly drained from him.

Chapter 44

Living with Angela and Greg was a revelation to Helen. She could see and feel the love and care that existed between them in their daily interactions. It wasn't that they were excessively lovey-dovey – they were probably just normal – but she had never seen an everyday, loving relationship up close before. She enjoyed spending time with them, but she also loved those times when she had the house to herself, when Angela was at work and Greg out learning how to make cheese or communicate in British Sign Language.

It was utter bliss not to be living with Brian. Nobody told her what to wear or what to eat, or kept tabs on where she was going. She had stopped cutting and colouring her hair and planned to allow it to grow long and wild and streaked with white. With the money she earned working for Kiss, Marry, Avoid, she had been shopping for a whole new wardrobe. Gone were the neat little twinsets, the classy, unobtrusive pearl earrings, the tailored slacks, the blouses buttoned to the neck. She no longer had to worry about meeting Brian's very specific stipulations – the line she had always had to tread had been incredibly fine, requiring her to look slim and attractive, yet modest and appropriate. These days she cared only about how the clothes made her feel. She had purchased several voluminous hand-painted tunics, some animal-print harem pants and even a pair of dungarees.

She had bumped into her old neighbour in town the other day and it had been a few seconds before Moira recognised her. When she did, she had given Helen the most enormous hug, grabbed her by the shoulders and said in tones of great emotion, '*Well done.*'

The only thing she missed a little was collecting Brian's prescription medications from the chemist on the High Street. She had enjoyed her small interactions with the handsome pharmacist, his eyes twinkling as he handed over the small brown plastic bottle containing Brian's anti-seizure drugs. The pills were round and white, and looked exactly like the aspirin she had been swapping them for ever since Brian came out of hospital.

She stroked the silky head of her new rescue greyhound. Angela and Greg hadn't minded her adopting Alecto – they'd encouraged it, in fact. Helen had loved the name Alecto since studying Greek mythology at school, and the fact that it was the name of the goddess of unceasing vengeance was nothing but pure coincidence.

THE END

Acknowledgements

Huge thanks as ever are due to my amazing duo of agents, Felicity Blunt and Rosie Pierce, the best corner-fighters ever, and to my editor Phoebe Morgan for her thoughtful edits and for being more responsive to emails than anyone else in the history of publishing.

To my parents, to whom this book is dedicated. They gave me a lot of useful information about mushrooms and the poisonous properties thereof for an earlier iteration of this book. None of this made it into the novel but suffice to say, if they ever die from mushroom poisoning, it will definitely have been murder.

Likewise Dr Sophie Flanagan, who provided me with some excellent and detailed insights into the medical side of things, poison-wise. Again, I'm sorry none of it made it to the book, but your time and expertise are nonetheless massively appreciated.

Thanks to Aisling for the loan of her gorgeous house in Rye, where some of this book was written, and to the team at Office Tribe, where a lot of this book was written. Thanks for creating such a peaceful and welcoming space.

To all my writing friends, especially the Ladykillers and the Bitches (you know who you are) – it means everything to have you along for the ride, whether it's smooth or bumpy.

Thanks to Natasha for the early read and spotting of

plotholes, and the rest of my squad – Claire, Catherine, Jane, Naomi, Rachel and always Hattie.

To you – thank you for buying, downloading or borrowing this book. It means so much to me when readers let me know they've enjoyed one of my books. I hope you liked this one!

And finally to my home team aka Family Plus Plus – Jon, Charlie, Arthur and Alma. The relationships in my books are often dark and difficult but thanks to you lot, my real life couldn't be more different. Thanks for your unwavering love and support.

Sashica